FENWICK

ALAN DEL MONTE

FENWICK

Copyright © 2020 by Alan Del Monte

Book Cover Design by Tara Seifrit - tarafydesigns.com
Book Formatting by Toula Magi - littlesunshinebooks.com

Published by:
Fishing Pole Publishing
Milford, CT

ISBN: 978-1-7326886-4-3 (pbk)
ISBN: 978-1-7326886-5-0 (digital)

Printed in the United States of America

For my lovely wife Jan: Always standing by my side and in my corner.

All was right with the world, or was it?

"There's been a Murder Down In Fenwick"

CHAPTER ONE

It was Thanksgiving time with the Tylers. Three months had quickly passed and Mary, Thomas and Lillith had successfully adjusted to their new school grades. Martha could not get over how well these three Tyler children handled change. She found herself thinking, "If only I could make whatever it is they have into a pill, it would be worth a small fortune."

As far as Peter Childers was concerned, no matter how hard Martha tried, she could not restrain herself from hugging him whenever the opportunity arose for orchestrating her position at Albertus Magnus, the unofficial sister school of the great Yale University in New Haven, and the perfect place for her to be in her new life as a Tyler. Martha was an ardent fan of the Ivy League, having graduated from Cornell and taught at Columbia in Manhattan. Columbia, however, was big city Ivy League, whereas in New Haven, Martha found herself simply bathed in the "Halls of Ivy." She was impressed by the high academic standards of Albertus Magnus and delighted in its close relationship between the college and the university. New Haven's air breathed Ivy League and Martha loved breathing it in.

And now, Martha was enjoying a whole new experience known as the insanity of the holiday season with the Tylers. Aunt Clara was busy orchestrating her Thanksgiving dinner plan. Martha had never known such joy attached to sheer bedlam. While at Cornell, she had gone to Philadelphia with her absolute best friend in the world, Lizzie Childers, for Thanksgiving, but anything less than a total orderly celebration was not acceptable to the wealthy, but oh so proper Clairmont family. Thanksgiving in New York was not much better. She had been invited to Ellen Gold's festivities, which were more like a glamorous business soirée where she would find herself, unintentionally, being served up as a table centerpiece. For the past few years, she chose to have Thanksgiving dinner at the Bowery Mission in Lower Manhattan, serving instead of being served. Her heart ached for all those of "want" as Dickens would say, existing in a place of such immense wealth.

Sam joined everyone at the dinner table. It was 6:30 and Aunt Clara was serving notice that, once dinner was consumed, no lingering at the dinner table would be allowed this evening. There was much work to be done. Aunt Clara stressed she was very serious about getting everything prepared for Thanksgiving Day. The mood at the table was light, but Martha sensed that something was bothering Sam. Not wishing to break the festive mood, she chose not to say anything just then. When dinner was finished, Martha and Mary took up their responsibility of washing and drying the dishes and pans. Thomas went with Injun Jim down to Old Saybrook to pick up the turkey and baked goods, namely the holiday buns and cookies at the last possible minute to ensure their freshness. Lillith went with Aunt Clara, to keep her company while she visited with the Ruckers, before returning back home to prepare everything for the pies she would be baking at the crack of dawn. There was church to attend tomorrow and then back home to get everything ready for a three pm Thanksgiving sit-down dinner. Yes, chaos, no matter how many attempts to gain control of it, was the order of the day for the holiday Tylers. Martha shuddered at the thought of what Christmas must be like.

Once the kitchen chores had been finished, Martha joined Sam out on the front porch.

"Okay, let's have it. What's bothering you, Mr. Tyler?" She asked.

"What do you mean?" Sam asked.

"Oh, please," said Martha. "I write books, but I also read them, you know. And you, my pensive husband, are someone I read quite well. Do you really think you can hide something from me? And before you answer that, just make sure you never try," she stated with hands placed squarely on her hips and a face filled with mock seriousness.

Sam simply smiled, lowered his shoulders as a sign of surrender, knowing she was right, then took her hands in his and drew her to his chest. It was one of the things that she so loved that he did. But then, there were so many things she loved that he did. Being up so close to him, being held in his strong arms and feeling his heart beat filled her with a pleasure she had never known.

"There's been a murder over in Fenwick," said Sam, softly. He held onto Martha as she made a move to pull back. "Sergeant Varnish called just before supper. He is positive someone was after Veronica Lansing."

"The Veronica Lansing, of stage and screen?" Martha asked.

"The very same," said Sam. "She lives over there."

"I had no idea," said Martha. "Why does Sergeant Varnish believe they were after her?"

"Her housekeeper and the local handyman were found murdered by a delivery boy delivering a full order of holiday foods from a local grocer. Evidently, she was planning to entertain guests for Thanksgiving and was supposed to be home. Varnish has begun an investigation into the two victims, but it doesn't seem likely that they were the intended targets. Of course, if they were there with Ms. Lansing, they would still have been murdered. Poor people, either way, they were going to die today. I have to go over to the crime scene to meet the sergeant. I won't be long. Can you hold down the fort for a while? I promise not to be too long."

"I'm going to hold you to that promise. I have been waiting all day to spend this evening with you. It's not very cold. I'll get some blankets and make sure the coffee is fresh when you get back so we can sit out here and enjoy the moon overlooking the harbor."

Sam kissed her tenderly then took his leave. Martha went back inside to get Mary and set the table for tomorrow's meal.

CHAPTER TWO

Sam drove south down route 154 to Old Saybrook and made a left turn onto the main drag. He continued straight ahead for about 1 and one and a quarter miles down to Saybrook Point where he made a right-hand turn onto Bridge Street, then followed along the road which wound its way along the coast of Long Island Sound. He continued across the causeway which separated the waters of the Sound to his left and a large pond, South Cove, on the right. Just after crossing over, he made a left-hand turn into Nibang Street, the private road leading into the secluded community of Fenwick where the rich and not wishing to be bothered lived. Everything about Fenwick led to the obvious conclusion that these people cherished their privacy. Nibang Street was the only road in or out. Fenwick was famous for its stately old homes in a sequestered setting whose defining architectural feature was characterized by their large grey weathered wooden structures, quite "beachie" in appearance. There was no mistaking it; this was a moneyed community which seemed to be speaking of a quiet, comfortable existence that bordered on the genteel. The homes were the type one might find among the well-heeled on Cape Cod. This was shoreline New England Americana. No Newport over-indulgence on evidence here. These homes were actually lived in the full twelve months of the year. The only absence Veronica

Lansing ever experienced was while she was on location making a movie or starring on Broadway. Other than that, she never strayed too far from her beloved Fenwick.

Veronica had been married to the famous screen actor, Matthew Fontaine, whom she met on the set of the movie "The Saint Louis Story". Their pairing on the silver screen began a whirlwind romance. From the moment they met, Lansing and Fontaine were inseparable. Their married life was the stuff of legends. And then disaster struck. The plane carrying Fontaine went down over Lake Erie. All the passengers were lost. Fontaine had just finished filming the outdoor adventure film "Wilderness Man" and was on his way to make a public promotion appearance in Buffalo. He was never seen again. Fontaine's death left Lansing devastated. She had not appeared in public or any production of any kind in five years. Rumors were circulating that she was about to end her retirement and begin rehearsals for a not as yet named Broadway production. Whatever the case, Veronica Lansing did not come home on this day and as of right now, she was still not there. No one knew where she was.

Sam followed Sergeant Varnish's instructions and made his way over to a very large wooden home sitting on the seawall with a magnificent view of Long Island Sound. He exited his police vehicle and began to make his way through the cluster of police and official vehicles when he spied Howard Grimes, the State's Medical Examiner, exiting the house and making his way down the steps towards his vehicle.

"Sam, my boy, I was wondering if you were going to make an appearance," said the dry witted State ME.

"I'm surprised to see you here," said Sam.

"Veronica Lansing is not exactly 'Mary everyday person'," Grimes quipped.

"The governor, himself, called to ask me to please look into it."

"And?" Sam asked.

"Oh, you're good," said Grimes, "a man of few words."

"What's it like in there?" Sam asked, pointing to the crime scene house.

"Beyond gruesome," said Grimes.

"Really? How so?" said Sam.

"My best guess is that whoever did this was not happy that the Lansing woman was not home to allow them to carry out their murderous plans. Both victims had multiple stab wounds, Sam, and I mean multiple. This was definitely overkill. Someone had to be near insane to do what was done to those two poor people. They were definitely in the wrong place at the wrong time. Be careful when you go in. There's blood everywhere."

Sam shook Grime's hand and thanked him. The ME would be able to tell him more after the bodies were transported up to Meriden. Sam climbed the steps and entered the house just as the handyman's body was being placed in a body bag. Grimes had not exaggerated. Truly, there was blood everywhere. But there was something else. Most of the furniture was overturned and many pieces had the fabrics slashed by what appeared to be angry knife strikes. Someone was really mad and had taken it out on anything and everything.

Sergeant Michael Varnish stood at the far end of the parlor talking to a councilman. Varnish was first generation Swedish-American. He stood about six feet tall with close cropped blond hair. He looked like a guy who had played football in high school, maybe even college. At Sam's suggestion, he had been made temporary Chief of Police until the new one could be appointed. Sam had spent some time with him over coffee at a local restaurant on a few occasions. It was obvious to Sam that Ethan Taft had taught him well. What impressed Sam most was that he began to realize how closely Varnish had observed and learned from Ethan. He seemed to have a very good grasp of police procedures and, more importantly, how to implement them in a town like Saybrook. The town council was so concerned about Sam's report to the state evaluating the way law was conducted in Saybrook that they were ready to agree to just about anything Sam suggested. Before a search could be made to attract and hire a new chief, Sam suggested giving Sergeant Varnish the opportunity to take charge. Varnish was local and that would eliminate the possibility of an outsider coming in and stirring up things, possibly upsetting the locals. There was another inducement that caught the imagination of the town council; bringing someone in from the outside would probably end up being lengthy and expensive. If Varnish could fill the bill, the need for a costly search could be avoided. The town council took a shine to the possibility of that happening. It appeared that Sam really liked Varnish. In its infinite wisdom, the town council figured it wouldn't be so bad if a state police captain were on friendly terms with their chief of police.

Varnish seemed pleased and relieved to see Sam.

"How's it going?" Sam asked.

"This is just awful, Sam," said the sergeant. My mom knows this lady. Her name is Abigail Turner. My mom is going to be devastated. Abigail is a single widow in her fifties who lives alone. She has two grown children, but both live far away. This is real bad, Sam, real bad. Abigail was just such a nice lady. She didn't deserve to die like this."

"No one deserves to die like this," said Sam. "And whoever did this does not deserve to live in a civilized world."

Varnish took Sam through the crime scene which seemed to begin in the parlor, move through the dining room and into the kitchen where the handyman met an equally horrible end. Sam came from money and was very aware of the value and quality of everything in the house. This was a very large home and every inch of it reeked of wealth. It appeared that the owner made sure that nothing, not even the smallest item was anything but the finest money could buy. Just then a strange thought worked its way into Sam's thoughts: "This person has never seen the inside of a thrift store." Of course, Sam was right. Victoria Lansing also came from money. The lady never spent a day in her life in the absence of luxury.

"Has anyone heard from Ms. Lansing?" Sam asked.

"No, not yet," said Varnish who showed some concern. "For all we know, this could very well be abduction and these two victims just could not be left behind as witnesses."

"Well," said Sam taken aback by that thought. "That's something I hadn't even thought of."

"Well, you know Ethan. He tried to think of every possible scenario," Varnish said.

"You're right, of course," said Sam. "It appears you've learned your lessons well, Sergeant."

Varnish gracefully accepted Sam's compliment.

"This is the first real crime around these parts since Ethan's death," said Varnish. "I never realized how much he taught me, how smart he was, Sam. Ethan was an amazing policeman. The more I try to think like him, the easier things get."

Sam was looking at Sergeant Varnish with newer eyes. He had been impressed with the young man up until this point, but what Varnish was saying was true. Nothing of any significance had happened since Ethan's death. And now, Sam was really impressed by the way the sergeant was handling the crime scene. This case could very well be the thing that proved he was indeed ready to take over the reins as Chief of Police for Saybrook.

CHAPTER THREE

As promised, Martha was waiting for Sam on the porch. The children had been tucked in. The coffee was just about ready. Sam told Martha all he had witnessed down in Saybrook. He also expressed concern that Veronica Lansing was nowhere to be found. There was emerging fear that she had been abducted. The woman was an actress. It was inconceivable that she posed a problem for anyone; certainly nothing to warrant the slaughter of two innocent people.

Martha got them both coffee and sat down with Sam on the rattan loveseat. She placed a blanket on both of their legs and smiled as Sam put his arm around her and drew near. Steam rose from their cups adding to the atmosphere of the late fall evening as the dancing reflections of the full moon rose and fell with the gentle rolling of the harbor tide.

There was a large crash that came from the kitchen followed by a large shout by Aunt Clara.

"I'm alright, you two," she bellowed. "You just keep doing what you are doing out there. It's too beautiful a night to be wasted."

Sam looked at Martha and tried to suppress a laugh.

"I just love her," said Martha. "I can honestly say there is never a dull moment around here."

"She saved us all," said Sam. "She's the reason the children are so tough. Aunt Clara refuses to be overwhelmed by anything, and all three of the children have benefited from that. A lot is going to be expected of them when they grow up. Arlen Templeton is a man of power and influence. They will not be able to escape the scrutiny coming their way as they mature. Aunt Clara has had much to say about the people they will become. I can never thank her enough. I confess, when Sally died, I was lost when it came to knowing what to do for them. I'm a policeman. My job requires most of my time. Thank God for Aunt Clara."

After a few moments, Martha and Sam began to embrace the silence of the night. They were content to sit very close to each other and allow the fresh cool breezes to carry their thoughts away. The warmth of their bodies being so close didn't hurt.

CHAPTER FOUR

The chaos had begun. Everyone was up and over at Aunt Clara's for breakfast. Aunt Clara had been up since four am. The pies were in the oven, the coffee was made and the pancakes were on the stove. The service at St. John's was at ten am. Aunt Clara pulled the pies out of the oven and placed them in towels on the window sills. Injun Jim took the twenty-three pound turkey, fully prepared, and placed it in the oven. It would be his job to keep watch over the house and the turkey in the oven until the family arrived back from service.

The congregation at St. John's Episcopal Church was more than ready to be in church giving thanks for the many blessings being pointed out by Pastor Linus Foster. A war was raging in Europe and Japan and our young men were valiantly fighting for the many blessings those at home were enjoying, namely, freedom, peace and the knowledge that those fighting over there were doing everything in their power to prevent a war from coming to American soil. Pastor Linus was in rare form. More than once the normally placid pastor allowed his emotions to escalate his voice to fever pitch. He reminded them that New England was the place where the celebration of Thanksgiving was first celebrated, and now hundreds of years later, we still set this day aside to celebrate the gift of God to us in these United States of America. Pastor

Foster kept reminding the congregation of the wars and the terrible toll of lost lives to preserve this great nation. He reminded them that this day was one for remembering all the blessings of their lives and the terrible price that had to be paid for those blessings.

As Sam and the family walked down the steps after the service, Sam noticed a Saybrook policeman standing there attempting to get his attention. Sam instructed the family to head home, assuring them that he would follow shortly. Martha and Aunt Clara made their goodbyes to Pastor Linus, took the children in hand and headed down Main Street.

The police officer introduced himself and told Sam that Veronica Lansing had returned home at two am. She had been to a concert at the Shubert in New Haven and then a party at the home of a wealthy New Haven benefactor of the arts. She was shocked to hear what had happened to her people and totally at a loss to know why something like that should occur in her home. Sam was relieved to hear that, at least, a kidnapping had not occurred nor the tedious investigation that would have followed, Lansing being a major star and the area's crown jewel to boot, was not necessary. It wasn't much, but it was much better than a kidnapping. Sam thanked the officer and headed home to join the family after being informed that Ms. Lansing spent the night with one of her neighbors.

Sam filled Martha in on what he had learned from the officer. They both agreed that it was too soon to draw any conclusions. There were a few unanswered questions that needed to be addressed before any attempts at motive could be found.

"Where did you leave off with Sergeant Varnish?" Martha asked.

"He's going to question Ms. Lansing as soon as possible and keep checking on the two victims to see if there's any connection there," said Sam.

"You think you will be involved in this case?" Martha asked.

"The governor called Grimes personally. I'm sure I'll be hearing from him, one way or another," said Sam.

Just then, the phone rang. Sam looked at the phone, then back to Martha.

"Wanta' bet?" said Sam.

CHAPTER FIVE

Another time-honored Thanksgiving tradition of the Tylers was for Sam to take the children to visit Arlen and Betty Templeton at noon. The Templetons would use any excuse to see and spoil their only grandchildren. Only Christmas could create more excitement for Mary, Thomas and Lillith. This would be Martha's first formal visit with the children's grandparents and she was just a little apprehensive. As Sam pulled his car onto the courtyard of the Templeton residence he noticed a large black Packard sedan parked there.

"That's odd," said Sam. "Their guests don't usually arrive until around three. Arlen likes to start later and go well into the evening."

"Well, you know how important the children are to him. I can't imagine anyone being here that would take his attention away from them," said Martha.

"You're probably right. There's only one way to find out, isn't there?" said Sam.

Sam parked the car and walked around to open the doors for Martha and the children. Squeals of delight rose up as Arlen and Betty appeared. Arlen always made a big display of joy when the children visited. It was not an act. He truly loved them and was so grateful for any time he and Betty could have them over for a visit.

After much hugging and kissing was completed, Arlen turned his attention to Sam, then Martha.

"So glad to see you, Martha," said Arlen. "You really should visit more often. Betty has a million questions to ask you about your books and New York, of course."

Martha thanked Arlen. He really seemed sincere and went out of his way to make her feel welcome. Betty could not wait to give her a hug before they all went inside.

"You're wondering about the Packard, aren't you?" said Arlen as he and Sam walked into the large Templeton home.

Sam simply smiled. "Knowing you, I'm sure you can't wait to tell me," said Sam.

Both men shared a laugh. Betty took the children into the parlor while Arlen directed Martha and Sam to the heated enclosed sun porch. Neither could believe their eyes. There, sitting regally in a large white rattan chair was none other than Veronica Lansing. The Lansing woman rose to greet them. She was taller than Sam or Martha imagined. Lansing stood about five feet nine inches tall with a figure that was trim and athletic for a woman in her late forties. She was also prettier in person.

"Sam, Martha, meet Veronica Lansing," said Arlen, with a special gleam in his eyes.

Veronica greeted them warmly, but it was obvious she was not in her most festive mood.

"I am so sorry to hear of your troubles," said Martha.

Veronica thanked her. "I am sure your husband has some questions he would like to ask me. I will be glad to answer them if it will aid him in finding those who did such a terrible thing in my home. But," she paused, "it is you, young lady that I really want to talk to. I just love your books. There is much talk in Hollywood that they may soon find their way onto the screen. I can't wait to see all the infighting that will surely be going on over who will play the female romantic leads," she said, showing a look of sheer delight.

Arlen took his leave to join Betty and the children. Sam spent a few moments with Veronica. It was obvious she had no clue as to the reason behind yesterday's occurrence. She was totally forthcoming, holding nothing back. After a few moments, Sam came to realize that the woman really had nothing to offer. At that very moment, Sam found himself holding out hope that Sergeant Varnish had something useful to tell him. He excused himself, went to the kitchen to get some coffee and then called Varnish down in Saybrook to see if he had anything to offer.

It was obvious that the children were having a great time with their grandparents. Sam could only imagine all the gifts they were getting. Betty bought everything for them at Saks Fifth Avenue in Manhattan and nowhere else. Sweaters, skirts, trousers, winter coats and anything else she could think of, that was Sam's gift to Betty Templeton. Sam had made it very clear that she had complete and total freedom to give them whatever she wished. The Templetons were so grateful to Sam for that.

Veronica took one of Martha's hands and led her to a seat near hers. It was obvious she was anxious to get Martha alone.

"Please forgive me, my dear," she said, but yesterday's events have really shaken me. It is so kind of you to provide me with a little diversion. I cannot believe my luck. I have so wanted to meet you. Here we are, neighbors, and I can't believe we haven't gotten together. I know you are busy teaching and dealing with your new family, and of course your writing, but I am so glad we could meet, even under such ghastly circumstances."

"I want you to know that I was completely unaware you were so close. I assure you I would have used any excuse to attempt to meet you, but now that we have met, I hope we will be able to visit and spend more time together. There was so much you can tell me about Hollywood and of course the Theatre. I'm sure you have a million fascinating things you can share with me," said Martha.

Martha was just what Veronica needed at this time. They spoke for about an hour and then it was time to take the children back home. Sam could see that it was going to take some effort to pry these two apart. Veronica's strong hug caught Martha completely by surprise.

"This is quite an amazing woman you have here, Captain," said Veronica, extending her hand to shake Sam's. "Thank you so much for sharing her with me. Please feel free to call me whenever you wish and please keep me informed about your investigation, if that is permissible for you. Abigail was very dear to me. Her loss is incomprehensible for me right now. But to have been murdered in such a horrible fashion, and in my home, makes it all worse than you can imagine."

Sam's look showed he understood her feelings. He thanked her for her time, gathered the children and all of their many gifts. They made their goodbyes with the Templetons and headed home. Arlen told Sam that he would be calling later to talk to Sam about Veronica. But now it was time for Aunt Clara's Thanksgiving culinary extravaganza. Holiday meals with Aunt Clara were a joyful, if not raucous, experience.

CHAPTER SIX

Thanksgiving dinner had been consumed. As usual, it was turkey with all the trimmings. Aunt Clara outdid herself. Accompanying the magnificent bird was Aunt Clara's famous stuffing, country style glazed ham, mashed potatoes in a bowl of giblet gravy, green beans in a cheese sauce, baked mushrooms filled with Aunt Clara's stuffing, cranberry sauce and mountains of dinner buns. A short rest was required before dessert was to be served. Sam took Martha and the children and made their way up Platt Street towards North Main Street and turned left, went over to Main, made another left and started heading down Main Street to walk off some of the overeating that had just taken place.

Wanda Loomis and her family, along with her brother Louis, who now operated Zuckerman's, were standing outside of the Black Swan. She too had decided to take her family for a little post-dinner exercise. Like the Tylers, they also had been guilty of holiday overindulgence. Everyone joined in on the conversation. The children were chatting away while the adults exchanged pleasantries.

Sam looked over at Martha and saw a strange smile on her face. He wasn't quite sure what she was thinking.

"Is everything all right?" He asked.

"Oh, Sam, thank you for this," Martha said as she took hold of his hand. "I have never been so happy. I love being here with you and the family, and everything about our life together. I cannot believe how happy you all have made me."

Just then, Martha felt a hand tugging at hers. It was Lillith.

"Oh, Mommy," Lillith said, "don't you just love it here?"

"More than you can ever imagine," Martha responded.

"I think God is pretty smart, don't you?" Lillith said. It caused Martha to pause with a questioning look on her face.

"What do you mean, honey?" Martha asked.

"Well, he brought you to us, didn't he?" Lillith answered.

* * *

Everyone just sat there at the table. No one seemed to be able to move. Aunt Clara had served up fresh baked apple, pumpkin and custard pies, all served with vanilla and chocolate ice cream and topped with homemade whipped cream. The adults had coffee, the children had cola. Injun Jim confessed he could not ever remember consuming so much food. He summed up everyone's thoughts when he claimed they were completely defenseless to exercise restraint for such a sumptuous meal. Sam noticed that for one brief moment, Aunt Clara actually smiled at James White Feather. Now that was something. Also, not lost on the adults was the fact that Mary and Thomas actually spent hours in each other's company without so much as a hint of an argument. That was really something.

Martha surveyed the scene. It seemed like hours had passed without her being able to suppress a smile that appeared to have taken up a permanent residence on her face. She shocked everyone when she announced that she would like to offer a prayer now, after the dinner. Everyone was touched as Martha thanked God for her family and her life and for the three wonderful children to bless her life. This was the first time any of them had ever heard Martha pray out loud. She made it perfectly clear that she now fully understood the real meaning of Thanksgiving Day.

Sam took Arlen's call around eight pm. Arlen informed him

that Veronica Lansing would be spending a few days with Betty and him. It seems that Betty and she were old chums. Their families were very close. Where she would go after that would be determined by how long it would take to restore her home after the police were finished with their investigation and her house could be thoroughly cleaned, painted and refurbished. The Lansing woman was more shaken than she let on. Her home was her sanctuary and it had been horribly violated. It was too early to tell, but she thought she might go into Manhattan and stay at the Waldorf. Arlen would keep Sam in the loop. Veronica had told Arlen to tell Sam that no matter where she was, he had full access to her. Of course, if he saw fit to bring Martha along, that would not be a problem. Sam laughed at that and thanked Arlen. He also thanked him, tongue-in-cheek, for the mountain of presents that he and Betty had showered on the children. Arlen hung up with a smile.

Martha listened well to all that Sam told her about his conversation with Arlen. The last little revelation concerning her joining Sam if he needed to see Veronica made Martha smile. They put the children to bed and sat in front of the roaring fire in their living room.

"I was wondering if you'd be interested in taking the family to the Christmas show at Radio City," said Martha.

"Wow," said Sam, who pushed back and ran his fingers through his hair. "What a great idea. You think we can still get tickets?"

"Have you met Ellen Gold?" Martha asked.

"Foolish question," said Sam.

"I thought it might be nice to go in on the weekend two weeks before Christmas. We can stay at the Plaza. The children would probably love to take a ride through Central Park. We can do lunch at Tavern on the Green. It's all right there. And of course, Santa at Macy's for Lillith. Then I thought we could go over to St. Patrick's, Saks and Tiffany's to see the windows and then Rockefeller Center. What do you think?" Martha asked.

"I only wish you had given this some thought," said Sam.

"What?" "Oh, very funny," said Martha. "Well, what do you think?"

"I think it's a good thing that you are such a rich successful author," said Sam. Before Martha could respond, he took her in his arms and held her close.

"We are so lucky to have you." he said. "But, honestly, between you and the Templetons, these children are going to be impossible to deal with."

"Is that a yes?" Martha asked.

"That's a yes," said Sam.

The brisk New England air was always inviting to her. She loved the cool crispness of it, the "good to be alive" feeling she always got when she left the house. Of course, it helped to be well wrapped against the cold, which she was. She felt warm and cozy in her camel hair Burberry coat, Russian sable fur hat, and the matching gloves and scarf that Aunt Clara had knit for her. Bundled up as she was, she would have felt comfortable at the South Pole.

CHAPTER SEVEN

Sam closed the car door behind Thomas, walked around, got in and started the motor. Without saying a word, he exited the grammar school parking lot and headed home. Neither he nor Thomas said a word. The trip took only a few minutes and now they were in front of Aunt Clara's home.

Aunt Clara, Mary and Lillith were waiting on the porch. Sam could not remember the last time he had been summoned to the principal's office because of a problem with one of the children. Thomas got out, angrily, and stomped up the steps to Aunt Clara's waiting arms. As soon as Aunt Clara held him close he began to cry. Sam followed him up the stairs and looked directly into Clara's sympathetic eyes.

"Mary told me what happened at school today," said Aunt Clara.

"Well, I wish someone would tell me," said Sam.

"Didn't anyone speak to you?" Aunt Clara asked.

"As I understand it, Thomas and his teacher had a spirited disagreement," said Sam.

"I'll let Mary tell you. She was there," said Aunt Clara.

"Thomas' teacher, Mrs. Callahan, took exception to Thomas disagreeing with her. Thomas is fortunate to be close to Grandpa Templeton, he talks to him on the telephone all the time. So when he heard his teacher telling the class something he knew was wrong, according to Grandpa, he could not restrain himself. You know Thomas. Well, Mrs. Callahan tried to bully Thomas, but he refused to back down. Grandpa Templeton told us never to back away from something when you know you are in the right," said Mary.

"You know this Mrs. Callahan?" Sam said.

"Yes, if you recall, I had her for fourth grade two years ago," said Mary.

"I don't recall you having any trouble with her," said Sam. "Why is that?"

Mary did not answer. She simply looked to Sam, then to Thomas and then back to Sam. Her eyes grew larger. It was as if they were saying "You really need to ask that question?"

It was a point well made. Thomas had a knack for driving people crazy with his constant questioning. Normally, it was harmless, but not this time. It concerned the war and Thomas did not like some of the remarks his teacher was airing before the class. He found them inappropriate. The teacher got so agitated that instead of sending him down to the principal's office, she angrily collected her things and left the building. The principal was both confused and mortified. She contacted Sam and waited desperately for him to come to see her.

The Tyler children were brought up to never be disrespectful to anyone, especially their elders. They were considered the nicest behaved children in the whole school. Everyone loved the Tyler children, everyone except Mrs. Callahan.

Sam was well aware of what the real problem was: Arlen Templeton. These were his grandchildren and no one wanted to arouse the ire of their grandfather. Arlen's affection for the Tyler children was near fanatical and no one wanted to lock horns with the most powerful man in town, especially when it concerned his grandchildren. Sam assured the principle that he would speak to his father-in-law and take care of the situation. But first, he wanted to get all the facts straight. He really wished Martha was home from Albertus Magnus to help him out.

Thomas began to plead his case. "Mrs. Callahan was bullying, Daddy. "She said the president lied to the people about not bringing America into the war. She said he probably turned a blind eye so that the Japanese could attack Pearl Harbor. He could then use that as an excuse to bring us into the war. I told her that was a lie and that our uncle was killed at Pearl Harbor and the president wouldn't allow something like that to happen. She said we were too young to understand such things and I told her I was old enough to know the truth."

Before Sam could say anything, Mary chimed in. "Mrs. Callahan always acts like she is so superior, like she knows so much more than anyone else. It's easy to bully fourth-graders. She got what she deserved, the 'old battle-ax'."

"Whoa, young lady. Battle-ax?" Sam said. "Where on earth did you hear that?"

Mary did not answer, but Sam had a pretty good idea where that comment came from. He looked menacingly over at Aunt Clara who could not help herself. She lowered her head and placed her hand over her mouth attempting to suppress laughter.

"Oh, perfect," said Sam. "Well done Auntie dear."

"Thomas, we'll talk later," said Sam.

"Are you mad at me, Daddy?" Thomas asked. "I bet Grandpa Arlen would have done the same thing."

Sam knew that was not quite the truth. Arlen would have done more, much more.

Sam took Thomas in his arms and held him close. "Of course not, Thomas, I'm not mad at you, son. But I do have to sort this thing out."

Sam was concerned about what things would be like for Thomas tomorrow and the rest of the school year in Mrs. Callahan's classroom, that is, if she came back the next day. He was worried that it might prove very uncomfortable for him. He didn't really know Mrs. Callahan. He had met her once at a parent-teacher conference when Mary was her student. But, then again, no one ever had a problem with Mary. Sam decided to wait for Martha to get home so they could agree on how to proceed. Then Sam smiled as a strange thought occurred to him. Mary had defended her brother. Could that be a sign?

CHAPTER EIGHT

Folks in the eastern part of the country were naturally focused on the news concerning the war in Europe. Obviously, the greatest number of people who migrated to New York and the East Coast were of western and eastern European ancestry, as well of those of the British Isles. Many still had relatives there and were naturally concerned for their safety. People of the Jewish faith had greater concerns as they were now well aware of the atrocities being carried out on the Jewish people by the Germans who admittedly sought to exterminate them.

It was at this time that the war in Europe and Africa began to take a painfully slow turn in favor of the Allied forces. Patton had become a national hero as had Montgomery who symbolized British tenacity and reserve. The Russians were proving to be the immovable objects to Hitler's near suicidal troop advances into a place the Germans had neither the experience nor desire to be. The weather in Russia was just plain brutally cold. And the losses being inflicted by the Russians were beginning to add further unrest in the military community that already was beginning to turn on Hitler. But the war really was a worldwide event.

"December 7th, a day that will live in infamy," were the dramatic words spoken before the joint houses of the American Congress by the President of the United States. The devastating attack on a sleepy, unsuspecting Pearl Harbor in the Hawaiian Islands had infuriated the nation which, until this point, had no quarrel with Japan. But now, a two-year-old child could have easily talked the Americans into declaring war on Japan and their allies in the west, the Germans and Italians. A once reluctant America was chomping at the bit to settle the score. And so, America did go to war. But wars of this magnitude are not won in a few days.

Amazingly, the Americans embraced the adjustments that had to be made on the home front. In cities like Bridgeport, one of the great war machine meccas, women were required to take their places on the giant machines vacated by the men who were marching off to war. Before long, the American soldier became canonized as G.I. Joe. But the soldiers were not alone in gaining a name that would be endeared to the free world. "Rosie the Riveter" became the poster girl for the women who labored tirelessly to support the troops by providing whatever machines or weaponry necessary.

A new craze sprang up on the West Coast. Japan's attack of Pearl Harbor, so close to California, brought an amazing and mostly unproven state of paranoia. Hollywood was already the world capital of the make-believe, so it was not so surprising that imagination swiftly began to take the place of reality and reason.

On one lovely Southern California evening, a famous Hollywood comedienne was driving her convertible home along the coastal highway, embracing the warm gentle breezes caressing her welcoming face. Suddenly, she noticed a series of blinking lights coming from about a mile out on the ocean. She was convinced that it was a signal being sent by a Japanese submarine. She immediately notified the police, radio stations, and of course, the Los Angeles Times. Instantaneous insanity erupted and from that moment on, every imaginable scenario that could be drummed up by the human mind reigned supreme in Southern California.

Unfortunately, this only fueled the fire and gave credence to the "internment camps" being set up and operated where those of

Japanese ancestry were being forced into bondage. This was a most sad occurrence. Many innocent Americans of Japanese descent were forced into disgraceful, deplorable conditions.

In the war effort, America possessed two military heroes of gigantic stature, one for each theater of operation. On the far eastern front, it was General Douglas MacArthur, a tall, self-assured, self-promoting individual who had spent much of his career in the Far East, and in the Philippines in particular. General Dwight David Eisenhower was the supreme commander of the war in the west. Ike, as he was affectionately known to his troops, was a gifted leader who shunned calling attention to himself. As far as the president was concerned, Ike was a blessing. MacArthur on the other hand, was someone who required tolerance and patience. Both were brilliant warriors who never considered the thought of defeat. Each was perfect for his calling.

As far as Thomas was concerned, Sam was guardedly proud of his little man who stood up for what was right. Mrs. Callahan was just one of a very large group of individuals who shared in the belief of the president's duplicity where our entrance to the war was concerned. Sam's main concern was in guiding Thomas through the storm that would surely follow. But he did not want Thomas to feel that because he was a Tyler and, of course, a blood relative to Arlen Templeton, that that would automatically entitle him to a *get out of jail free pass*. Sam had witnessed the difficulties being experienced by many of his wealthy school chums who simply could not handle the hard realities of life unless mommy and daddy, along with their money, were there to protect them. He was absolutely committed to making sure that was not going to happen to Thomas. Fortunately, Arlen stood right by his side. This was a good thing.

CHAPTER NINE

Sam and Matt D'Onofrio of the New Haven Police Department were enjoying their coffee an' at Willoughby's on Chapel. Sam called him to see if he had heard any rumblings concerning the dual homicides at the home of Veronica Lansing. The Lansing woman had been to the Shubert Theater that evening and then the home of Warren Carstairs, a well-known millionaire and patron of the arts. The whole thing just made no sense. Sergeant D'Onofrio had to agree.

The two old friends talked about the war and how much they missed the summer baseball games between the rival police departments of the shoreline towns between New Haven and Saybrook. Now, many of their comrades had gone off to war, and sadly, some had given their lives for their country.

"Phone call for Sergeant D'Onofrio," came loudly from the back room. Matt took the call, but was informed that it was for Sam. It was the governor's office, requesting Sam go immediately to Hartford.

"How can I refuse?" said Sam, with just a touch of sarcasm.

"It's two thirty in the afternoon," said D'Onofrio. "By the time you get there and get back home it will be quite late."

"Gives you a good idea what the phrase 'public servant' stands for, doesn't it?" said Sam.

D'Onofrio laughed. "Yeah, we are at his Majesty's beck and call," referring to the governor. "It must be something really important for the governor to make you come up there now. He's usually out of his office by three. This will definitely interfere with his afternoon golf game."

"Your treat, right?" said Sam as he got to his feet and headed out the door to his vehicle.

"Wow," said D'Onofrio, "everybody's servant, and benefactor too."

Sam knew the best route to take would be to head over to Route #15, a highway with no traffic lights. Better known as the Merritt Parkway, Route #15 was the only true highway in Connecticut, running north and south through some of the most rural parts of the state. It connected to the Berlin Turnpike at about midpoint of the state. On a good day, it made for a very enjoyable ride. To reach Route #15, Sam would have to take Dixwell Avenue to cross over to the other side of New Haven. With any luck, that would take about ten minutes. The trip to Hartford from there, if all went well, would take at least an hour. The best he could hope for was to reach Hartford by five pm. It would already be dark. If the meeting with the governor lasted only one hour he might get home before eight pm He would have to take Route #9, a road that had few traffic lights. In fact it had no illumination. Sam was less than enthused at his prospects. He found himself wondering, could this Lansing woman be that important?

Along the way, Sam found himself thinking about his most unlikely friendship with a New Haven police officer. Matt D'Onofrio's early years did not resemble anything like Sam's. Matt was a tough street kid who grew up in the Grand Avenue section of New Haven. The area was ninety percent Italian and one hundred percent tough. It was said that if you reached twelve years of age and not had at least three major fistfights, you had never left your home.

Sam, on the other hand, grew up with both money and prestige, two things the D'Onofrio family had no knowledge of. Matt was working class, Sam was first class. Sam went to Avon and UMass. Matt went to the school of hard knocks. Sam's regard for D'Onofrio was born out of the knowledge that he was as honest and as hardworking as any police officer Sam had ever met. And he was smart too, street smart, which is something Sam greatly admired in him. Through the years, D'Onofrio proved to be one of the most respected police officers New Haven had to offer.

The governor stood to his feet as Sam entered the room. He was not alone. Sam was surprised Buckley was not there.

"Come in, Captain, so glad you could come on such short notice," said the governor.

"I assumed it was pretty important for you to track me down, Governor," said Sam, with an earnest, friendly tone.

"You were right, Captain. Allow me to introduce Captain Palmer and Commander Mickelson of the U.S. Navy," said the governor.

"Gentlemen, this is Captain Samuel Tyler of the Connecticut State Police."

Sam and the officers shook hands. Everyone took their seats. Just then, Buckley came rushing unceremoniously through the door.

"Sorry I'm late, gentlemen, traffic from Boston was heavy," said Buckley. "Sam," Buckley continued, "these two naval officers here have some information that the governor and I are convinced has something to do with the double homicides down in Fenwick."

Sam looked over in the direction of the two naval officers. Commander Mickelson did the talking. The commander was older and shorter than the captain, but spoke with the kind of authority one would need to captain a Navy vessel. He looked to be in his late 40s, with hair graying at the temples. He had a slight Midwestern accent.

"Three days ago," he began, "Commander Wilson Boland, of

U.S. Navy Intelligence, left Washington by train for a meeting in New York City with high-ranking officers of the Army and Marine Corps. We knew he was planning to make a side trip to Saybrook to spend the holiday with his sister before going on to New York for his meeting on Friday. The commander never showed up for his Friday meeting and we have not received any word from him. That is not procedure. Given the commander's exemplary service record, I fear something has happened to him. He simply would not do something like this unless something wrong had happened to him."

Sam hesitated to respond. He attempted to process this information before asking any questions.

"Would it be permissible for you to tell me the nature of his business in New York?" Sam asked.

"All I can tell you, Captain, is that the commander had in his possession some highly classified documents detailing three possible campaign scenarios for the war in France and parts of Germany. If these plans get into the wrong hands, it could cause much concern for our troops over there. The plans themselves are merely proposals, but more importantly, they show our thought process for the war in that area. If these plans ended up in the hands of German intelligence, they would be able to surmise and hypothesize scenarios we might be considering. In essence, they would be privy to our general beliefs and attitudes for warfare in that campaign arena. This would not be a good thing."

"How does all of this have anything to do with the deaths in Saybrook?" Sam asked.

"Commander Boland is the brother of Veronica Lansing. It was she whom he was planning to visit," said Commander Mickelson.

Things were starting to become much clearer to Sam. At least now, he had something to go on. It wasn't much, yet, but it was a whole lot better than nothing. Well, maybe not a whole lot better.

"As I see it, we don't even know if the Lansing woman ever

met up with him, and more importantly, we need to find out how anyone could have known his plans to go and spend Thanksgiving with his sister," said Sam. "And, whoever did know obviously planned to go to Fenwick and deal with him there. We are going on the assumption that the killer or killers were very angry that they missed him. Now, I'm wondering if he were there, given the ferocity of their actions, would everyone, including Victoria Lansing, have been dealt with in the same way. We still don't know what their intent was, but I am pretty sure they all would have been killed," said Sam.

The commander gestured that he was in complete agreement with Sam's line of reasoning.

"Commander Thomas, down in Milford, said you were smart, Captain. He wasn't mistaken. I'm glad you are the person we will be dealing with. I'm sure you understand the gravity of the situation," said the captain.

"You can bet on that, sir," said Sam. "The Lansing woman attended the theater and a private party in New Haven the evening of the murders. I'm assuming she had a room at the Taft Hotel. That would be her style. It's possible she and her brother met up there. In any case, New Haven looks like a good place to start to try to find out if whatever happened to the commander took place there. Of course, that's going on the assumption he reached New Haven and made contact with his sister. I have a very good working relationship with the New Haven Police Department. I assure you they are top-notch. I know they will work tirelessly to aid in this matter."

"I don't have to tell you that the person I answer directly to is the president himself, do I?" said the commander.

"Of course not, commander, but now that you have, I understand completely. There will be much scrutiny, here in Connecticut, I'm sure. We won't let you or the president down," said Sam.

"I'm confident you won't," said the commander. "By the way, Captain Tyler, the president appears to be a fan. I think I can see why. Whatever you need, and I mean whatever you need, you call me directly," the commander said as he handed Sam his card.

The two officers got to their feet, shook hands with everyone and left. All during that time, the governor never said a word. And even now he waited for Sam to speak. When Buckley started to say something, he was waved off by the governor. It was Sam's moment.

"I won't let you down either, sir," said Sam to the governor. "I am well aware of the pressure you will be under during our investigation. I'll pull out all the stops on this one. I really did not like what I saw over in Fenwick. If I have anything to say about it, no one is going to come into our state and get away with acting in such a barbaric manner. Those two innocent people did not deserve the horror inflicted on them."

"I know you will, Sam," said the governor, finally, in an uncharacteristic quiet tone. "We too are grateful that you will be the one to be handling the investigation. And one more thing; the Navy commander's offer goes double for us, Sam. Whatever you need...."

CHAPTER TEN

It was shortly after five thirty pm when Sam pulled out of the capitol parking lot. He drove across Hartford, heading southward towards Route #9 and home. It was already dark. The road conditions were good. The skies were clear, sporting a three-quarter moon that bore a slight orange tint. Many stars were in view, suggesting a clear, crisp autumn evening.

Sam reached Route 9 and began the long ride back to Essex. After a while, he realized he was not observing the forty-five mph speed limit. His mind was fixed on the story Commander Mickelson had related to him and the governor. He understood the incredible importance of locating Commander Boland and those secret documents.

No mention had been made of Victoria Lansing seeing her brother in New Haven. Sam had to wonder, did the commander ever meet up with his sister in New Haven? He'd have to contact D'Onofrio and ask him to go over to the Taft and see if the commander had been there. He would need to find out when Victoria Lansing changed her plans and how she got word to her brother who obviously did not go to Fenwick; or did he? That was one more real possibility, one he had not thought of until now. Things were getting complicated. But of course they were. No matter how seemingly implausible the thought, a war of espionage kept finding its ugly way into Sam's life and jurisdiction. He smiled to himself knowing Martha's reaction to all this; another book, perhaps?

By the time Sam pulled into the driveway he had literally worn himself out hashing and rehashing everything he knew up to this point, over and over in his brain. He sat for a long moment before exiting the car. He looked up in time to see Martha coming down the back steps from Aunt Clara's to greet him.

"Oh, boy," Martha said, as Sam wearily got out and closed the car door. "It appears my big strong handsome man has had himself quite a day."

"That's not the half of it," said Sam. He kissed his wife, placed his arm around her and headed up towards Aunt Clara's kitchen.

"Just in time for dinner," said Aunt Clara. "We were about to give up on you."

"Suppertime, children," Aunt Clara called out to Mary, Thomas and Lillith who were in the parlor. They came running into the kitchen, greeted their dad and immediately took their seats at the table. It was nearly an hour past their suppertime. But it was Saturday night. Eating a little later would not have a negative effect on them for Sunday morning. Sam prayed over the food and a lively evening of dinner and conversation began.

After dinner, Sam took the children home and he and Martha got them settled into their rooms before bedtime. He joined Martha down in the parlor and fixed a fire. With a warm fire and some red wine he began to tell her all that had happened up in Hartford. Martha listened with great interest and told her husband how confident she was that he would get to the bottom of things. Her words were pleasing to Sam's weary ears, but he was sure he could see the wheels churning around in Martha's brain; those *"this would make a swell idea for a book"* wheels.

* * *

It was Monday and the holiday weekend was over. The children were back in school and Martha was on her way to the train station to get the train to New Haven for work. Sam called Matt

D'Onofrio in New Haven to fill him in on his visit with the governor.

"Conspiracy and sabotage seem to follow you around, paison'," said D'Onofrio.

"Yeah, just what I need right now," said Sam. "This is such a special time for the family. We do so many things together during the Christmas season. The children really look forward to this time. And I guess I do too."

"Well, at least you've got help, my friend. I'm sure Martha will be able to pitch in," said Matt.

"You're right, but I was hoping we could enjoy the season without any outside distractions. This is Martha's first Christmas with us. I was kind of hoping...," Sam's words trailed off.

"That's some lady you got there, my friend. What little I know of Martha, she'll probably have a ball with all of this," said Matt.

"You know, you're probably right. But listen, I need you to go over to the Taft and see if the Lansing woman did stay there, and see if she had any visitors, namely a Navy commander."

"You got it, Captain. And by the way, next time you call me, ask for Captain D'Onofrio."

"Are you serious?" Sam exclaimed. "That's great news. Congratulations, Matt. I can't wait to tell Martha,."

"Thanks, pal. Listen, I got a good friend in Manhattan. I'll have him check to see if anyone saw this Commander Boland. I'll check with the railroad to see who the conductors were on that run up from D.C. It may take a few days, but I'll get some names and as much information as I can for you. Cheer up, Sam, it's 'Christmas Time in the City'."

Sam laughed and placed the receiver down and disconnected. It was a comfort to know that Matt would be handling the New Haven investigation for him. It was also great news to hear of Matt's promotion.

Sam got in touch with Commander Mickelson to see if he could arrange to get passage to Washington and get clearance to meet and interview everyone who would have knowledge of the missing commander's itinerary. Mickelson liked the idea a lot and told Sam to go to Saybrook Point as soon as he could. A transport helicopter out of Sikorsky in Stratford would be there to pick him up and bring him back to Sikorsky. From there, he would join Sam and fly to Washington to give Sam whatever assistance he required.

Sam called Martha over at Albertus Magnus and told her he would be going to Washington D.C. He would call her later to let her know if he would be staying overnight. He went home and quickly packed an overnight bag and headed to Saybrook Point. He called Sergeant Varnish of the Saybrook Police Department to meet him there and take charge of his cruiser. Varnish agreed and looked forward to bringing Sam up to speed with his investigation into the background of the two victims.

CHAPTER ELEVEN

Late September had produced an extraordinary occurrence. Ezra Tinsley's career and life were considered dead in the water, as the saying goes. The poor man seemed totally lost. He hardly left his home and when he did it was mostly under the cover of darkness. Allison's indiscretions, leading to her acts of scandal and treason left him devastated and covered in shame. It seemed to him that he had been deserted by the whole world. In all fairness, nothing that transpired during that time was his fault. The truth was, he truly tried his utmost to rein in his rebellious daughter, but everyone knew that Allison was utterly impossible to deal with. Allison did, however, possess one great talent. One which she achieved a one hundred percent success rating in. Everyone disliked her. In fact, you would be hard pressed to find anyone who could tolerate being in her company for more than a few minutes. She possessed a magical ability to offend and annoy. Ezra never stood a chance with her.

At midday, on a Tuesday in late September, as Ezra was returning home from a court appearance in New Haven, his driver noticed a female sitting on the front porch. He pulled the car around and parked. He got out and walked around to open the door for Ezra and then realized who the unscheduled guest was. It was none other than his ex-wife, Mary Ellen Tinsley, Allison's mother.

Ezra exited the car and stood still for a long moment. He had no idea why Mary Ellen would be here. The ex-Mrs. Tinsley had been enjoying a most comfortable life of leisure in San Francisco. The Tinsley family, thanks to its immense wealth, had seen to it that she was well taken care of, that is, as long as she did nothing to cause any trouble for Ezra or the Tinsley family. As long as she played ball, as the saying goes, she would live a life very characteristic of a gay divorcé.

They met halfway up the walk and an awkward silence ensued. Ezra dismissed his driver. Now he and Mary Ellen were quite alone.

"Oh, Ezra," said Mary Ellen, breaking the silence. "I am so sorry to hear of all your troubles."

Ezra remained silent. He really did have nothing to say. At least no words came to mind. After all that had happened, he never imagined seeing Mary Ellen again.

"I know you are questioning why I am here," said Mary Ellen.

Ezra simply gestured yes. He did not have the strength to have a confrontation with his ex-wife. Finally, he spoke.

"Is there something wrong in San Francisco? Is the money not enough?" He asked.

"Oh, Ezra, the money is more than enough. When I realized you were left all alone to face these troubles, I had to come back. I am so angry with myself for ever deserting you. Our life together was so uncomplicated; I never envisioned something like this happening. We had it so easy. But now, I realize that a wife of someone of your stature and position must anticipate the possibility of life not always being so devoid of real problems. Won't you let me stay with you, at least until you get back on your feet again? No strings attached, no payoffs, just allow me to do what I should have been doing all along," said Mary Ellen.

Ezra suggested they go up and sit on the porch.

"Aren't you enjoying your life in San Francisco?" Ezra asked.

"If you mean the parties and social functions, I guess you

could say yes. But being there made me realize that all the money in the world could never take the place of life with someone you love and want to be with," said Mary Ellen. "If I went on another date with one more eligible bachelor, one of our social standing, I think I would scream. The whole social scene is so superficial, so pretentious. I couldn't stand it any longer. I missed Connecticut so. I missed you, Ezra, even though I don't expect you to believe me."

"I never thought I would see you again," said Ezra. "I really do have a pretty good idea why you left me."

"You do? Well, I'm having some trouble with that," said Mary Ellen. "I really believe that I just took so much for granted and became so detached that I lost sight of what life is all about; family first."

"I guess I tried too hard to make life too easy," said Ezra. "I guess I never learned how to be comfortable with wealth that I did not earn myself. Inheriting wealth sounds fine, but there is a huge price to pay. One never feels worthy, never gains respect for one's self."

"Whatever happened to Jeanne?" Mary Ellen asked.

"Ah, the illusive wife number two," said Ezra. "The mayor's life, here in Essex, was too boring for her. Of course, Allison did not make things easy. Jeanne foolishly believed she could win Allison over. Allison simply steamrolled her. She didn't just leave, she ran."

Both started to laugh. It had been a very long time since they shared a light moment.

"It's so good to see you laugh," said Mary Ellen. "I'm pretty sure moments like this have been few and far between for you."

For the next two hours they sat in the backyard and just talked. It appeared as though Mary Ellen really wanted to come back and stay by Ezra's side, no matter what the outcome. Ezra didn't know what to think or believe, but Mary Ellen was the only woman he had ever truly loved. When she left him, he was crushed. Marrying his second wife, Jeanne, was probably an attempt to escape spending time alone with Allison, who was beyond obnoxious. Allison, all by herself, could be sufficient cause for any wife to run for the hills. And now, Allison was gone, probably to face a firing squad or electrocution. The wishes of the whole Tinsley family were, "the sooner the better."

Wanda Loomis nearly fell off the bar stool she was inhabiting when Mary Ellen and Ezra came through the door of the Black Swan.

"Holy . . . What in the world," said Wanda, not believing her own eyes.

It was not common knowledge, but Wanda was one of the few people in town who was totally loyal to Ezra. Through the years, he had always chosen Wanda to cater any event he was responsible for. That was just one way Ezra showed his loyalty and support for local businesses. Many of the wealthy inhabitants of the town chose to employ the services of fancy caterers, most of whom had to travel some distance. But Ezra would not be one of them. He even used Wanda's services for private parties held in his home. Wanda never forgot all that he had done for her and her family. She also knew what a good public servant Ezra was.

The common belief was when the wealthy had someone in their family they did not want in the family business, they would encourage them to run for political office. The whole country seemed to be full of such people. Ezra may not have had business potential for his family, but he was an absolute first rate mayor and Wanda was one of his staunchest supporters, even after the Allison mess.

After a few brief moments of obligatory social banter, Wanda took Mary Ellen aside to find out what she was up to. Wanda's first thoughts were to accuse Mary Ellen of coming back when Ezra was at his lowest point. She was well aware of Mary Ellen's lucrative arrangement with the Tinsley family. But having your hands on all the money instead of waiting for your monthly payoff deposit to arrive could be very attractive. After all, Mary Ellen was a Radcliffe girl. And Radcliffe girls knew where the money was. That was a major part of their education.

Wanda sat transfixed as Mary Ellen filled her in on her shallow, aimless existence in San Francisco. She never thought she would have a second chance at a relationship with Ezra, even one that might include Allison. But the recent turn of events and scandal convinced her to come back and try her hardest to win Ezra again. That conversation led to a most unlikely chain of events, one almost unheard of during times such as these.

Finally, Ezra decided to take Mary Ellen back. He was so lonely and defeated; he felt he had nothing to lose. How right he was. Mary Ellen served notice that she was going to stand by him no matter what. That decision fueled Wanda's fire to talk Ezra into running for reelection. Ezra thought she was crazy. Actually, the whole world thought it crazy. But when the Tylers heard about Wanda's idea and pledged their support, Ezra found new life.

There were only two locals who could be persuaded to mount any kind of campaign to oppose Ezra. Wanda, with Aunt Clara's help, launched a relentless campaign calling in every favor they had to get the townsfolk to forgive and forget and to get solidly behind Ezra Tinsley who was innocent of any wrongdoing. The truth was, Ezra really had done nothing to deserve any punishment. Interestingly, a huge sum of campaign money came in from the Tinsley family of Boston to support whatever was necessary to ensure a victory. There was, however, the understanding that their name was not to be involved in this whole affair. Heaven forbid they take the high road and stand with one of their own. Public opinion in times like these was very important to them. The last thing the wealthy needed was a scandal. It was rumored that the two opposing candidates had been persuaded to accept sizable offers to launch the weakest of campaigns. It was also rumored, and of course, never substantiated, that anyone defeating Tinsley would find rough going with Arlen Templeton. No one knew if these rumors had any substance and no one really wanted to find out.

This election drew statewide attention, even some national. Electing a mayor who had fallen from grace and who had a member of his family involved in treason during a time of war was serious business. The governor decided to take action and instructed the State Police to maintain a presence at the polling stations. Sam's ranks were spread thin. It was absolutely imperative for the governor to make sure no one could make any claims that the election was not conducted all fair and square and legal.

The turnout on Election Day was light, and Ezra won the election. Every newspaper in the state trumpeted the town of Essex for showing the true forgiving spirit of America. The impossible had been achieved. The million to one shot had come in. Ezra Tinsley was once again the mayor of Essex, Connecticut. And for one small moment in time, in one small quiet town in Connecticut, all was right with the world.

CHAPTER TWELVE

Sergeant Varnish stood in front of Sam's vehicle raising his arms to shield his eyes from the tremendous rush of air created by the descending Sikorsky transport returning Sam from his trip to Washington DC. The helicopter made a graceful placing of its tires onto the Saybrook tarmac. It was a strange conflict of opposing forces; roaring beating rotors and tacit shock absorbing landing wheels guiding the large carrier to a safe, gentle landing.

Sam signaled to the pilot, shook hands with Commander Mickelson and exited. He made sure to keep low while moving the way to safety. He shook hands with Sergeant Varnish and then turned to watch the fine craft gracefully lift off, turn and head south toward Stratford.

"How was your trip, Captain?" Varnish inquired, half yelling over the roar of the propellers.

"Groundbreaking, but not very informative," said Sam as the roar moved away.

Varnish gave him a "What does that mean?" look.

Sam laughed. "Ride back with me and we can talk," said Sam.

Varnish motioned to his officer to follow them back to the station.

Sam started his motor, moved slowly out of the parking lot and drove towards town and the Saybrook Police Department.

"When I left, you told me you were going to fill me in on the two victims. Well, I'm back. What did you find?" Sam asked.

"Well," said Varnish, "I learned something, but I'm not really sure it means anything."

"For instance," said Sam.

"The Turner woman has been here a long time, just as Miss Lansing told us. It appears the two women had a close relationship. The handyman, on the other hand, has only been around for a little while. The previous employee just upped and disappeared. The male victim has only been here for a little over three weeks. But I don't know if that helps us. He was of Italian ancestry and moved here from the Bronx in New York about two months ago," said Varnish. "It's sad to think of someone finally getting the chance to leave the city to come to the peacefulness of the country and then die like that."

Sam thought for a moment. "Seems unlikely he could figure in on this, especially since he ended up getting butchered."

"That's what I figured," said Varnish. "My feeling is, for now, anyway, we still consider him an innocent bystander."

"Okay," said Sam, "but do me a favor. Send everything you have on him over to Captain D'Onofrio over at New Haven PD.

"Captain?" Said Varnish.

"Yeah, I guess you didn't hear the news, he just got promoted," said Sam.

"Wow," said Varnish. "That's great news. He's a top-notch police officer."

"I agree," said Sam, "and a good guy to have on your side. Send it off to him and I'll contact him later."

"Right away," said Varnish as he got out of Sam's car at the Saybrook Police Department building.

"Thanks again for watching my vehicle," said Sam.

Varnish gave a "thumbs up" signal and walked into the building.

Sam headed up Route #153 to Essex to meet up with Martha

to fill her in on his Washington trip. There were only three people who knew the commander's plans. Commander Mickelson arranged for all three to meet at the Judge Advocate General's headquarters in Andover, Maryland. Sam interviewed each one separately with the help of a stenographer who promised to type the notes up and have them delivered by courier the next day. Sam thanked her, but wasn't sure anything he learned there would help his case very much. He would have much preferred she would be delivering something he could actually use in his case. Of course, having things documented ensured that he would be able to review them if necessary or if anyone of the three came under suspicion at a later date. He planned to have Martha go over each one and get her take on them as well as to familiarize herself with the case so far. And so far, the case was nowhere.

Commander Boland was a loner. He was not married and did not appear to have anyone in his life, including close friends. He was someone who was experienced in handling sensitive documents. He was well respected and considered above reproach. The three people Sam interviewed claimed they knew him only on a strictly business level; military business. One of the three people interviewed was an attractive woman in her late twenties, but she wore an engagement ring. The ring was not from the commander. She was merely part of the secretarial pool at Naval Intelligence.

As of right now, all three appeared to be just what they claimed, members of the navy infrastructure who were at Commander Boland's disposal. On face value, it appeared that none were on an intimate level with him nor did they have any social contact with him whatsoever.

Sam sat with Martha in front of the fire attempting to wind down from a twenty-four hour period that produced a lot of activity but achieved very little. There was a growing excitement in the family as Christmas season was now in full swing. The upcoming trip to New York City just added to the already annual Tyler Christmas season excitement and expectations.

Christmas Eve belonged to Arlen and Betty Templeton. Their house was nothing short of a *winter wonderland* for the occasion. The Templetons had no fewer than four huge parties, one every weekend, leading up to Christmas. A never-ending stream of wealthy, important and powerful made their way up to Essex to celebrate life and the season with Arlen and Betty Templeton. But as far as the Templetons were concerned, it was Christmas Eve with Sam and the children that was the highlight of the season. And they did everything in their power to prove it to their family.

Martha sought to take Sam's mind off the investigation by telling him all about her plans for the New York trip that was only two weeks away. Sam was pleasantly surprised at how much thought she had put into the trip and the care she had given to make sure there was something for everyone, especially each of the children. He marveled at how much effort she had put into getting everything ready.

This time of the academic year was stressful for the professors as they had to prepare their students for finals knowing how disruptive the holidays were for academics. For Martha to prepare herself for finals and still be able to plan and carry out a whirlwind weekend in New York was greatly appreciated by both Sam and Aunt Clara. Sam was convinced that this was going to be one of the best Christmas holidays for the Tylers in a long time. There was only one small problem. There was the matter of that murder down in Fenwick.

CHAPTER THIRTEEN

Sam was sitting in Aunt Clara's kitchen just about to begin his second cup of Joe to start his day when the telephone rang. He didn't even bother to look up choosing rather to savor the rich aroma rising from his piping hot cup.

"It's for you, Samuel, a Howard Grimes," said Aunt Clara.

Sam got up, reluctantly, and walked to the hallway to retrieve the telephone.

"Howard, how nice of you to track me down," said Sam. "Did you call over to my home?"

"Why bother," said Grimes. "You're never there. You sure you really live there?"

"How well you know me, Chief State's Medical Examiner," said Sam.

"Just watching over the taxpayers' money," said Grimes.

"Wow, a true public servant," said Sam.

"No one knows the pains I take, Captain, to ensure the public welfare," said Grimes.

"And no one really cares either, my martyred friend" said Sam. "Now, if we are finished with the self-sacrifice award segment of our conversation, how about you honor me with the real purpose for this call," said Sam.

"Okay, if you insist on being such a killjoy," said Grimes. "I have something I want you to see. Can you come up to Meriden?"

"You mean, now?" Sam asked.

Grimes did not answer, but Sam could hear his breathing getting louder.

"It's that important?" Sam asked.

"Let's just say that I believe it would be more meaningful for you to see what I have to show you than for me to just tell you about it over the telephone. Besides, you could use your siren to get here much faster. Think how much fun you'll have with that, to say nothing of the excitement you could cause for all the folks you'll pass along the way."

Now it was Sam's turn not to speak. He so loved verbal jousting with Grimes. Sam believed Grimes was the only person in the state who truly got him.

"I'm on my way."

One hour later, Sam was looking at photos taken of the bodies of the two Fenwick victims.

"I wanted you to see these," said Grimes, "because they suggest something very unusual."

Sam didn't speak, but his body language told Grimes he was ready to observe and learn.

"You'll notice that some of these entry wounds are clean and tidy. I measured them for thickness because they give us a very real possibility of knowing the exact kind of weapon used in the killing. There are three clean wounds, all with the same dimensions, five centimeters by six centimeters by fifteen centimeters. They tell us the height, width and length of the weapon. It's safe to assume that the weapon used was a knife.

"Now we examined all of the knives found on the Lansing property. Every knife there is of French origin. All are much too thin to have been used. I've gone over whatever database I could use, which was not much, to try to find out the origin. My conclusion is that it is one that is standard issue for the German S.S."

Sam still remained silent. He sensed Grimes was not through.

"It appears that once the killer struck with precision, he or she

51

went on a maniacal tear, viciously cutting up the victims. I am convinced only one person did this."

"Both victims?" "How?" Sam asked.

"The second victim was killed in exactly the same way," Said Grimes.

"That would imply that the two victims were not killed at the same time. They were killed separately. No way of knowing how far apart the attacks occurred," said Sam.

"Right you are, Captain. That's the way I see it. So my guess is that the killer was both professional and a lunatic at the same time," said Grimes.

"Wonderful," said Sam. "I'm assuming your best guess is that whoever did this was German," said Sam.

"What else?" Grimes said. "They say that the S.S. is comprised of the Nazis' most dangerous and fanatical members.

Sam's dry reaction: "Wonderful."

Sam knew he had just enough time to get to Saybrook railroad station to meet Martha coming in on the 6:10 out of Manhattan. He pulled into the station just in time to see Martha exiting the platform. She quickly made her way over to his car and got in. She leaned over and kissed him and then settled back into her seat.

"Have I got news for you," she said.

"Good news, I hope," said Sam. "I've already used up my allotment of bad news for the day."

"While I was about to leave school, I had a few minutes to spare. So I called Veronica Lansing. She's staying at the Waldorf," said Martha.

"Why did you call her?" Sam asked.

"I just wanted to touch base with her and ask her advice on a few questions I had for our trip, but I got more than I bargained for," said Martha.

Sam looked over at her with questioning eyes.

"Sam, Veronica Lansing does not have a brother," Martha said.

"What?" said Sam, nearly driving off the road.

"That's right, she has no idea who Commander Boland is. What's more, she had no plans to meet or entertain anyone from the military over Thanksgiving," said Martha.

"Why on earth . . . ?" came Sam's unfinished response.

"This doesn't help much, does it?" Martha asked.

"Well, that all depends," said Sam. "Before, we had nothing and now we have less than nothing. I guess you could call that progress of sorts if you wanted."

"I'm sorry, honey," said Martha. "I hate to be the bearer of bad news, but now that you know the truth about his supposed visit, you won't be running into any blind canyons."

"Thank you. I'm glad we found out now," said Sam. "It appears I have some calls to make. The good news is, when you've got nothing, any place is a good place to start."

It had been dark for hours, a proper setting for Sam's mood. Somewhere along the line, someone or something was going to have to produce a starting place. Boland was a fraud. But just how much of a fraud was he? Was he really Commander Boland? Either he was, or he had successfully carried on a brilliant deception for who knows how long.

Sam put in a call to Commander Mickelson. The commander was having dinner over in Georgetown. His assistant would attempt to locate him and have him call Sam back. Next Sam called D'Onofrio over in New Haven. It seemed logical that one of the conductors on the Washington to New York train would have seen Boland and possibly even spoken to him. A shot in the dark? The wildest at best. No one had to tell Sam how important it was to the soldiers fighting, over in France, that he keep these plans out of enemy hands. There was only one thing standing in his way. He was nowhere.

Sam spoke to Matt first. He explained everything to him. It was all negative, but it was all there was. Matt would put in a call to his friend on the NYPD and have him find out when the conductors would be in New York. There was a three-hour long layover before the return trip to Washington. Time enough to question anyone if there was someone to question. Sam told him that he would have Commander Mickelson contact him to coordinate their efforts with the railroad to try to find anyone who may have seen or had contact with Boland, or whoever he was.

Mickelson called about an hour later. Sam could not even look at his food until they spoke; he was too anxious. Mickelson was stunned by the news. Sam suggested he investigate Boland's history, but also find out everything he could, concerning the three people he had interviewed while in Washington. Mickelson promised to tear their lives apart and know everything about them. He would check everyone's background, clearance and history back to the fourth grade if he had to. Sam had a feeling that Mickelson would do just that. He seemed to be someone who took his commission very seriously.

CHAPTER FOURTEEN

During all the confusion, Martha's latest book had been released, just in time for the holiday shopping season. Early indications were that it was going to be another smashing best seller. The critics raved, assuring a huge amount of sales. It gave Martha and Sam an excuse to go to New York so that Sam might get an opportunity to interview anyone who had seen Commander Boland. It would have to be a whirlwind trip, but Sam knew he was grasping at straws right now, and sitting around his office at headquarters, waiting for any breakthroughs would drive him crazy.

Word came from D'Onofrio that three conductors on that particular run were scheduled to be in New York the next day. Two lived in Queens and the third was from Baltimore. All three would be at Penn Station on 34th St. at seven am, three hours before the ten o'clock for Washington, D.C. was scheduled to leave. If it were possible, Sam would have run the whole way.

Ellen Gold was ecstatic. Having Martha make an impromptu visit to New York was nothing more than a fabulous early Christmas gift for her. She immediately set up a book signing at the New York Public Library on 42nd St. and 6th Avenue at Bryant Park. Only Ellen could pull something like this off. It seemed a lot of people owed Ellen, and Ellen knew how to collect. She managed to place ads in the New York Times and Daily News while getting word to the major radio stations to alert their audiences of the event. The stations were only too happy to oblige. The media recognized the importance of reporting anything considered good news during these trying times. Martha had already agreed to an evening appearance with the whole family when they came to New York for their Christmas weekend visit. Ellen worked feverishly to pull everything together. No one could remember ever seeing Ellen Gold smile this much.

Martha had only one morning lecture class on her schedule. She would not be due back on campus for two days. Time enough for her and Sam to do what needed to be done. Sam picked her up at school and brought her to the New Haven Police Department where Captain D'Onofrio would take charge of his vehicle.

Ellen booked them into the Waldorf. Nothing was too good for her star author, who just happened to be the wife of her favorite cousin, who, as it so happens, is America's "darling of the moment." Harcourt maintained a suite of rooms at the famous Waldorf for their important visitors. The suite just happened to be available. It provided Martha with all she would need to prepare herself for the evening festivities. Ellen agreed with Sam that he should not attend and ruin the family function planned for the next week. Sam had contacted NYPD as soon as he got to the suite. A meeting was set up at Navy headquarters at the United Nations building overlooking the East River.

Sam met with members of Naval intelligence, the FBI and the NYPD Detective Bureau to coordinate efforts to find out if Commander Boland had been seen and, if possible, have some clue to his present whereabouts. All three conductors were contacted and told to be at New York Central offices at Penn Station at seven am. Once again, a stenographer would be present to record all their conversations.

The meeting went well, considering the possibility of a turf war between all the government agencies involved. All had a respectful distrust for one another, but Sam wisely implored them to think of all the young men in France counting on their successful prevention of dangerous materials getting into the hands of the Nazis. That seemed to do the trick, but only time would tell. Everyone in the room knew of Sam's recent successes and that none other than the president of the United States gave him his full backing. No one wanted to take the president on.

Sam joined Martha and Ellen in their suite at the Waldorf. The impromptu book signing appearance was a huge success. Some of New York's wealthiest families were in attendance, as well as Veronica Lansing who added star power to the affair while professing great affection for Martha Frost. Let the world know that Veronica Lansing was an adoring fan. Ellen was grateful for Lansing's presence; she was staying at the Waldorf while her home was being repaired. Had she not showed up would have sent a bad message. But Ellen, being Ellen, had to wonder if Lansing had aspirations of starring in an up and coming movie planned for Martha's first book, that being the role of one of Martha's most important characters, Stella Dean. Whatever the reason, Victoria Lansing's presence put a major icing on the cake for the evening.

Sam and the ladies enjoyed a nightcap and the telling of all that had happened that evening at the book signing. Sam gave them a watered-down version of his meeting with the government agencies. Being well aware of Ellen's penchant for theatrics, he was not about to give his cousin any ammunition for print in the Times. He was also concerned that Ellen might not know that any involvement by her might place her in grave danger. Ellen had a talent for giving the appearance that she knew much more than she really did. The Nazis would not be privy to that information. If they went after her for any reason, she would be helpless to avoid certain danger, possibly even death.

After Ellen left, Sam filled Martha in on his meeting. The truth was that the real reason they were in New York was for Sam to try to get important information. Still, he made sure that Martha knew how happy he was for her to have so much success. Martha realized how thoughtful her husband was. She felt truly blessed. They turned in early so Sam could get a good night's sleep for his all-important meeting at Penn Station. Martha made sure everything would be ready for Sam in the morning, including a six o'clock breakfast. Naval intelligence would have a car waiting in front of the Waldorf at six forty-five to take him to the meetings.

The third man Sam interviewed was Henry Walters, a tall, thin, elegant black man who definitely remembered Commander Boland. The first two men Sam interviewed had not seen the commander. Commander Boland even engaged Walter in some enjoyable conversation. Walter remembered the commander even talking about places on Long Island. He never did mention his purpose for being in New York, saying only that he had business here. The two men talked about places of interest in Manhattan, but somehow, got into a conversation about Long Island. Boland seemed to know a good deal about OHEKA Castle and the Gold Coast, a wealthy Long Island community just outside the borders of Queens where many of the country's wealthiest lived. He also inquired about Montauk at the farthest reaches of the island. Immediately, Sam's mind went to a place not mentioned, but also out near Montauk, Gardeners Island. Sam's case in Bridgeport and at Charles Island, in Milford, made him aware of the fact that Gardeners Island was another major location where it was believed Captain Kidd visited and buried treasure. Sam made a note of it and intended to make a thorough research of Gardeners Island when he got back home. It could mean nothing, but what else did he have, really?

Something also came out of the interview which shed a whole new light on the case. The commander intimated that there was a woman in his life. That bit of information set Sam's pulse racing. He thanked Henry Walters and told him not to discuss anything about this meeting with anyone. The fact that there were ten other people in the room while the interviews were going on, all of whom appeared to be important government agents, made a large impact on Walters who was not about to take all that lightly. Sam was pretty convinced that Walter was scared enough and honorable enough to follow his orders.

As soon as Walters was out of the room, Sam looked directly at Commander Mickelson.

"The female secretary," he said.

"Joan Peterson?" Mickelson asked.

"Yeah, Joan Peterson or whatever her name is. Don't ask me why, but my gut tells me she's involved. Find her and everything you can about her and do it quickly. She's all we've got and I'm telling you that something is telling me she is involved."

"I'll get my people on it immediately," said Mickelson. "I'll fly out this morning and take charge in the search personally. I'll get back to you, Sam."

Mickelson made a quick exit. Sam asked that NYPD do all in its power to get photos of Boland into the hands of the police departments from New York City to the Hamptons. It would be an enormous undertaking, but the stakes were high enough to expect full cooperation and an intense manhunt. Boland had to be found and the documents he was carrying had to be retrieved. A full-scale manhunt was now in effect in New York.

"Happy holidays," said Sam, to himself.

CHAPTER FIFTEEN

It was gray and overcast, with a forecast for flurries. Ezra Tinsley sat alone with his thoughts in the backseat as his driver navigated the narrow two-lane road leading to Fort Dix, New Jersey. Ezra had tried on two occasions to visit with his daughter since she had been placed there awaiting execution for crimes against the government. Both times, she had refused to see him. Then, suddenly, she seemed to have had a change of heart and requested that he, and only he, come see her.

Fort Dix is a sprawling military complex serving as one of the most important training facilities for the United States Army. Like all installations of its type, it is in a remote location. Thousands of young men have passed through its gates to be trained to go off to war. Because there is no facility for females convicted of war crimes or treason against the United States, it had been chosen to house Allison Tinsley until she could be taken to a federal penitentiary for execution.

Ezra's heart was heavy over the horrible series of events that led up to his rebellious daughter's actions. Somehow, he had clung to the belief that she did not fully grasp what she was doing at the time, and was most certainly, ignorant of the consequences of her actions.

Once through the main checkpoint, his driver drove as instructed to a remote area where the jail was located. Ezra got out and made his way up the three wooden steps leading to the stark, windowless concrete structure that looked as ominous as it most probably was. It was very much in character with the joyless weather conditions surrounding it. He entered and was greeted by two military police who took him down a long colorless hallway to the office of the captain in charge of the facility. Ezra found the captain to be professional, but totally indifferent, almost contemptuous of him for visiting a prisoner who had committed such a heinous crime against the very country the captain had committed himself to serve, even to the death.

Two guards escorted Ezra to an area that had been set apart from the rest of the stockade to isolate the prisoners. Allison was to have no contact with the other prisoners or anyone else for that matter. She was in total solitary confinement. Ezra entered the 10 x 10 room and found Allison already there, seated. The room was bleak with sparse wooden furniture; one table and two chairs. A single overhead lamp hung from the center of the room, directly over the table. Ashley was chained to the chair as well as shackled in both her feet and hands. She waited for Ezra to be seated before she looked up into his eyes to tacitly acknowledge him. They sat motionless for a few moments, neither speaking. Finally, tears began to stream down Ezra's face. He refused to wipe them.

"Thank you for coming, father," Allison said, finally.

Ezra smiled weakly, but did not speak.

"My time is coming to an end and I did not want to die without speaking to you, just one more time."

Ezra tried to speak but no words came out.

"I have had some time to think about the pain I have caused you," said Allison.

Ezra was surprised by that revelation.

"Before I am gone, I want to set the record straight between us. First, I want you to know that I am at peace with my fate. The chaplain here is a kind and gentle man who has led me to the Lord. They tell me that it is easy to find God in places like this. The reality is, when you have nothing to prevent you from facing the truth, it is much easier to accept. The chaplain and I have spent many hours together and his love for God and for me is very comforting for me. I have never seen such love or devotion. I read the Bible from morning till night. It has given me a peace I have never known. For the first time in my life, I feel like there is something to look forward to each day." She paused for a moment and then said, "I know where I am going, father, and I want you to share in my peace."

"Oh, Allison," was all Ezra was able to say. He was totally overwhelmed by his emotions.

"I've always felt that I was cursed, even from the time I was very little," Allison said. "But I never really blamed you or my mother. No, neither of you played any part in my fate. I realized I was a Tinsley, a family which I have come to loathe over the years. As a young child, I realized how cold and heartless our family is. I was so confused. The only way I could rebel was to be as defiant as I possibly could be. Somehow, I believed that I could combat hatred with more hate. I now understand you, daddy, and how hard it must have been for you to live with the awful Tinsley reputation when you had no choice but to do so. But you really had no choice. You were expected live up to the legacy of the Tinsley men. And as far as my mother is concerned, no one should blame her for deserting us after all the misery I put her through. I took everything out on her. How futile she must have felt to be faced with the reality that the only child she birthed into this world was someone like me. Father, I don't want you to be sad. It's for the best that I go. My death will spare you a life of living hell.

"I was glad to hear that you were reelected. I know how much you love being the mayor. And, also, that you and mother have reconciled. That is so good. I wish you both the very best. Be happy for me, daddy. I am going to a far better place knowing all of us will be the better for it."

Allison turned and motioned to the guard that she was ready to leave. She and Ezra were not allowed to touch one another. Her guards took hold of her and directed her out of the room. Slowly, Ezra got to his feet and, accompanied by his guards, made his way back to the main office and out to his waiting car as if he were walking in a daze. He didn't say a word as he got in and settled himself while his driver closed the door behind him. He then broke down and began sobbing uncontrollably.

CHAPTER SIXTEEN

Sam was sitting at Aunt Clara's kitchen table enjoying his first cup of morning coffee while all around him there was total chaos. The children were scurrying about gathering their books and warm winter coats as they prepared for Injun Jim to walk them over to North Main Street to catch their school bus. There was much animated conversation about the upcoming trip to New York and, of course, Christmas. Aunt Clara was busy directing everybody in an attempt to establish some sense of order. Martha came through the door with her large leather briefcase filled with all her work materials.

"Wow, it's really going to be a cold one today," she said. She leaned over to kiss her husband, but made short work of it as she made a beeline for the coffee pot. Sam just stared at her with an expression of *really? That's it?* Martha fixed the coffee and came back and sat down at the table with Sam who was still looking at her, but saying nothing.

"Is something wrong, honey?" she asked.

Sam remained silent.

"By the way," said Martha, ignoring Sam's silence, "what are your thoughts concerning this whole Long Island mystery? Do you really think this Commander Boland or whoever he is was really heading there?"

"I don't know," said Sam. "In fact, you could use that same answer for just about every question out there where this case is concerned."

The children came over and kissed Martha and Sam, then headed out the door to meet a waiting Injun Jim.

"Long Island has a very rich history of pirates, millionaires, smugglers and even Masons," said Sam.

"Grandpa Templeton is a Mason," said Thomas as he was about to go out the door. "Ask him to tell you about his tunnels, daddy," he yelled from the porch as he was about to meet up with Mary, Lillith and Injun Jim and walk up Pratt Street towards North Main.

For a moment, Sam sat stunned at Thomas's revelation.

"Do you know anything about this?" Sam asked Aunt Clara.

"There's been rumors going around here for years, but I'll be darned if I know anything," she said. "Your father-in-law's such an important man, I wouldn't be surprised either way. That Arlen Templeton has always been a man of mystery. It wouldn't shock me to learn he is a Mason. One thing's for sure, a man like Arlen would never advertise it if it were true. Lots of folks don't trust the Masons. I'm pretty sure Arlen would keep that kind of news to himself. Of course, you could ask him. I doubt he would keep the truth from you. You know how much that man respects you."

Sam didn't say a word. He simply got up and headed for the telephone in the hall. But the phone started ringing before he could get there. He motioned for Aunt Clara to take the call, which she did.

"He's right here," she said and handed the phone to Sam. It was some Commander Mickelson, calling from Washington.

"I'm beginning to think your instincts are right, Captain," said Mickelson. "We fished the Peterson woman out of the Potomac last night and were able to identify her body. She was stabbed several times which makes me pretty convinced that she was killed by the same person. If that's true, it looks like this killer really gets around."

"Either that or there is more than one person who likes to kill in the same manner," said Sam.

"You may be right, but, for now, I'm going to assume that there is just one killer; one that's really dangerous."

"What's your next move?" Sam asked.

"I'm going to do what I said I was going to do. I'm going to tear her life apart and quickly. This killing just shows me, we need to move full speed ahead."

"I've got a few things I need to check out here. I'll call you if I get anything," said Sam.

"Fair enough, captain, said Mickelson. "I'm really beginning to get worried we've got a real homicidal maniac on our hands. The stakes just got higher, if that were possible."

"Smooth sailing, sir," bade Sam.

Sam told Martha the news as quickly as he could and went back to the telephone to put in a call to Arlen Templeton. Just then, Injun Jim beeped the horn letting Martha know he was back and ready to take her to the Saybrook train station to catch the 9:10 to New Haven. Martha walked over to Sam to kiss him goodbye. It appeared she realized the last one was just a little abrupt. She made sure this one was quite satisfying.

"I'll see you tonight, big guy," she said with a playful wink of her eye. Sam smiled and watched her go out the kitchen door.

Sam was lucky to catch Arlen at home before he left for his office in New Haven. Arlen told him to come right over. He'd have the coffee on.

"What's got your interest in the Masons?" asked Aunt Clara.

"So far, I've been going on inhibition and hunches. For some reason, as soon as I heard Long Island mentioned, it got me to wondering. I can't believe that Charles Island is the only island the Germans were interested in. It's common knowledge that Captain Kidd is not the only pirate who buried treasure off the coast of

Long Island and off the coast of Massachusetts. Surely, the Germans are aware of this and if they are truly interested in finding treasure to aid their war effort, they might have a network in place to find them. If this is true, there would be places for Commander Boland to go to for sanctuary and for passage back to Germany. It seems the pirates and the Masons have a connection. The Masons are famous for building intricate hiding places right in plain sight. It's just a feeling, Aunt Clara, but feelings are all I've got to go on, right now."

Aunt Clara said she understood and wished Sam good luck as he left for his meeting with Arlen.

CHAPTER SEVENTEEN

Arlen handed Sam his coffee and motioned for Sam to join him in the study. Of all the rooms in this large, gracious and interesting home, the study was Sam's favorite. It was all dark wood and books; loads of books. Arlen possessed a huge collection of first editions of works of the great authors as well as those of little-known, but incredibly interesting authors from all over the globe. One of the walls was filled with framed photos of Arlen with everyone from Albert Einstein to Leopold Stokowski. The walls were done in a rich hunter green bordered with white crown molding. With plush leather seating, it was one of the most comfortable rooms Sam ever experienced. Both men sat and sipped their coffee.

"Umm," said Sam.

"Puerto Rican," said Arlen. "Most people don't even know that Puerto Rico has some of the finest coffee beans in the world. If I had my way, we'd annex the place just to gain a monopoly on them. But then, I'm sure you are not here to hear me explain the origin of my coffee beans."

"The Masons," said Sam to a slightly surprised Arlen. I'm interested in the Masons of whom I have been told you are one."

Arlen smiled. "Who told you such a thing?" Arlen asked.

"Thomas Tyler, your adoring grandson," said Sam.

Arlen smile broadened. He didn't speak but rose from his chair and motioned for Sam to keep his. Arlen walked over to behind his desk, opened the drawer and took something from it. He walked over to Sam and handed him the large, heavy ring bearing the crest of the Masons.

"Twenty three years," Arlen said. "I am a Grand Mason and proud of it. Why are you so interested in the Masons?"

Sam held the ring and kept admiring its weight. "That's really something," said Sam.

"And it interests you, why?" Arlen asked.

"There is a Navy commander who has disappeared," said Sam.

"Boland," said Arlen.

Sam was not surprised. "Of course you would know," he said.

"Not as much as you, son, but enough to know there is great concern over the man's whereabouts. After Veronica Lansing's narrow escape, you should've known that I would be interested in this affair, especially because it happened in our own backyard."

"Commander Boland has very important papers, very much like war games documents containing possible strategies for combating the Germans on the French-German front. If the Germans were to get their hands on them it would certainly make them aware of our thinking. It would allow them the advantage to prepare for whatever we have in mind. The lives of many of our young men are resting on our stopping Boland and retrieving those documents before they can be viewed."

"Thank you, Sam. I appreciate you telling me this. But how do the Masons figure into all this?" Arlen asked.

"That's an interesting question," said Sam. The best answer I can give you is that maybe they don't. Here is what I can tell you. A woman in the secretarial pool in Andover might have been instrumental in aiding Boland to obtain and escape with those documents. Unfortunately, we will not be able to find out anything from her. She was murdered and her body thrown into the Potomac. It was retrieved last night. I have a strong suspicion she and

Boland were close. It's even possible they were romantically in-volved. It appears that the killer of the people over in Fenwick wanted to make sure she was unable to give us any aid. The killer wanted to make sure she did no talking. It's just speculation, but speculation and my instincts tell me that Boland is in Long Island where the Masons have been instrumental in building many of those enormous estates on its Gold Coast. The Masons are some of the most gifted people in the world at building secret passage-ways and bunkers. It's also common knowledge that pirates and Masons have always had a close relationship. I have not ruled out the buried treasure theory yet. And who better to devise secret hiding places than the Masons? I'm grasping at straws, here, but I do not know where else to turn. The president is counting on me to help solve this thing."

Arlen was looking at Sam as though trying to make up his mind about something.

"By the way," said Sam, "Thomas suggested I ask you about your tunnels. Do you really have tunnels?" Sam asked

"I do," said Arlen. "I want to show you something, Sam."

Arlen went over to one of his shelves and retrieved a large book. He walked back to his desk and placed it down, opened it and held a large folded sheet of paper up to show Sam.

"Come over here," he said as he unfolded the paper and laid it down flat on his desk.

Sam went over and looked down at the drawings on the page. He immediately recognized it to be a large scale drawing of what was now Main Street, Essex. But some of the buildings were not on the map. They were too new. The drawings seemed to be at least one hundred years old, maybe older. Arlen pointed to two buildings at the top of the page which appeared to be churches.

"I'm sure you know these two buildings," said Arlen. He was pointing to Our Lady of Sorrows Catholic Church, a narrow con-struction with a high pointed steeple. Originally known as the first St. John's Episcopal Church, it was the first church to hold services in Essex village. A most interesting fact concerning it was that it was moved, in its entirety, from down in Saybrook to this very spot; a major feat. A short distance to the right of it was the Methodist Church. They stood side-by-side, high on Zion Hill, overlooking Essex and the harbor.

Arlen moved his finger down and placed it on a large parcel of land Sam immediately recognized. It was now occupied by the very house he was standing in. Arlen then used his fingers to draw an imaginary line to the waters of North Cove, very near the place where the British attacked Essex during eighteen hundred fourteen.

"There is a boathouse down at the Cove that has been replaced and still occupies the original site." Arlen tapped the spot with his fingers a few times and then retraced his imaginary line to its starting place.

"I'm sure you know that my home now occupies the space that you see here. Originally, there were two large barns constructed here, just after this rendering was completed. A tunnel was constructed to act as a passage to allow townsfolk to go to and from the Cove after the siege of eighteen fourteen. To this day, very few people know of its existence or how to access it."

"But, what about Thomas? Aren't you afraid he might draw attention to it?" Sam asked.

Arlen just laughed. "Thomas has never seen it or even knows of its exact location. I told him about the tunnel but he doesn't really know of its existence. I think he rather enjoys thinking of it as a make-believe place of fantasy, kind of like in Peter Pan," said Arlen.

"But it does exist," Sam said.

"Would you like to see it?" Arlen asked.

"Absolutely," was Sam's immediate response.

Arlen walked past Sam towards the doorway leading to a private bathroom just off the study. He placed one hand on the second shelf down and with the other pushed the unit back towards the wall. There was a clicking sound and then the whole bookcase slowly rotated out exposing a passageway. Arlen took two flashlights from an earthen shelf, handed one to Sam and bade him follow. They began walking and made a slow descent until they reached the end. It took only a few moments to complete the trip. Arlen then moved a small stone which allowed a view of the boathouse interior. It was deserted. The door to the boathouse was padlocked, ensuring no one could gain entry but its owner. Arlen held the only key. He pushed the stone into the wall and it opened a passageway just large enough for a grown man to pass through. Sam had lived here his whole life and never knew of its existence.

CHAPTER EIGHTEEN

Sam and Arlen made their way back to the study, but Arlen was not finished. Once again, he directed Sam's attention to the church buildings up on Zion Hill.

"The attack by the British in eighteen fourteen is something the people of Essex or Pottapauk, as it was known then, would not ever forget. It took many years for the townsfolk to trust the British along with those Americans who still had ties to them. The Methodists and the Episcopalians were friendly to each other. Religious freedom was most sacred to those folks. So they constructed a tunnel system between the two churches to help each other should their congregations come under persecution. That gave aid and comfort to both sides. I wish I could give you a happy ending, Sam. Unfortunately, there was another problem, a very serious one.

"As you are well aware, many of the so-called great American families amassed their enormous fortunes in opium and slave trade. With Massachusetts to the north and New York to the south, Essex seemed like a likely place for those seeking to help the people being transported as slaves. The conditions those poor people were exposed to were deplorable. And here they were, being treated as less than human by many of those who came to America for religious as well as personal freedom.

"The clergy in the area banded together to make Essex a place of refuge for anyone seeking to escape a life of slavery. The tunnel you just came from is part of a system that goes all the way up to Zion Hill to link up with those two churches. The system had two purposes. Someone could seek asylum in the churches and then be taken away by boat during nightfall. Or, boats could transport folks here to Essex where they could be cared for by the churches. From here there were two destinations they could escape to. Some went north to Canada while others went west by the Underground Railroad: a network of folks who would hide and protect them along the way. Slavery was a terrible thing, Sam, but the amounts of money that could be made was staggering. Sadly, many bedrock families who are revered in this country made their fortune over the backs and blood of many who were not so fortunate.

Sam was greatly impressed by what Arlen said and needed a minute to take it all in. "And the other tunnel system?" he asked.

"It goes right through here, Sam, and connects with the one I just showed you. The wall at the top of my tunnel gives way and opens to make the escape tunnel complete," said Arlen.

* * *

Once again, Martha found herself in the Yale library. One of her favorite pastimes was being hunkered down in a library doing research for whatever she was working on. This time it was for something to aid Sam.

"I know this is crazy," he told her, "but I have to make sure Veronica Lansing is really innocent. I need to know if her absence the night of the murders was totally by chance or if she has said anything in the press to reveal a hidden agenda against America."

Martha understood that he was only doing his job, and a darn good one to place even the great Grande Dame of stage and screen not above suspicion.

"I know you'd just love to become friends with her, but let's make sure she's not in the loop here," Sam said.

Here, among all the books of great knowledge and young scholars, who would someday take a significant role in shaping the nation's future, Martha felt a sense of belonging like nowhere else. It did not take long for her to have very special feelings for this amazing institution and its Gothic architecturally inspired design that was so different in appearance and atmosphere from all the others of the Ivy League. Someone had told her that there was a network of tunnels beneath the surface of the main campus linking it all together. These tunnels would allow certain faculty and administration to reach anywhere they needed to go on campus without ever going outdoors. She knew that Sam would find that fascinating, but, for now, she was here on another quest.

Martha poured over every article she could find concerning Veronica Lansing spanning a ten year period. There were so many that she began to feel overwhelmed by the sheer number. Every issue of the trades, gossip columns, society pages, magazine articles and media interviews lay before her. After three long hours staring down at print, she decided to take a break. It was then that she began to sense the uncomfortable feeling that she was being watched by someone, just as she had been once before. Slowly, and without obvious movements, she stretched and began to observe her surroundings. She got up and made her way deliberately to the women's restroom, stopping every few seconds discreetly to see if she could discover if, indeed, anyone was watching her every move. She washed her hands and exited the restroom and made her way back to the table she was working at in much the same way she had left it. She noticed nothing and no one. But that did not convince her that she was not under surveillance.

One more hour later and she concluded that as far as she was concerned, Veronica Lansing was squeaky clean and absolutely innocent of anything to do with the homicides that had taken place in her home. The thought of that made her smile. And then another thought invaded her mind; one she was sure was shared by her husband. Veronica Lansing was an amazing actress and an extremely intelligent woman.

CHAPTER NINETEEN

Enzo Pasconi, the new handyman who had been savagely murdered in Veronica Lansing's home, gave an address, as his previous
address on his application for employment. It was in the Italian
section of the Bronx, affectionately known as Arthur Avenue, the
area that started from East Fordham Road to Crescent Avenue
where St. Bartholomew's Children's Hospital sat. Arthur Avenue
was the name of the main thoroughfare that served as the hub for
all the buying and selling activity in that section of the Bronx.
Block after block of grocery stores, meat markets, bakeries, and
pastry shops lined both sides of the street. Here, one could pur-
chase all types of household goods from pots, pans and dishes to
percolating coffee pots, as well as those dedicated to the making of
the perfect cup of espresso.

Close by was the Pelham Parkway section where Italians and
Jews lived in close harmony to insure the safety of their neighbor-
hoods against unwelcome intruders. The Morris Park Association
was formed for that very purpose. Notable neighbors were the
Bronx Zoo and the Bronx Botanical Gardens. Both attracted great
throngs of visitors and possible trouble.

Captain Matt D'Onofrio had a cousin who was a New York
City police detective who had grown up in the Bronx. Matt contacted his cousin Phillip D'Onofrio, whose father was the brother

of Matt's dad. Detective D'Onofrio knew the Arthur Avenue section well. He had spent many a Saturday afternoon, in his youth, escorting his mother and two sisters up and down Arthur Avenue as they went about the weekly ritual of food shopping. If the children behaved, their mother would treat them to a pastry at her favorite pastry shop. If not, they would have to answer to their father. Disobedience did not happen very often.

Matt had two choices for reaching Manhattan. He could take the 9:14 out of New Haven, which lumbered along stopping at every city along the way until it reached Stamford and then proceed non-stop to Manhattan. His other option was to take the Merritt Parkway, Connecticut's only real highway, to connect with Westchester County, take the Cross County Parkway through Yonkers and then hook up to the Henry Hudson Parkway passing through the affluent Riverdale section before riding parallel to the Hudson River all the way down to the bottom of Manhattan. He did have one thing in his favor: the weather was unseasonably mild for this time of year. For Matt, the choice had been simple. He pulled out his New Haven Register and eased back in his seat as the 9:14 to New York City pulled out of New Haven right on time. An hour and one half later the train crossed over the river from the Bronx to Manhattan and came to a halt at the 125th Street Station. About a minute later, the train picked up speed and was soon entering the vast tunnel system that would take him underground to his destination, Grand Central Station.

Matt knew what to expect. As soon as the train came to a complete stop and the doors were opened, every passenger made a mad dash out and up the long concrete ramps to the upper level. A smile of amusement crossed his face as he slowly rose and made a civilized exit from the train. He followed the path of the crowd, but at a leisurely pace.

He emerged from the tunnel and entered the vast cave-like concourse area taking note of the large number of humans scurrying in every direction. One complete wall, separated in the middle by a large exit to 42ⁿᵈ Street, housed all the ticket windows. Each set of windows sat beneath a giant schedule reader board notifying the people which trains were or were not on time and the departure time of many others. Matt made his way over to the circular information booth in the center of it all to ask directions to the Vanderbilt Street exit. He was directed to the western section of the station where he climbed a marble staircase that would take him to Vanderbilt. He walked about one hundred feet down a passageway that brought him out to the street where his cousin stood leaning against his police automobile appearing to be in no hurry to go anywhere.

The two men caught sight of one another and embraced warmly. After exchanging a little back and forth kidding, Matt entered the car at his cousin's request and sat back and enjoyed the detective's expert navigation through the insanity called Manhattan traffic.

Once Detective D'Onofrio reached the FDR Drive on the eastern shore of Manhattan, he drove north to the far reaches of Washington heights, crossed over the East River, on to the Cross Bronx Expressway and traveled east for a few miles until they reached the Webster Avenue exit, which he took. From here, he drove north on Webster Avenue until he reached East Fordham Road and made a right-hand turn and headed south westerly where the multitude of shops and restaurants of Arthur Avenue began to appear. They passed the Vincent Ciccarone Playground, a grassy neighborhood park that sat surrounded on all sides, sandwiched between four streets making a square and completely enclosed by a large iron fence. The southernmost tip of the park sat on 187ᵗʰ Street and their destination.

D'Onofrio pulled his car into a no parking spot in front of Little Italy Fruit Market, parked and bade his cousin exit and join him. Matt did as he was told.

"Wow," said Matt as he surveyed the busy scene.

His cousin merely laughed.

"Just a little different from New Haven, wouldn't you say?"

"You got me there," said Matt, "Where are we going?" he asked.

The detective led them to the pizza shop called Zero Otto Nove, about twenty paces back up Arthur Avenue, across a driveway that led to parking in the rear of the buildings.

"Pizza?" inquired Matt

"And good conversation," said the detective.

Both men sat down at one of the tables and waited for the proprietor to make an appearance. When he finally did appear, he merely looked at the detective and asked,

"Eddie B?"

The detective nodded affirmatively.

"Ahshpetta" (wait) said the man.

Both men had coffee while they waited for an answer from Eddie B., whoever that was.

"He'll see you now," said the proprietor, finally.

Both men got up. The detective asked what they owed for the coffee.

"It's on Eddie," he said. "Better go, he is an impatient man."

The detective waved good-bye, "A salut." he said.

"A salut," the man answered back, with a voice lacking in sincerity.

CHAPTER TWENTY

The detective led the way through the alleyway to the next street behind and parallel to Arthur Avenue. They walked down to 2966 Hoffman Street, climbed the steps and rang the third bell from the top. Seconds later a buzzer rang to let them in.

The hallway was dimly lit. There were stairs leading up to the next two levels, but they would not be necessary. A large wooden door to their right opened slowly. A middle aged woman wearing a house dress, an apron and tightly bunned hair looked at both men and then backed away into the apartment. They took this as a sign to enter, which they did, cautiously, with the detective in the lead.

"What can I do for you two gentlemen of the law?" asked a man who was in his early fifties and still in his pajamas sitting in a large stuffed chair holding a cup of espresso.

"Nice to see you too, Eddie," said the detective with just the right amount of sarcasm.

After exchanging a few cutting pleasantries with each other, Eddie rose from his chair and embraced the detective who returned the gesture. Both men had a good laugh and then settled into their seats. Matt and the detective sat on a couch that was surprisingly comfortable and appeared to be rather new. Matt looked around and made a note that everything in the apartment seemed to be new and of very good quality. Eddie took note of Matt's actions.

"Fell off of a truck," he said with a look of apology. "What are the odds?" he asked.

Matt was about to respond, but was prevented from doing so as his cousin placed his hand on Matt's arm.

"Eddie Bartolamo, Eddie B. to his friends, is the President of the Sanitation Union for the City of New York," said the detective. "He is also a lifetime member of this community. Nothing happens around here that does not reach Eddie's ear."

Matt sat back against the soft cushions of the sofa. He realized that Eddie was the "man." It would serve no useful purpose to disrespect him. Eddie might not be a mobster, but he had to have close ties with the "boys" to hold his position of authority.

Without asking, the woman reappeared and brought a tray of cups of espresso for Eddie's guests. She quickly vanished.

"There was a guy who claimed he was from here who was murdered up in Connecticut. He wasn't there very long, maybe a few months, and he claimed to be from 187th street and Arthur Avenue."

"Five Ninety," said Eddie. "Upstairs from the bank."

The detective smiled a knowing smile.

"What was his name?"

"The name he gave was Enzo Pasconi. We have no way of knowing if it was real or not."

"Why the interest?" Eddie wanted to know.

"Matt," said the detective, prompting him to answer Eddie's question.

"He seems to be somewhat of a mystery man. He got the job under very strange circumstances. Right now, we are gathering as much information as possible, trying to see what we can come up with," said Matt.

"So you got zilch!" said Eddie.

"Yeah, that and not much else," said Matt.

Eddie let out a laugh.

"Hey Philly boy," he said to the detective, "I think I like this guy."

"That's great," said the detective in return, "cause I know he really likes you."

Everyone laughed.

"The teamsters want me to help you out, Philly," said Eddie. "As you know, we usually don't like to give aid to the badges, but it seems like this thing goes pretty deep and people I know are very concerned about that murder and about some secret plans that have gone missing."

Matt sat back as his cousin expressed shock at Eddie's words.

"When the Indians attack, the settlers circle their wagons. America is no different from Japan when danger comes calling. We may not see eye to eye, but in times of trouble, we forget all that and deal with anyone foolish enough to start a war with us."

"I told you I liked this guy," said Eddie. "Give me a minute."

Eddie dialed a number and told the man on the other end to expect the two officers and to give them all the aid necessary.

"Go to five ninety. One of my boys will meet you there. Show him a picture and tell him the guy's name. He'll know if he is legit or not."

Once again the woman magically appeared, walked over to the door and opened it. It was an unmistakable sign.

"Grazie," said Phil. "I owe you."

"Yes, you do," said Eddie. "Say hello to your mother for me. Tell her she raised a fine son, even though he chose the wrong side." He smiled, but did not get up.

Both men thanked him and left.

CHAPTER TWENTY-ONE

After they exited the building and descended the steps down to the street, Matt began to laugh uncontrollably.

"What's so funny?" Phil asked.

"What a character that guy is," said Matt.

"Hey, don't laugh, that guy is pretty big stuff, let me tell you," said Phil.

"Okay, if that's the way you want it," said Matt, "but what a scene, straight out of a movie."

"Why do you think it's so funny?" Phil wanted to know.

"It's almost noon and that guy is still in his pajamas. And the personal maid, that was priceless," said Matt.

"Hey, careful Cuz. Eddie B. is not someone to fool with," said Phil.

"Yah, he's real big stuff alright. If he's such a big shot, why is he living in that apartment? What's so special about that place? It's not such a big deal," said Matt.

"It is if you own the whole building, and the one on either side," said Phil.

"For real?" said Matt, shocked by the revelation.

"As real as it gets, my country bumpkin cousin," said Phil.

"Well, don't I feel like an idiot," said Matt.

"If the shoe fits," joked his cousin.

"Oh, thank you very much, Mister New York Slick," said Matt.

Just then, Phil pointed to a very skinny man standing in front of the bank at 590 187th Street. As they drew closer, Matt could see that he was someone in his late forties, nervously smoking his Chesterfield, seemingly marching in place.

"You guys from Eddie B.?" he asked when they approached.

"Yah," said Phil. "I'm Detective Phillip D'Onofrio, N.Y.P.D. and this is Captain Matt D'Onofrio, New Haven, Connecticut, P.D."

"Eddie didn't say nothin' about no cops," said a very nervous thin man.

"And you would be?" asked Phil.

"Joey," the man responded.

"You have a last name, Joey?" Phil asked.

"You don't need to know my last name. What is it I can do for youse guys?" Joey asked.

"Okay, Joey," said Phil with a 'have it your way attitude.' "I want to show you a picture of a man who claimed he lived upstairs until about six months ago."

Detective D'Onofrio motioned for Matt to show Joey the picture of the deceased handyman.

"He don't look so good," said Joey.

"That's 'cause he's dead," said Matt.

"Well, that explains that," said Joey.

"How 'bout we stay focused, Joey. Do you recognize him or not?" Phil asked.

"Never seen him. The people living upstairs been there twenty-five years. Got no son, no nephews in this country, anyway, and don't take in boarders," said Joey.

"Are you sure?" asked Matt.

"As sure as anyone who lives next door to them for twenty-five years. They're in one and I'm in two. There are only two apartments up there. This stiff never lived here," said Joey.

"What now?" Matt asked Phil.

"Eddie B. says I am to take you gentlemen around the neighborhood to see if anyone knows anything," said Joey.

"Lead on," said Phil.

For the next hour Joey led the two policemen throughout the neighborhood. They went in to the shops, visited people in Caccione Park, stopped people on the street who Joey knew; no one knew the deceased.

Finally, Matt and Phil had enough.

"Thanks, Joey, you've been a great help," said Phil. I'll be sure to tell Eddie how helpful you were," said Phil.

"Make sure you do," said Joey. "Eddie takes care of his people. Especially the ones who help him out," said Joey. "So excuse me, gentlemen, but it's past my lunch time and there is a bowl of minestrone waiting for my attention."

Without any more banter, Joey turned and made his way quickly towards his apartment.

"Come on," said Phil to Matt. "Can't send you home on an empty stomach."

Phil led Matt back up Arthur Avenue to Roberto's. Most of the restaurants on the avenue had been there for years. Roberto's was no exception. White tablecloths and waiters dressed in black greeted them. The waiters also had been there for years. One of the house specialties was lamb chops with a side order of black truffle linguine and goat cheese ravioli. Phil ordered for both of them and they ate and enjoyed each other's company. Just before they finished and paid the bill, Phil got a call from headquarters. He excused himself from the table and walked over to the bar area to talk to his commanding officer. He had just finished, hung up and sat down and ordered espresso when he was again called to the phone by the bartender. He excused himself a second time, and went to the phone. Matt could not help notice that this conversation was heated and was causing his cousin to become embarrassed. He finally hung up and rejoined Matt.

"Trouble?" Matt inquired.

"The worst kind," Phil said.

"My mother. I am to take you to a few shops before you go back home, so you can bring some things to your mother. She says she'll be disgraced if you go home empty-handed. I tried to tell her you were here on official business. That didn't matter to her. Come on, let's get out of here."

Phil led Matt down the Avenue and crossed over to a bakery called Madonia.

"They make the best black olive bread," he informed his cousin. He ordered a loaf of black olive and another of the house bread. Next, they went to Marrone's Pastry Shop and ordered a box of pignoli nut cookies. They were not done. Phil took Matt into Peter's Meat Market to buy two large sticks of sopressata, a table sausage to go with a pound of pecorino table cheese. They took the bags and boxes and headed to Phil's cruiser. Matt was sure they would be heading back. He was wrong. Phil drove over two blocks on 187th to Artuso's, famous for their biscotti. Phil got out and told Matt to wait. He would be right back. One pound of mixed biscotti from Artuso's was placed in Matt's lap.

"Do yourself a favor. Don't fight it. Italian mothers are impossible. My mother would skin me alive if I did not do this. As far as she is concerned, her honor is at stake," said Phil.

Matt stayed silent as Phil put the car in gear, made a left on E. Fordham Road and began their trip back to Manhattan.

CHAPTER TWENTY-TWO

It was around three in the afternoon when Matt and his cousin crossed the 2nd Avenue Bridge to take the Harlem River Drive down the East River to Police headquarters in lower Manhattan.

"What are your thoughts, Cuzz?" He could see Matt wrestling with those thoughts.

"Well," Matt began, "we now know that the handyman probably never set foot in the Bronx, and certainly never lived in the Arthur Avenue section. So, once again, we got squat. We got a guy who shows up in Saybrook pretending to be an Italian off the boat. He just happens to come into town right when the local handyman mysteriously goes missing. No one knows where the handyman is and now we know that we know absolutely nothing concerning his unfortunate replacement. I don't doubt the guy was really Italian and let's face it, Mussolini will do anything the Nazis tell him to do, so it's a safe bet that he was sent here by our enemies."

"Even though he was murdered?" asked the detective.

"Yeah, even though. I am thinking this guy was placed here to aid the killer who probably got pretty angry when his plans did not work out. Let's face it, the stakes were high and the killer probably has to answer to someone whom he would not want to cross. Phil, you should have seen the crime scene. I am telling you, it was some of the worst homicide photos I have ever seen. Whoever killed him and that poor woman turned it into a slaughter. The ME in Connecticut still has not been able to conclude just how many wounds they had. Their blood was everywhere. The force of the attacks on their bodies was fierce. Whoever did this was quite strong and pretty high-strung, believe me."

"So we're talkin' overkill, here?" said the detective.

"Of the highest order," said Matt, who suddenly became silent and took note of all the buildings along the drive.

"Jeez," he said, finally. "How on earth do you deal with a city this big? I sometimes find New Haven a little overpowering. Manhattan is beyond my scope."

The detective just laughed. "Believe me, Cuzz, after you live here a while, it really becomes doable. I've been here all my life. To me, it's just one big neighborhood, one very big neighborhood."

Matt also laughed. He just looked over at his cousin, but said nothing.

"There are some people waiting to see you downtown. I think they are naval intelligence. They have a report to give you to bring to your State Police buddy in Connecticut."

"Do you know what's in the report?" Matt asked.

"Not a clue." He answered.

"Sit back and enjoy the ride, Matt. You will find out soon enough."

Detective D'Onofrio's words quickly came true. No sooner had he and Matt entered police headquarters, down in the financial district, Matt was ushered to a conference room where six members of the armed forces intelligence agency were seated and waiting.

Matt took the seat offered him on one side of the table while the six others faced him across the cheaply covered 12 x 3 foot conference table. The lead man, Admiral Wilson Blake, introduced the five other attendees whose names Matt quickly forgot. The five were high ranking officers of the Army and Navy.

Matt noticed the leather-bound folder placed in front of him. It was entitled Top Secret.

"We have been instructed to show this to you, Captain D'Onofrio, and to make sure we answer any questions you may have. You will be taken back to New Haven by an armed guard where you are to give this report to Captain Tyler of the Connecticut State Police. You are to show this to no one else. Captain Tyler will take charge of it. This report comes from the highest possible authority. There is also a letter of instruction informing you that all of the New Haven Police Department will now follow Captain Tyler's orders to the letter. Your mayor and all elected officials are being notified as we speak."

At that moment, Matt D'Onofrio gained a full understanding of just how serious this whole matter was. He could not think of a better man to be in charge of this operation than his good friend Samuel Tyler. He held Sam in the highest regard. He knew him to be honest, intelligent and someone committed to the defense of his country. And now, he opened the report upon the admiral's instruction.

Anti-Mussolini underground forces in Sicily have informed the US Naval Fleet off the coast of Italy that the Bavarian Brothers who vacated Charles Island off the coast of Milford, Connecticut, have been given sanctuary at the Vatican. This was discovered by a group of powerful Sicilian cardinals violently opposed to Italy's involvement with Hitler. There is a rapidly growing atmosphere of hostility towards the Pope's allowing these people to come under the protection of the Vatican. It is believed that it is Hitler's plan to annex all of Europe under German control. This will lead to the extinction of the Vatican and Papal Order, and replaced by non-religious tolerance and obedience only to the Nazi Party. Hitler is a great fan of the Illuminati.

The Pope, understanding the gravity of the rebellion, acquiesced to the pressures and had the order transferred to a castle in

France, owned by Prince Edward of England, suspected of sympathizing with the Nazis.

The Sicilians got word to the Mediterranean Fleet which then transmitted the news to the American Forces who in turn informed members of the French Resistance Forces. Although the French castle was being guarded by a small squad of elite German soldiers, it was quickly overrun by French Resistance Forces. Captured, along with the Bavarian Brothers, was documentation strongly suggesting that there were huge amounts of pirate gold buried on two islands off the northeastern coast of America. The first was on Gardner's Island, a very large island just off the northern tip of Long Island and west of Montauk Point. The other was on Naushaun Island located off the southern tip of Cape Cod, Massachusetts.

The report drew a conclusion that these two islands had a connection with Charles Island in Milford, Connecticut. Lines drawn connected all three islands forming a strange triangle which vaguely resembled a secret Masonic symbol. There was one more piece of information that really caught Matt's eye. An island north of Naushaun Island in Nova Scotia called Oak Island was said to have been visited by Templars during the time of their persecution by the French. It suggested that they followed the sea routes taken by the Vikings as they left Scotland seeking a location to bury an enormous fortune which many authorities believe truly exists. At one time, in their glory days, before the persecution instituted by King Louis IV of France, the Templars were one of the wealthiest entities on the planet.

Hitler was, himself, a fanatic in his beliefs that the pirates and the Templars were really one, and as one, they buried their treasures in many places, none of which has yet to be discovered.

Matt noticed a second report that was bound and tightly secured. It would take a sharp object to free it. "The second report can only be opened by Captain Tyler. He will then read it and fill you in on what it says. Any questions, Captain?" said the admiral.

"How soon do we leave, sir?" asked Matt.

"Immediately," said the admiral.

Two armed guards were brought into the room to escort Matt back to New Haven. Matt followed them down to the street and joined them in a black, four-door Cadillac limousine. Matt with his boxes of Arthur Avenue bounty sat in the back between the two guards while another guard sat up front. The soldier in the front surveyed the scene, and once satisfied with what he saw, motioned for the driver to head out, which he did instantly.

Matt was surprised when the large vehicle was guided over the Brooklyn Bridge and headed in a northeasterly direction where it picked up the Belt Parkway heading along the coast. Matt seemed a little uncomfortable.

"Relax, Captain," said the soldier in front. "We are going to Idlewild to take you to a small plane used to transport the brass quickly and comfortably wherever they need to go. It's a six seat twin engine Cessna kept in a secluded hangar. The fewer people who know of its existence the better."

"Will we be flying into New Haven?" Matt asked.

"Deep River, sir," the soldier answered. "Your Captain Tyler will be there along with Navy Intel. He will open the second report and fill everyone in. From that point, he is the guy in charge. He must be some pretty important man to have the president so sure that a civilian can handle this sort of operation."

The soldier was looking for a response from Matt. Matt simply folded his arms, smiled and settled back into his seat. It wasn't long before they were making their way through the airport, passing the main terminals and heading to a remote hangar quite a distance from the commercial terminals.

The limousine made its way inside the hangar and Matt and his three escorts got out and boarded the plane. Without much fanfare or hesitation, the pilot taxied out of the hangar and onto a remote runway near the water's edge that could only be used by a small plane. Within moments they were lifting up into the clouds and heading for a rendezvous with Captain Tyler in the field at Deep River where Sam had been introduced to the secret gliders by Arlen Templeton.

CHAPTER TWENTY-THREE

Up in Deep River, the temperature was not quite as inviting. Still milder by most winter standards, the wind had begun kicking up causing it to feel much colder than the actual temperature. Sam stood shivering alongside Arlen Templeton as the two waited for the twin engine plane transporting Captain Matt D'Onofrio to return from New York City. Night was quickly falling, promising to make things much colder. Standing nearby were six very somber looking naval officers, a group that included Commander Anthony Thomas, the naval officer who was in charge of the facility under the Villa Rosa in Milford. He and Sam had developed a close relationship following their successful collaboration thwarting an enemy attempt to bomb the huge gas storage tank in Bridgeport harbor. Commander Thomas was very vocal in his whole- hearted support of Sam being chosen to head up the ongoing investigation. Considering the fact that there was so little to go on, Commander Thomas knew it would take many entities, working together to coordinate successful efforts to insure the Nazis were prevented from gaining critical American military strategy that was either stolen by the naval imposter Boland or captured along with him. It was Commander Thomas' opinion that Sam possessed the intellectual and social skills to get all parts of their cooperation with one another for the sake of the American war effort in Europe. Even though the stakes were high and their country needed them, petty jealousies between many factions had to be recognized. Everyone wanted to be the white knight, the hero of the day when the very day was in great danger of being lost, courtesy of their foolish ignorance.

Just as the light of day was about to disappear, the twin engine became visible above the trees and made its descent onto the open field. The last thing anyone was expecting to see was Captain Matt D'Onofrio exiting the plane with his arms full of boxes of Arthur Avenue treasures.

"Why did you say the captain was going to New York?" asked an amused Arlen Templeton as the naval brass looked on in disbelief.

"I guess he didn't want to waste the opportunity to bring back some real New York Italian," quipped Sam.

Captain D'Onofrio hastily made his way over to where they were waiting.

"Well Matt, I see your trip was fruitful," said Sam.

"More than you can imagine," said Matt. "I have important documents for you, courtesy of the United States Navy. I have been instructed to give these to you for your immediate attention. I assume that is why the Navy brass is here."

Sam had been made aware that a meeting with the Navy was immediately required and quickly took note of Matt's confused look over the presence of Arlen Templeton.

"I am aware of the gravity of the task before us, and I can think of no one better to help me decipher certain delicate pieces of information for which I am, regrettably, ignorant. Arlen is my father-in-law, my children's grandfather and one of the most patriotic Americans I know. He is also the possessor of a brilliant mind and has access to people and places I may need to get things moving along with very little time wasted trying to break down walls. Besides, he is an old poker playing chum of the President. Surely that can be of immense aid. And, I trust him with my life."

Matt had to agree. Sam had made sure that his comments to Matt were spoken quietly before the naval group joined them. It was agreed that they would adjourn to the Griswald Inn to go over all the material sent from New York.

All the arrangements had been made. Arlen Templeton had seen to that. Nine very serious men entered the Griswald Inn, at the far end of Main Street in Essex. The 'Gris' as it was known to the locals and fans, had a registry that said it opened for business in 1776 and laid claim to the title of one of the oldest, if not the oldest, continuous running Inns in America. The Gris never made any pretense to modernize or upgrade the way it presented itself to the throngs of satisfied guests, who joined the legion of repeat customers wishing to escape their busy lives and steal away to a place that took them back to a time when America was young and in many ways innocent.

Arlen could easily have used his considerable influence with the military to commandeer the dining room, but that was not his style. Instead Arlen secured the dining room by assuring the inn-keeper that he would match the proceeds usually taken in for that evening of the week, while treating all the guests and dinner patrons to dinner on Arlen in the bar. Fortunately, the normally busy bar did not have any entertainment scheduled for the evening which meant only the local regulars would be in attendance. Still, Arlen made sure that their first drink was on him.

Sam and the group were led to the dining room where they began rearranging tables and chairs into a circle signifying the way this meeting would play out. Sam would open each report, read it, and then pass it around to the naval officers. Matt would be filled in later, but would be present to get a pretty good idea of the content. For now, his job was to make sure that no one outside of the group wandered in accidentally. Sam was relatively sure that Arlen had a pretty good idea of the contents of the reports.

Sam opened the leather-bound briefcase containing three separate documents. He had no idea what they contained, but he would not have long to find out.

The first dossier Sam saw had a document attached, alerting him that all the information he was about to study was believed by the high command to be absolutely essential towards the unraveling of this mystery which must be solved with the utmost speed. Sam was to spare no one and nothing towards that goal. He was also informed that his was of a civilian nature, but would place the military at his disposal whenever necessary. He was to report only to Admiral Blake who would supply him with a coded phrase that only the two of them would know. Sam was to respond to no one else, even if they should discover the coded phrase.

CHAPTER TWENTY-FOUR

Dossier One

Charles Island on Long Island Sound, just off the coast of Milford, Connecticut is believed to be one of three islands Adolph Hitler has great interest in. All three are believed to have treasure buried on them by Captain Kidd and various other pirates. When lines are drawn to connect the three, they form a triangle which is a most significant symbol of Mason involvement.

The first island is located directly across the Sound at the far end of Long Island in the vicinity of Montauk Point. Gardener's Island sits in a land surrounded inlet. It is six miles long, three miles wide and has been owned by the same family for well over three hundred years. Lion Gardener obtained it by royal decree from King Charles I of England. It was the first colonial settlement of the State of New York. Over the years, the Gardeners have welcomed guests from every stratum of society. It is rumored that most of the island is uninhabited and the vegetation made it easy for pirates to come and go undetected. One end of the island, in particular, served as a harbor to accommodate invited guests to dock and come ashore. It was the part of the island where most activity occurred. The coast of the island measured twenty-seven miles, not all accessible by craft, with a long stretch of a very narrow finger-like protrusion stretching from the southern tip south-westerly towards the western tip of Long Island.

Local legend states that Captain William Kidd came to Gardener's Island in sixteen ninety nine on his way to Boston to answer charges branding him a pirate as opposed to the privateer he claimed to be. It is said that Kidd was welcomed by John Gardener who granted Kidd permission to bury some of his treasure there with the expectation that Kidd would be freed and return to get his treasure. Neither happened.

It would be quite easy for Germans to gain access to Gardener's Island as it is quite remote and taking control of the island would not take much effort. It is not being monitored by the military at this point. It is also believed that very few people live on the island. Any attempt to protect it by the locals would be futile.

Sam finished reading and passed it along to Commander Thomas.

Dossier Two

Naushon Island, just off the coast of Cape Cod, is another island that has been owned by one family for over one hundred twenty years. It is seven miles long and is part of the Elizabeth Islands. It is the largest of the Elizabeth Islands and like Gardener's, it is inhabited by very few. Long before the Forbes family took possession of the island, John Murray Forbes purchased it from James Bowdoin III, of the Bowdoin family, who had owned the island from 1776 when father James Bowdoin II, the Governor of the State of Massachusetts, took possession of it. Ownership before that was anybody's guess. Some evidence suggests Indian inhabitants were there. Nonetheless, Kidd and other pirates or privateers, whatever they were, had unlimited access to it and are rumored to have buried vast treasures there. Many have searched, none have been successful.

This brought clarity to the unknown elements of all the information of the first two, while expanding the mystery far beyond anything Sam had envisioned until now.

Dossier Three

Evidence obtained from the Bavarian Order in France suggests that a small island off the coast of Nova Scotia, Oak Island, contains greater treasures than the other three islands combined. If what the Bavarian Brothers claim can be believed, it would help to explain why the Vatican gave them aid and shelter, especially as it was discovered that the ten non-Bavarians who cohabited Charles Island with them, were held captive by them and then cast adrift in the North Atlantic. They were never heard from again.

According to the Bavarians, who were trying to make a deal with the resistance fighters, the Templar Knights fled France in 1307 to escape the tyranny of King Philip IV. Up until that time, the Templar Knights had become the wealthiest and most powerful entity on earth, possessing a navy of more ships than any country. While the Templars existed in places other than France, it was in France where they became the most powerful.

Louis IV's attempts to capture, torture and learn the whereabouts of their treasures forced them to escape to Scotland, Switzerland and Spain, among others.

It was in Scotland that they learned of the voyages of the Vikings to the New World over sea routes high in the North Atlantic. It is believed that the Templar Knights became tradesmen to escape tyranny and find autonomy among the people with whom they lived. One of the trades they invested their energies in was in masonry. Before very long, they became the masters of that craft. Thus, the Masonic Order took root. These men became the master builders of their day and created an organization that would offer a place of refuge for those who would oppose government tyranny and control.

It is believed that, following the routes of the Vikings, they traveled to Oak Island and placed their vast treasures there. By this time, they had learned to devise many architectural designs that would thwart any attempts by fortune seekers to gain possession of their hidden wealth.

No one knows for sure why they would choose to travel across an ocean to a small, seemingly insignificant island in such a remote place, but as is well known, the Masons gained a foothold in North America and many experts believe that they have made incredibly large contributions to some of our most important buildings, including the general layout and architectural design of our nation's Capital. George Washington was himself a Grand Mason and it is documented that under his guidance, Washington DC took form with the Masons being the chief architects. Their symbols are everywhere and no one can dispute the evidence of their design influence.

Sam passed the final report along and sat back, closed his eyes and let all he had read sink in. It wasn't easy.

"Three American islands reported to have pirate treasure buried somewhere on them. An island in Canadian waters that is believed to possess one of the greatest treasures in the world. Templar Knights becoming Masons. The Masons becoming a secret society while also becoming some of the most significant architects and builders the modern world has ever known."

These were Sam's thoughts as he tried to digest all of what he had just learned. And these thoughts were beginning to give him a major headache as he challenged his brain to produce an answer to the biggest question of all: "What on earth has all of this got to do with someone impersonating a naval officer, who was either kidnapped or is part of a plan that killed two seemingly innocent people in a place far removed from anything that could remotely connect it?" He had not yet been told by Matt that it appeared that Enzo Pasconi also was an impostor. Meanwhile, all this was doing was adding fuel to the fire that was a headache gaining strength with each passing minute.

After everyone had read the material, Sam opened the discussion to the group hoping someone, anyone, could share information that would be of some help. The discussion opened to the group. If nothing else, a few good ideas would be most welcome. All Sam got for his trouble was six blank U.S. Navy faces staring back at him. Finally, he adjourned the meeting, allowing the naval officers to get back to their stations. He spent a few extra minutes with Commander Thomas. They both agreed to keep in close contact with each other as things progressed. Considering how little, if any, progress had been made, Sam was searching for a more appropriate word. At this point in time, progress was not a word that could honestly be associated with this investigation.

Arlen took his leave, having set up an appointment the next afternoon with Sam in New Haven, after Sam had a chance to get together with Matt, who had to travel back down to New Haven. Sam watched Matt's tail lights disappear up Pratt Street, spent significant energy turning his body towards Aunt Clara's and proceeded to drag himself up the steps that led to her kitchen.

CHAPTER TWENTY-FIVE

Sam walked across the lawn, looking forward to seeing Martha and the children before the children went to bed. Coffee at Aunt Clara's had helped to rejuvenate his spirits.

"Hey Dad," yelled Thomas, as Sam made his way into the kitchen, "Mrs. Callahan has taken a leave of absence. She says she is not feeling well. I'll bet it was Grandpa Arlen that made her sick."

The children laughed. Sam did not. He looked to Martha who remained expressionless. Sam had a feeling she was waiting to see what his reaction would be. Sam let the laughter subside. The children sensed he was not amused by Thomas' revelation. Lilith made her way over to Martha and pressed her body into Martha's legs. Apprehension was in the air. After a few moments of silence Sam spoke.

"Thomas, I would like you to come into the parlor with me."

"Oh boy," said Thomas, fearing the worst.

"Thomas didn't mean anything Daddy," said Mary. "He is just happy that old...," Mary caught herself and thought better about saying anything else. The look her father gave her encouraged that silence. Mary looked over to Martha who motioned for her to come join her while Thomas followed his dad into the parlor. Sam and Thomas took seats in the plush chairs facing each other, separated by a beautiful oak and glass coffee table that had been in the Tyler family for over seventy years.

"I'm sorry Dad," said Thomas. "It's just that Mrs. Callahan is so darn mean, it feels good to have her see how it feels."

"I will never tell you how to feel, son, or that you can't get angry with someone, especially if you have good reason," said Sam.

Thomas looked at Sam with a, 'so what did I do wrong, then?' look.

"Your grandfather is a very powerful man. He would never go out of his way to make fun at someone's expense. Mind you, I'm not saying he would not want to. What I am saying is that he has too much dignity to allow himself to stoop to someone else's level. It is true that Grandpa Arlen can make someone sick; I'm sure he has on more than one occasion. We both know he is a very powerful and influential man. But, Thomas, he is also a very highly respected man, not so much for his power, but for his ability to show kindness when he has all the power and his refusal to belittle someone whom he has just overcome with his power. Do you understand?"

"Yes, Daddy, I think I do. Aunt Clara always reminds us that we are Tylers, and the Tylers have a responsibility to act with dignity," said Thomas.

"That's right," said Sam. "And you and your sisters are also members of the Templeton family. You three have a greater responsibility to rise above the crowd. Never forget this. It will have a lot to do with the path you choose in life and just how successful you will be on that path."

"I'm sorry, Daddy. I should not have been so happy to see Mrs. Callahan feeling bad."

"But, it did feel good, didn't it?" Sam asked.

Thomas started to smile. Sam joined him.

"Remember, son, what you felt was natural. And also, the most important thing to remember is how you handle those feelings. People always respect and admire those who consider the other person's feelings. But there is no denying it really did feel good, didn't it?"

Again Thomas smiled and then jumped into Sam's beckoning arms. Much was going to be expected of Thomas. He alone carried the Tyler name. It was an enormous responsibility for a ten year old who just happened to be the only living Tyler male other than Sam, and the only male heir of the Templeton fortune. Yes, it was an enormous responsibility.

* * *

Martha and Sam sat on the plush living room sofa in front of the roaring fire Sam had fixed once the children had gone up to bed.

"You really are a great dad, you know?" Martha said. "You managed to reprimand, teach a valuable lesson and then show your son how much you love him. That really takes in a lot of territory. I'm proud of you, Mr. Tyler."

Sam smiled. "I think you are going a little overboard in the fatherly assessment department," he said.

"I lived with my father for seventeen years of my life and not once did he show me anything like what you did with Thomas. No, he was so caught up in his own world that all I would ever get from him was a look of disappointment or impatience. Heaven forbid he should speak kindly to me or hold me in his arms like you always do to the children. I can tell you without any doubt, either way, children never forget. Yes, the children will live their lives under much scrutiny, but the love they have been shown all these years will carry them through just fine."

"Thank you," said Sam very softly. He realized that in Martha he had gained a true soul mate. Her validating his efforts as a father meant everything. Sam was always questioning himself, wondering if his job was denying his children the childhood he so wanted them to have. Martha's words of encouragement helped ease his conscience.

Sam's demeanor turned serious.

"What's troubling you?" Martha asked. "How did your meeting with Matt and naval Intelligence go?"

Sam took a deep breath, held it and then let it explode out.

"I have never seen a case where absolutely nothing connects. The murders in Fenwick, the disappearance of a naval brass imposter who has extremely dangerous military documents, the death of a female from the Navy secretary pool who may or may not have helped the imposter, a handyman who lied about his last place of residence and whom no one seems to know. (*Matt was able to get word of that to Sam*). And finally, a president that wants me to help make sense of it all. Other than that, I'm feeling quite confident."

It had not taken Martha very long to become familiar with Sam's dry wit as a means for him to deal with his frustrations. She leaned over, put her arms around his neck and kissed him gently on the cheek.

"Even the president realizes how capable my big, strong, handsome, intelligent husband is. Let's not forget what an intelligent person our president is," said Martha in a reassuring tone.

"Wow," said Sam. "Get out the shovels, it's starting to get piled high in here."

They shared a laugh which helped break Sam's somber mood.

"Okay, husband, let's have it. What was your meeting all about?" Martha asked.

Sam filled her in. It took some time as he labored to make sure he made a full and complete disclosure. Sam knew how well Martha could fit the pieces to a puzzle and he greatly valued her assessment of all the pertinent information. He paused on occasion to make sure his recollections were completely factual. Once done, they sat for a few moments in silence. Martha was rolling everything Sam had revealed to her around in her brain. She had to admit none of anything seemed to connect.

"How can I help?" Martha asked.

"By asking to be of help," Sam responded.

"You knew I would. But I don't want to get involved unless that is what you want," said Martha.

"Many different sources are going to come into play before this whole affair comes to light. I have already secured Arlen's help and now I have yours. You are the only two people on this planet that I can count on, the only two I can trust to let no other agenda influence our work," said Sam.

"So I'm in?" asked Martha.

"All the way," said Sam.

* * *

Sam was just finishing his second cup of coffee at Aunt Clara's, when the children came running up the backstairs and burst into the kitchen.

"Daddy, Daddy," they breathlessly yelled in unison, "the soldiers are here!"

Martha joined Sam as he walked to the back porch to see what the children were yelling about. Martha had been on the telephone talking to her dean at Albertus Magnus about a change in scheduling her last lecture hall session before Christmas break.

As Sam and everyone reached the back porch, they were met by two Army officers who were standing in front of a large black four door Packard Sedan accompanied by two military Jeeps, one in front and one in back. One of the officers stepped forward.

"Sorry to bother you sir, but we have been ordered to escort you to a meeting with Admiral Blake," the officer said.

"Exactly where is this meeting to take place?" Sam asked.

"I am not at liberty to tell you sir, until you are in the automobile provided for you and we are underway," the officer said, pointing to the Packard. "The admiral will be calling you at this number and will supply you with the necessary information. I suggest you go back into the house now and wait for his call."

Sam hesitated for a moment to let the message sink in. He then gathered the family and did as the officer suggested. In two minutes, at eight thirty am., Aunt Clara's phone rang. Sam answered it and immediately recognized the voice of Admiral Wilson Blake who spoke the password Sam had been instructed to memorize and respond to when the admiral wished to make contact with him. Sam assured everyone that it was alright, and that he would be accompanying the soldiers to meet the admiral. He took the children to the back porch and signaled to Injun Jim, who had been standing on the side wondering what was happening, to take the children to school. He kissed Martha, who was taking the Buick down to New Haven to do some research for Sam at the Yale library, and then have an early dinner with Peter and Liz Childers before heading back to Essex. He blew a kiss to Aunt Clara who stood there, arms folded and none too happy about the goings on. Surprise guests or visitors were not something she took kindly to. Aunt Clara never saw the need for last minute or unwelcomed impromptu changes of plans.

Sam settled into the large Packard back seat next to one of the soldiers. The lead soldier closed the door behind him, got into the front and ordered the driver to proceed. Before they reached North Main Street, Sam had been informed that Admiral Blake was at Yale with members of the Joint Chiefs of Staff, up from Washington with some late breaking news that he felt would be vitally important to Sam's investigation. At this point, Sam would be willing to go to the North Pole if he could gain even one ounce of information that would help jump start his investigation. At this very moment, Sam had absolutely nothing to aid him in this case. In all his years on the State Police force, he had never been faced with an investigation that was so completely devoid of anything to help gain a successful conclusion to a crime committed on his watch.

After forty minutes of driving through every coastal town between Essex and New Haven aided by motorcycle police escorts from every one of those towns meeting them at the city limits and escorting them to the next, they reached New Haven and Yale. Sam was ushered into the university president's office on the Yale campus, where Admiral Blake and six members of the Joint Chiefs of Staff were waiting in a conference room off the main corridor. The seriousness of this meeting was immediately evident to Sam as he took note of the ten uniformed officers of the United States Marine Corps who were there to make sure no unwanted visitors would interrupt this meeting with Sam.

Admiral Blake introduced the members to Sam and then they all took their seats. No refreshments of any kind were offered. The admiral motioned for the U.S. Army General to issue his report. But before the general could begin, Sam made a request.

"I'm sorry sir, but would it be possible to get a cup of coffee, cream no sugar before we begin? I have not had breakfast today, but coffee will suffice."

The Admiral tried to suppress a smile as it was obvious the brass was not happy with the interruption. He ordered coffee, Danish pastry and muffins to be served ASAP. Everyone waited in aggravated silence until the order showed up, about ten minutes later. The ice quickly thawed as the brass fell all over themselves grabbing the baked goods and coffee. And finally, the general began. He addressed Sam as the others were already aware of all of the information.

"I am going to present you with three separate reports, which we believe when added together present some very interesting conclusions. First, I'm going to fill you in on events from the Russian front, which have only been partially released to the press for reasons I will make clear. Once again, Hitler has underestimated the spirit and resolve of those he chooses to fight. We truly believe he mistook the passive resistance of the Jewish people in his country as an attitude typical of all those around him. Those poor people could not allow themselves to believe something so horrible could exist among their own countrymen. The atrocities committed against them by their own neighbors, was simply something they could not allow themselves to imagine to truly be happening."

Hitler considers the Russians to be sub-humans. He has made strong note of this in many of his speeches. When his panzer divisions began their Russian campaign their early success seemed so easy and seemingly unstoppable that they were emboldened to become more aggressive in the belief that the Russians would just lie down and die before their incredible might. They were wrong. Many people are under the impression that the events at Stalingrad turned the tide for the Soviets. Nothing could be further from the truth."

Sam was startled by this disclosure.

"It was at Kharkov and later, Kursk that the Soviets overcame seemingly impossible odds to stop the German advances and drive them all the way back to where they began, back beyond the Dnieper River. Strategically, those battles were considered stalemates, but in terms of damage and lost tanks, the losses by the Germans were devastating, to say nothing of their spirits being crushed by an enemy that outwilled them. It is one thing to defeat a foe that offers little or no resistance, it is quite another to try to take someone's homeland by force.

"But it was all not spit and blood on the part of the Soviets. The Germans deployed a very intelligent strategy to maintain their advances. They kept reforming their divisions and rebuilding their forces by combining and advancing, not allowing valuable time to be wasted while pushing forward. But the Russians had an ace up their sleeve; they had produced a new tank, the T-14, which was no match for the panzers in one-on-one combat, but were of such a simple, basic design that they could be repaired and placed back into use in an amazingly swift time. The Germans never really knew the size of the Soviet forces they were combating, as the new Soviet tanks kept reappearing, creating the illusion that the Soviets had an inexhaustible supply of tanks. Eventually Field Marshall Prokorouka, of the German Reich, pulled his men back to avoid total annihilation by his enemy. Of course, he could be forgiven for his miscalculations, but acting on the information he had, he made the right decision. The Soviets would have fought down to the last tank and the German losses would have been alarmingly high. Prokorouka decided that nothing there was worth the possibility of that occurring. He then convinced Hitler to call off this Soviet offensive, code name The Citadel, before their losses reached a point where they could not recoup their strength.

"Hitler was devastated. Prokorouka was the second general who had disobeyed his orders on the Soviet front. He knew both Prokorouka and Field General Getman at Stalingrad had made the right decision, but their open defiance as he perceived it, was an alarming turn of events. What kind of message would this be sending to his other generals? Hitler was becoming increasingly paranoid that he was losing control and that he was becoming vulnerable to assassination attempts from within his own forces.

"Hitler is a man who believes in prophesies and the occult. Somewhere, in the back of his mind, he envisions that the discovery of a huge fortune hidden by the Templar Knights when they fled France would make him a king in the eyes of his people, who brought him to power because of the horrible bankrupt state of the German nation as a result of reparations paid for their creating World War I.

CHAPTER TWENTY-SIX

Sam spent hours in discussion with the members of the Joint Chiefs to get their individual opinions. He concluded that these men were in general agreement with the findings so far, but each had his own slant on the case before him. All agreed that if organized crime was involved in any way, things could get much more difficult. The "mob" as they were known, controlled the unions. The unions controlled New York, specifically the docks. Now would not be a good time to take these men on if that were the case. They were all keeping their fingers crossed. At this point in time, America did not need to fight another war. Germany and Japan, our opponents who were doing a good enough job of dividing our forces over vastly separate parts of the globe, didn't need any company from within America to make things more difficult than they already were.

Sam had received a message from Martha that she would be dining with the Childers and would be heading back to Essex around six pm Sam got permission from Admiral Blake to have his men bring him to Consiglio's, one of the best Italian restaurants in New Haven, located on Wooster Street in the Italian section, to meet up with Martha. Going home with her was just what his head needed after such an exhausting day. And the sooner he filled her in, the better. Admiral Blake instructed his men and Sam met Martha, Peter and Liz at Consiglio's for dessert. He surrendered to the fact that a real meal was not in the cards today.

For the longest time, Sam's social circle consisted of his family, his Essex neighbors and colleagues. They were enough for him. He never felt as though he were missing anything. Sally's death made demands that he change his focus to be the hands on dad with little time for anything else, considering his heavy workload. Only his barrack's commander had more responsibility. When the commander retired, Sam had to carry a double load until a new commander could be chosen. It should be noted that the governor wanted him to take the post, but Sam loved being a police officer and could not see himself tied to a desk, no matter how important the desk was. It was far removed from the action. The governor accepted Sam's turning down the post, but got his way by announcing that due to the war and a belt tightening economy, appointing a new commander was not essential. He made this decision to include all the State Police barracks in the state. But everyone knew his main objective. Title or no title, the governor wanted Sam and so he got his man.

It had not been that long since he and Martha had been in the company of the Childers. It seemed like only a few moments after he joined Martha, Peter and Liz that they were all laughing, talking up a storm and enjoying each other's company. He could not get over how comfortable he was with Martha's dearest friends. Yes, Pete was a bit of a stiff, but something about Martha really loosened him up. By the time Sam got there, all the walls had come down.

After an hour of merrymaking, the party broke up, everyone hugged and Martha and Sam got in the Buick and began heading back to Essex. Martha bade Sam tell her all that had transpired with his meeting with the Joint Chiefs. For a good half-hour Sam gave her a general overview of all that had been discussed and all the new information that was piling up, but sadly going nowhere.

Martha had to control herself because the day had taken an unexpected turn and she was just bursting to tell Sam all the information she had discovered. Sam finished and asked Martha what she had learned.

"I spent a couple of hours over at Yale and was getting frustrated," she began. "I decided to take a break and go over to Loft's, on Chapel, to get a coffee and raisin bran muffin. I called Liz to touch base with her. She was really excited that I called. She told me Peter had been looking for me over at the library and was upset when he could not find me. Peter wants you to come by the apartment. He has a little surprise for you. He's so anxious to share something with you."

"Slow down." Martha said. "What could that surprise be?" Sam wanted to know.

"You'll have to come over to find out, but Peter tells me you won't be sorry and may not need to go back to Yale after you hear what he has to tell you."

"So, did you go to their apartment?" Sam asked.

"How could I not?" Martha responded. "I couldn't wait to get there."

"And?" said Sam.

"And?" said Martha. "Peter came over with one of his students. I had called Liz in the morning to firm up our plans for later, but she was in the shower so I spoke to Peter. I told him the reason I was coming down to the library. He told me he would relay my message to Liz."

"Who was this student and why would Peter bring a student to meet with you?" Sam asked.

"The student's name was Sheldon Fiedler, of Cold Spring Harbor on Long Island. Young Shel, as he is known to his classmates, is studying pre-law. When I told Peter about my interest in Gardener's Island, he could not wait to go and locate the Fiedler boy and bring him to me."

"It seems you are a magnet for attracting secret societies. Shel told me an amazing story about this fabulous area out on Long Island called the Gold Coast. It seems that it has the greatest concentration of moneyed families in all of America. He claims there are scores of castles, huge homes that rival those of Newport, Rhode Island. The main difference is that these great homes are not seasonal residences, but the place where the elite live year round. These castles, as it were, sit on huge tracts of land. Many are said to have been built by men who are suspected of being Freemasons. If that is true, you can rest assured these homes are overflowing with secret passageways, secret rooms and hiding places. It is possible your fake naval officer is hiding on one of these estates. He was last seen in Manhattan."

"He could be anywhere," said Sam.

"Yes, and one of those places could be out on Long Island," said Martha. "When the depression hit, many of those people went belly up. That and income tax sure cramped their style. But, there are still many very wealthy people living out there. And, some have been suspected of being sympathizers with a socialist form of government, namely Germany. Some have ancestral ties to Germany. Their lives and activities are being looked into by the F.B.I. and a special task force set up by the N.Y.P.D. But these things take time and time is something we have very little of. Sam, I think we should follow this line of thinking. Remember, Gardner's Island is on Long Island and Naushon Island is right across from there in Massachusetts. It is not too difficult to go from the coast of Long Island over to there. Tomorrow I will begin researching this island off Nova Scotia and I will gather everything I can to try to find evidence to substantiate the claim that while in Jerusalem, the Knights Templar discovered the revered treasure of King Solomon. How does that sound?" Martha asked.

At this point, Sam's defenses were gone. All he wanted to do was to assault his mattress at home and spend the next month in solitary confinement. What Martha proposed was the absolute best possible plan to go forward. Sam readily agreed with her. But, he was so tired and mind weary, that he would have gone along with anything anyone told him. Fortunately for him, it was reassuring to know that it was Martha who had come up with the plan. He would go to sleep knowing that when morning came, whatever he had agreed upon with Martha would be the best possible route forward.

CHAPTER TWENTY-SEVEN

Sam was sitting in his office at the State Police Barracks when he was informed that Detective Phillip D'Onofrio of the N.Y.P.D., was on the phone. He looked at the clock and noted that it was one pm. He picked up the receiver to take the call.

"Captain Tyler here," said Sam.

Detective D'Onofrio introduced himself.

"I wasn't expecting your call until tomorrow," said Sam.

"Here in New York we operate on double time, and not by choice," said the detective.

"Have you made any headway with your inquiries?" Sam asked.

"Yah," said the detective, "and much more quickly than I anticipated. It seems that organized crime, New York style, gets antsy when accused of possible espionage and crimes against the country."

"I'll bet," said Sam. "So what did you learn?"

"First, I went over to the Bronx to meet, once more, with one Eddie Bartolamo, the president of the New York City Sanitation Union. When I told him why I was there, he was not very pleased."

"What was his problem?" Sam inquired.

"Well, he was not too happy that I requested he put me in touch with someone from the Bartolo crime family in Brooklyn. He feigned ignorance as to any relationship we might assume he had with the 'boys'. I helped him see that it would be in his best interest to comply as he would not want to become a person of interest if he could avoid it."

Sam let out a laugh.

"I see that your powers of persuasion are finely tuned."

"I do the best I can," said the detective. "But understand, I would not want to be the one who had to go to these people and tell them that they might have visitors from the U.S. Military. The Bartolos are not what anyone would call a refined bunch."

"Was that his chief gripe?" Sam asked.

"Oh, no," said the detective, "it seems that there is some bad blood between the Sanitation Department and the military where Long Island is concerned."

"Did he tell you what caused the bad blood?" Sam asked.

"He nearly spit at me he got so worked up. It seems that one of those huge homes, in fact probably the largest of them all, Cold Spring Harbor, the home of the late Otto Kahn, the great Wall Street banker, was headed for foreclosure and demolition. But as luck would have it, the Welfare Fund of the New York City Department of Sanitation purchased it and its employees enjoyed the building and its grounds, a whopping four hundred forty three acres, as a recreation facility and getaway from nineteen thirty nine to nineteen forty.

"However, that enjoyment was short lived. Sanita, as it had been renamed, came under fire from the residents of the town of Huntington, who proclaimed that they did not want 'those kinds of people' in their town. They chose to go the tax-exempt route and forced the issue in the New York State Supreme Court. They won a victory when a judge granted a restraining order to expel the sanitation people once and for all. Of course, they had to use the tax-exempt excuse to go to court. Huntington claimed that New York City had no right to make the facility a tax-exempt property. And, they won. Even Mayor Fiorello Laguardia was powerless to gain victory for their cause. It might also be noted that the judge was born in the neighboring town of Babylon, Long Island. And so the sanitation people only got to enjoy solitude for one summer. But every one of them will tell you that it was one of the greatest summers of their lives. The town of Huntington won, but it did not make many friends with the people of New York City. But you have to understand that the people of Huntington and the surrounding cities are inhabited by some of the wealthiest people this country has. Alienating these folks would be suicidal for anyone with political aspirations. So much for 'vox populi.'"

Sam was quiet for a moment, and then asked. "So why are Eddie B. and his people mad at the military?"

"It just so happens that in March of this year the mansion was reopened by the United States War Shipping Administration as a school for maritime radio announcers.

The inability of our military to prevent the attack on Pearl Harbor by a whole Japanese armada thousands of miles from home infuriated Congress and President Roosevelt. They were at a loss to explain how the Japanese were able to catch our fleet so totally by surprise. The ineptitude of the military cost the lives of so many of our men, to say nothing of the catastrophic loss of ships in a single day. Something had to be done and someone had to do it. And so, the sanitation people were once again infuriated that they had been kicked out on the pretext that the estate was supposed to be demolished. And there it was, alive and kicking for the military's use. Eddie B. and his people were beyond consolation. They wanted blood but knew that there was little chance of that happening. One more thing, it is rumored that the Brooklyn 'families' were compensated by the grateful elite of Long Island. Let's face it, if this is true, any chance of having the property returned went up in smoke."

"All of this went down when?" Sam asked.

"I finished up with Eddie late yesterday afternoon and came back to my office to run down some other leads. I gave up about an hour ago. I was called into a meeting with my captain and called you as soon as I could get away. Sorry to say my leads were either dead ends or not readily leading to anything helpful. But I am not giving up. It may take some time. Oh, and just so you know, one of the things I am waiting on is to hear from the Bartolos concerning Thomas Ragetti. I spoke with a low level wise guy from their organization. It may take some time for them to respond. And that's about all I have for now."

"I appreciate your efforts, detective. It may be wishful thinking, but I feel like we are finally getting somewhere. I see the tide turning. But as the saying goes, '"the wheels of justice grind slowly,'" said Sam.

"Yah, 'grind' is a good word. I'll keep you in the loop if anything comes up," said the detective.

"Much appreciated," said Sam, who said goodbye and hung up.

* * *

Sam got in touch with Martha who was down at Yale researching the history of the area of Long Island known as the Gold Coast.

"You can't believe a place like this actually existed over the last forty years." She said. "Sam, there is so much wealth here it is truly staggering. Even now, after the crash and income tax, there is probably more wealth here than in any other place on the planet, forget about America. It's a veritable who's who of mega wealth. I've been at this for about four hours and am going to meet Lizzy for lunch. I'll stay here till they throw me out and spend the night with Peter and Liz. I already called Aunt Clara. She was only too happy to have the children all to herself. She'll get their clothes from next door and they can stay the night with her. How are things going for you?"

"Not bad," said Sam. "I just got off the phone with Matt's cousin in New York, Detective Phil D'Onofrio, and he had some interesting information. We're still in the dark here, but I have a feeling we are approaching the dawn."

CHAPTER TWENTY-EIGHT

Sam was about to enter his State Police cruiser when one of his officers called out to him to tell him he had another phone call. Sam looked at the officer who just stood there but made no gesture.

"It's the military again, sir," the officer explained when Sam walked back inside the barracks. "I did not want to shout that out to you."

Sam thanked him, told him it was alright and went to the telephone in his office. He picked up the receiver and found himself talking once again with the admiral.

"We need your presence in Brooklyn asap, Captain. Commander Thomas is heading your way. The Commander has commandeered a private yacht the Safe Harbour out of Port Milford to meet you at the public beach in Westbrook. Commander Thomas will ferry you across the Sound to Rocky Point where you will be taken by transport to the Brooklyn Navy Yard for a meeting with myself and Edward Harriman, the president's chief of staff. Some very interesting things have come to light. Please proceed to the public beach asap. The commander will be waiting for you. There is a small launch that will take you out to the Safe Harbour. Time is of the essence, Captain. Do not delay." The admiral hung up without waiting for Sam's response.

Sam took the phone from his ear, held it out and just stared at it.

"Aye aye, Admiral," he said. "There's only one of me," he deadpanned. Sam was committed to serve his country no matter what the cost, but he was beginning to get a good idea of what military life was all about. Thinking was not a major requirement when you were a subordinate. As he exited the building and hurried to his car, he could not help wondering if he could embrace such a life. Giving orders was great. Taking them without question was quite something else. These were necessary evils as far as the military was concerned, but for someone who made decisions only after careful consideration of all the variables, this could be pure torture.

It did not take very long to get from the State Police Barracks to the public beach. As Sam pulled into the public parking area completely empty at this time of the year, he saw the Safe Harbour out in the bay and a small craft with an outboard motor, with its lone owner, waiting on the shore. Sam parked and approached the small craft and made his way briskly across the sandy beach. The dampness filling the air was not enjoyable.

"Captain Tyler," said the fisherman. "I'm Ned Parker, sir. It will be my pleasure to take you out to the Safe Harbour. They are waiting for you, Captain."

Sam shook Parker's hand, got in the boat and sat as Parker backed out into deeper water, came around and headed for the Safe Harbour.

Commander Thomas welcomed him aboard the thirty-six foot wooden beauty and led the way down to the cabin, which was mercifully warm. The short trip from beach to craft was quite chilling. The seas were calm, but Mother Nature was not going out of her way to make it comfortable. The commander told Sam that it would take approximately ninety minutes to reach Rocky Point, where a small convoy would be waiting to take Sam to the Brooklyn Navy Yard for his meeting on the newest U.S. Navy Battleship *Iowa*.

Sam and the commander spent the whole ninety plus minutes going over every inch of the information they had. As they reached their destination, both men agreed that they were nowhere as far as the investigation was concerned.

Sam shook the commander's hand, exited the Safe Harbour and climbed into an army transport vehicle inhabited by twelve army personnel. There would be no Packard limousine this trip. Instead, Sam and the servicemen were huddled under the canvas which was the only thing between them and twenty-four degrees of winter cold. Sam could not believe his bad luck. This was by far the coldest day of winter to date. But, he could not decide what was colder, the outside temperature or his investigation.

One frigid hour and a half later, the convoy made its way into the Brooklyn Navy Yard, a place Sam had never seen. He exited the truck and took in the terrain. He was struck by the enormity of it and of the magnificent battleship staring him in the face. He was quickly ushered up a gangplank and onto the first of the *Iowa* type battleships of the U.S. Navy, the U.S.S. *Iowa* with its 16" guns looking ominous even in a resting state.

Sam was led below deck to a spacious compartment that caught him off guard. He was not expecting something so refined on a battleship that housed incredible artillery with awesome striking power manned by upwards of twenty-six hundred sailors.

The commander and Sam were introduced to Edward Harriman by Admiral Blake. Harriman was a balding man in his mid fifties who appeared a little on the soft side, physically, to Sam's eye, but there was no mistaking the expensive clothes his body was housed in. Sam knew the difference between what bureaucrats wore for clothing and what the wealthy adorned themselves with. Harrison seemed modest but extremely intelligent. Everyone sat around the oval table which took up the center of the space.

"Thank you for coming on such short notice, Captain, but I felt it paramount that we meet without further delay," said the Chief of Staff.

"You are probably wondering why on a battleship and in Brooklyn, no less."

Sam smiled letting him know that was exactly the question he had in mind.

"Well, this is the first of the new battleships America is producing. The First Lady christened her last year. Besides its many points of interest, it also bears the honor of having transported the president to Algeria on his way to Tehran for a meeting with Winston Churchill and Joseph Stalin, hence the more spacious and elegant quarters. That meeting was absolutely essential to the war effort. She is now here to prepare for her next assignment as part of the Pacific Fleet."

"I had to be in New York for briefings and came across some startling news. But first allow me to inform you that we can eliminate Thomas "Little Tommy" Regetti as having any involvement here."

"How did that happen?" Sam asked.

"It appears that Mr. Regetti, in the flesh, showed up at F.B.I. headquarters in Manhattan early this morning. He had no idea who our Enzo Pasconi was, but he assures us it was not him. As Pasconi is dead, we figured we'd take the man at his word. It was probably one of the very few times in his life that Regetti saw that happen."

Both Sam and Commander Mickelson enjoyed a laugh at the Chief of Staff's wry comment.

"Are you familiar with an area on Long Island known as the Gold Coast?" Harriman asked.

Commander Mickelson was not, but Sam had just discovered its existence. Sam told Harriman that he just had been made aware of it by a professor at Yale who was a friend of his wife. He further relayed that at this moment, Martha is at the Yale Library researching everything she can find about this Long Island Gold Coast.

Harriman paused for a moment, as though in deep thought. Then he smiled and acted as if a light had just gone on.

"Of course, Martha Frost. Let me tell you, Captain, your wife is the darling of the congressional wives in Washington. I can't wait to tell my wife that I met the man who is married to the famous Martha Frost."

Sam just stood there and weakly thanked Harriman. Not knowing the man, he was unsure how to respond.

"I'm sure Marty will be very pleased to hear that she is well regarded in Washington."

Now it was Harriman's turn to feel awkward. "Oh, Marty yes, I see," he said.

But before he had a chance to continue, Commander Mickelson had something to say.

"You know, sir, Sam has become quite well known in certain circles himself," he said. "Actually, the captain has gained quite a reputation for himself."

It was all Admiral Blake could do to keep his composure, realizing that Sam and the commander had just completely stolen Harriman's thunder. But Harriman was a seasoned politico. He quickly gathered himself and took charge of the meeting.

"On his meeting with Prime Minister Churchill, the president and the prime minister had a separate conversation which did not include Stalin or anyone else for that matter.

"It seems that the Wellingtons have a lineage that goes back to Germany. They are from the House of the Hanovers, of decidedly German heritage. When Queen Victoria married Albert, the son of Ernst, Duke of Saxe-Coburgand-Gotha, she embraced the Hanovers. Her son, Edward VII, was the last to carry that name to the grave. George V changed all that in 1917, after twenty-four GOTHA double engine German bombers bombed London during WWI. It was George's intention to eradicate any possible link between England and Germany and to ease tensions which were keenly felt by the British people at that time. Wellington sounded so much more British.

"When George's son, Edward, became king, the monarchy was placed in a terrible state of affairs. Absolutely no one in the British intelligence community believed Edward capable of reigning over England, which was attempting to rebuild itself after WWI. Edward's chief attribute was his elegant appearance and high fashion sense. He displayed little strength of character, so necessary for England at the time and fell in love with a twice divorced American woman of highly questionable character. When it appeared that the royal family was powerless to force Edward to give up this tawdry relationship, they had no recourse but to instruct Parliament to accept Edward's abdication so that he could, as he stated, 'marry the woman that I love'."

Edward was no longer king, but that was not the end of his negative influence. He and Wallace Simpson, the woman he loved, were known to have visited Margonette Provost of the very wealthy Long Island Provosts of banking and shipping money. Provost was a very close friend of Wallace Simpson. Her home was a veritable meeting place for a select number of Americans who embraced Fascism. Edward spoke openly of his favoring this form of government. He and Wallace-Simpson even visited Hitler in Germany and were said to have found favor with the 'Fuhrer.' In an interview with the F.B.I., a monk in an American monastery, once known as Duke Carl Alexander Wurttemberg claims that he knew for a fact that the Duchess, as Wallace Simpson was now known, had slept with a German ambassador, Joachim von Ribbentrop, in 1936 and that he was convinced that the Duchess was still in contact with Ribbentrop and was even leaking secrets to him.

The Duke and Duchess settled in France and as late as February, 1940 a German minister claimed that the Duke had leaked British war plans. Churchill went nearly insane with anger over the outright stupidity and treasonous behavior and had the Duke and Duchess banished to the Bahamas. The only reason they complied was that Parliament was convinced by Churchill to strip the Duke of his title, land and monetary allowances should he refuse. The Duke acquiesced, but still proved to be a thorn in the side of Britain.

French forces have recently taken Bavarian monks prisoners when they raided an estate owned by the Duke. The estate was being guarded by a small force of German soldiers. If Churchill could have gotten his hands on the Duke, at this point, I doubt anyone would have prevented him from strangling him.

If the Provost family estate, the Twin Eagles, in Lloyd Harbor is truly host to sympathizers to the German cause, it could very well be the place where our vanished naval imposter is hiding. The Twin Eagles, a 62 room mansion that sits on a thousand acre plot of land, is said to have been built by a Masonic group and has a myriad of secret passageways and tunnels that provide escape routes to the sea. It is very possible that Commander Boland, or whoever he is, is there and is waiting for the chance to escape by sea to Germany. We have a naval presence off the South Shore, which borders on the Atlantic, but it is impossible to know if the

Germans have submarine activity there, which we suspect is possible."

"Is there any evidence to suggest that Boland is on Long Island?" Sam asked.

"No," said Harrison, "but follow my line of reasoning if you will. Boland was supposed to go to Fenwick to the home of Veronica Lansing. He was claiming to be a relative. Ms. Lansing has denied he is a relative or that she even knows him. Of course, we know that Boland is not his real name, and that as far as we know Veronica Lansing is an only child, born in England and whose parents are deceased. Scotland Yard assures us that they have thoroughly investigated Lansing's family and that she absolutely is an only child. It appears that her father passed away shortly after she was born and that her mother lived her whole life in the same town and at the same residence and that there is no way she could have given birth to another child. She never left and was never away for any amount of time. If this is true, we have to assume that Boland was not going to leave the Lansing residence alive and probably knew this, which is why he did not go and explains the anger of whoever was sent to get the information he was carrying and kill him."

"Is it possible that Veronica Lansing could have suffered the same fate?" Sam asked.

"That is possible, but as of yet, we can find no plausible reason why she and her home were ever brought into the picture in the first place," said Harrison.

"Then that is the answer to all of this," said Sam.

Harrison looked confused.

"How do you come to that conclusion?" he asked.

"Answering that opens up the whole mystery. Right now, it appears that there is no reason or connection. That tells me that there is a reason and a connection, one that will provide the answers we need. Until we unlock that mystery, we are up a blind alley. We must find the answer and fast."

CHAPTER TWENTY-NINE

Sam was weary from all the travel that day and the long ride home from Brooklyn. The military vehicle Sam was being transported home in, a Chevy four-door coupe, made a right hand turn onto South Main Street off of Route #154 when Sam began to notice a chaotic traffic situation at the bottom of Methodist Hill near Champlain Square, Mayor Tinsley's residence. There appeared to be an inordinate number of vehicles parked haphazardly with no drivers in sight. The scene in front of him quickly brought him out of his funk. Then Sam noticed one of the local teenagers heading his way.

"What's all the commotion?" Sam asked the boy.

"Fire up at the Methodist Church. Someone tried to burn the nativity scene on the lawn," the boy responded.

"What?" yelled Sam. He informed the driver, an army private that he would go on foot from here. He gathered his things, thanked the driver for the ride and sent him on his way. Sam made his way up the hill and through the large throng of emergency personnel and what appeared to be half the town folks, some of whom were at the Methodist Church meeting to discuss plans for their Christmas pageant and other related holiday activities. He found Mayor Tinsley, who was wearing a fireman's hat that said "Fire Chief " on it.

"Sam, my boy, thank God you are here," said the mayor.

"What's going on Mayor?" Sam asked.

"I'm not sure, Sam, but I'm starting to get a bad feeling. This is the second fire this week at the Methodist Church. A couple of days ago, there was a fire in the kitchen downstairs in the church hall. Thank goodness the pastor smelled something and called it in. We are only a volunteer company Sam, but these boys responded immediately and prevented some serious damage," said the mayor.

Just then Trooper James Colson, the State Police trooper, who is assigned to the Essex Police station approached Sam and the mayor. The town of Essex has a provision in its charter to pay the State of Connecticut to have a State Police presence in the town. As it was, Essex only had a two man police force. Most of the time, the trooper's presence was only a deterrent. They were not there to enforce the laws of the town of Essex, but rather to be of assistance should it become necessary. Of course, in time of emergency, they were to take whatever action necessary. Their training made them much more capable of taking the lead in those times. The town of Essex was most grateful when they did.

"Have you interviewed anyone who might have seen something suspicious?" Sam asked Trooper Colson.

"No one seems to have seen anything, sir," said Colson.

"Anything to report?" Sam asked

"I spoke to the pastor who said he heard a loud bang coming from the hall. When he came downstairs to investigate, he noticed the fire in the kitchen. He was so rattled he grabbed the fire extinguisher and put out the flame before it could do much damage."

"Did he see or hear anything else?" Sam asked.

"He was much too concerned with the fire to notice anything else," the trooper said.

"Okay," said Sam. Try to help restore order and see if the parishioners want to continue with their meeting. If they do, I want you to stay here to make sure they are safe. If not, send them on their way and see if you can lend any assistance to the police. Then go back to your post. I'll contact you later."

The trooper did as he was instructed. Sam walked back over to where the mayor was standing.

"Nothing like this has ever happened here, Sam," said the mayor.

"Has anyone heard of any problems the church has had with anyone?" Sam asked.

"I'll have a talk with the pastor to see if they have been having any difficulties with anyone," said the mayor.

"Very good," said Sam. "It looks like you have the situation well in hand, mayor. I'm glad you were able to continue on as mayor. I believe the townspeople made a very wise choice. You are good for this town, sir. Keep up the good work."

The mayor was pleased to hear Sam's encouraging words.

"Thank you, Sam," said the mayor. "That means a lot to me coming from you. But let's not forget that I wouldn't be standing here if not for Wanda Loomis. She really turned the tide in my favor," said the mayor.

"Just shows she has good taste," said Sam with a smile.

The mayor smiled back.

"Samuel," said the mayor, "I sincerely mean it when I say you have no idea how much that means to me." The mayor could hardly utter the words. It was obvious that Sam's opinion of him was extremely important.

Sam placed his hand on the mayor's shoulder, then turned and headed back down the hill towards home. Along the way he had a chance to speak to some of the locals. He saw Wanda Loomis outside the Black Swan and congratulated her for helping Tinsley regain his office.

"He loves this town and he loves his job, Sam," said Wanda. "No one is going to put more effort into keeping this town a great place to live and bring up a family."

Sam had to agree. He gave Wanda a hug then headed for home. He smiled to himself on the way, being grateful for a small break from the investigation, which had now officially consumed him.

Aunt Clara was standing on the back porch with Injun Jim as Sam came up the driveway.

"Welcome home, son. What's all the fuss?" she asked.

"A fire up at the Methodist Church, I fear they have made an enemy," said Sam.

"That's the second one this week, Sam," said Aunt Clara.

"So I hear," said Sam. "Do you know of anyone who has some sort of problem with the church or its pastor?" Sam asked.

"No, but it sure appears as though someone is looking to make trouble for them," said Aunt Clara. "Dear Lord, the church wasn't damaged was it?"

"For goodness sake, Samuel, it's Christmastime. Who could be that cold to start trouble with them during the Christmas season?" said Aunt Clara.

"The church is fine," said Sam. "But, it does appear as though someone is taking issue with them."

"The world sure is changing, Aunt Clara," said Sam with an air of disappointment. "It appears that the problem is taken care of, for now, but I'm concerned we haven't heard the end of this. I'm going to have my men who are stationed at the police station to keep a lookout for any suspicious behavior. I assume the children are in bed?"

"All snug as a bug, nephew," Aunt Clara assured him. "You look very tired. Go home and get a good night's rest. I'm sure whatever problems there are to create this awful situation will still be here in the morning waiting for you."

Sam smiled a wry smile, kissed his aunt and said goodnight to her and Injun Jim and then headed home. He was amazed at how many nights he was experiencing this walk across the lawn that felt like he was carrying a piano on his back. With great effort he dialed the Childers' residence and told Martha the news about the fire and that he would be waiting for her in the morning to fill her in on his trip to Brooklyn. After he looked around and decided that no one was going to help him climb the stairs to his bedroom on the third floor, he began the laborious trek upstairs and the promise of a waiting mattress.

* * *

Sam had asked Aunt Clara to ring him in the morning so he could have breakfast with the children before they went off to school. After her call, he quickly jumped out of bed and showered, dressed and made his way across the lawn. It was a royal raucous gathering as the children jockeyed for Sam's attention wanting to know how his case was going and if he remembered the upcoming trip to New York City was only eight days away. Sam did his best to hide his apprehensions and the stress he was under to make sense of this investigation. As if he didn't need anything else to add to the pressure he was under, he knew that it would be very difficult to take the family to New York and not have his mind elsewhere.

Aunt Clara came into the kitchen and informed the children it was time to get their things and head off to school. They grabbed their books, hugged their dad and bolted out the back door to a waiting Injun Jim. Aunt Clara was already on the back porch and hugged each one and told them how much she loved them. She then went into the kitchen and warmed up Sam's coffee and poured a cup for herself. She sat down at the table with Sam.

"The children are sure all fired up over this trip to New York," she said.

Sam smiled and took a large gulp of his freshly warmed coffee.

"I know you are under a lot of pressure, Samuel, but don't let it get the best of you. The good Lord will see us through all of this. He knows what you are going through and I truly believe no foreign enemy is going to be allowed to damage America," said Aunt Clara.

"Well, while He's at it, I sure hope some answers start appearing because I have never been so in the dark," said Sam.

"Have a little faith, nephew. You would never have been put in charge of this whole thing if you were not given the tools to handle it. I have complete faith in you," she said.

Sam sat back in his chair. The thought occurred to him that he was allowing himself to be swallowed up by an avalanche of maybes and possibilities. He was expecting Martha to be home at any moment. All of a sudden he felt a charge of adrenaline. He and Martha would do a suspect board even though there were no real suspects. The only way to make headway was to spread all that he knew before him to try to narrow down the puzzle.

"You know, Aunt Clara," he said, "this may sound crazy, but I believe we are only days away from cracking this thing. Thank you."

"Thank me? For what?" Aunt Clara wanted to know.

"Clarity," said Sam. "Clarity."

It was at that very moment that Sam became convinced, in the absence of any clear reason that this case would be solved before the trip to New York was to take place. Burned into his brain was the thought that he could not allow America's enemies to succeed on the home front. No, it was time to lay all the pieces out and set a plan of attack in motion. Heaven help anyone who called himself an American who might think that for a moment they would be allowed to do anything to place our fighting boys in harm's way. Not if Samuel Tyler had anything to say about it.

Sam was not a person who condoned violence, but in the case of those who committed crimes against America, he promised himself that he would be present at their trial and execution.

* * *

Martha came into the kitchen and hugged Aunt Clara and then went to kiss Sam, who had gotten up to greet her.

"I'll leave you two alone to gab," said Aunt Clara. "I hear my driver pulling into the driveway. Injun Jim is taking me down to Saybrook to get some fresh fish for tonight's dinner."

Aunt Clara made her exit and Martha got herself a cup of coffee and sat down with Sam to hear all about his time at the Brooklyn Navy Yard. Sam filled her in on all that had occurred and that he felt they were ready to go on the offensive with this case. Martha had only two lecture hall classes before Christmas break. Her decks were cleared for her and Sam to get aggressively active to try to solve the strange case before them. But first, Sam had to follow up on the fire at the Methodist Church. He said he would be back in an hour or so, giving Martha a chance to freshen up and relax and place all the information she had gathered at Yale to present to him.

Sam's first stop was to meet Mayor Tinsley at the Black Swan. Wanda made sure there was plenty of freshly made coffee for them.

"Sam, I can't help feelin' as though someone is sending a message here. I really don't believe someone wants to burn that church down. It seems awful fishy to me that the pastor heard a very loud noise coming from down in the church hall. It's almost as if someone wanted him to find that fire," said the mayor.

"I think you're right, Mayor." Sam said. "To follow that up with a fire set on the church lawn makes me think that the pastor or the church, for that matter, has found himself an enemy. I'm not feeling comfortable knowing many people, especially children, will be in the church and possibly in danger. We have to find out if anyone knows of any problem that exists between the church and any group or anyone. We can't be too careful here. I'm hoping this will not cause any problems for the parishioners during this holiday season."

"Right you are, Sam," said the mayor. "What do you have in mind?"

"We're spread pretty thin when it comes to law enforcement here," said Sam. "I can have my man cover the church for at least four or five hours. But he would have to respond if he were called away. I was wondering if you could round up a few volunteers to keep a watchful eye on the church. I'll deputize them so that they will be official, but with the express understanding that they were there to observe and report. Under no circumstances are they to carry any weapon or try to take action on their own."

"Right you are, Sam," said the mayor. "We don't want anyone getting themselves hurt over some foolish notion that they are law enforcement officers."

"Absolutely," said Sam, "to say nothing of the possible legal liabilities should that happen."

"Oh, dear," said the mayor, "that would be terrible."

"Yes, awfully expensive and terribly complicated if someone were to get really hurt on your watch, sir."

The mayor began to respond, but stopped himself. He seemed to be envisioning the worst scenario. One could say that the mayor froze in his tracks.

Sam said his goodbyes and headed over to the town hall on West Avenue where the Essex Police Department was housed. A state police trooper was stationed there. Sam went to meet up with Trooper Dolan who was awaiting his arrival. Sam talked to the trooper and after getting his report on the fire, he informed Trooper Dolan that he was to begin keeping surveillance on the Methodist property from five to ten pm. He would be relieved at ten, but was not to leave until he knew his relief was in place. If no one showed up, he was to immediately inform Sam. The trooper understood and assured Sam that he was ready to do his duty.

Sam had a lot of confidence in Dolan. He had been on the force for six years and took the assignment in Essex in stride. Essex is a sleepy town nestled in the Connecticut River Valley, hugging the shores of the Connecticut River where tranquility and the safety of those who lived there were of paramount importance. Sam knew that Dolan would be perfect for the evening watch. He had been in a patrol car for most of his time in service, patrolling the area around Hammonasset Beach in the service of the good people of Connecticut. The chance to be stationary in a town like Essex, not very attractive to most on active duty, suited Dolan just fine. He got to know many of the townsfolk and integrated himself well within the community. Sam was secure in the knowledge that Dolan took this assignment personally. Having done all he could do at the time he headed home to work with Martha.

CHAPTER THIRTY

On the way home, Sam made another stop at the Black Swan to get some take-out for him and Martha.

"Two cheeseburgers on soft buns, a large order of French fries, two bottles of Coca Cola; food for the soul," said Wanda.

"And so healthy," said Sam, with a voice dripping with sarcasm.

"Well, it's all over town that you live dangerously, Sam," quipped Wanda.

"You mean I'm the talk of the town?" Sam asked.

"Yah, a regular celebrity," quipped Wanda. "And right here, in our neck of the woods. Could we be any luckier?"

Sam had to laugh at that. He picked up the bag of food with one hand and grabbed the two bottles of soda by the necks, raised them in a salutatory manner and left. Wanda simply smiled and shook her head.

Martha was waiting for Sam in their dining room, having placed all the materials they had on the large, but seldom used, dining table that seated twelve comfortably with both leaves in place. They sat and began to eat their lunch while staring at all the material placed before them. When they finished eating, Martha took the dishes and went into the kitchen to quickly wash them, discard the paper bag and napkins and rejoined Sam.

"There is a lot, isn't there?" said Martha.

"Yes and no," said Sam.

"I guess you are right," said Martha.

"I see you have divided everything by category," said Sam.

"I thought it might be easier to proceed if we at least had some semblance of order," said Martha.

"What are your thoughts?" Sam asked.

"We don't really know Commander Boland's intentions in all of this. Or should I say the man who claims to be Commander Boland," Martha said.

"Go on," said Sam.

"My instincts tell me he is military or he could never have fooled so many people. He is probably very intelligent or he could never have retained all the knowledge he would need to pull off his deception for so long. I truly feel, based on what little we have, that Nazi sympathizers on Long Island would provide him with a safe haven and the means to make his escape."

When Martha became pensive Sam asked, "What's wrong? Why are you hesitating?"

"I'm finding it difficult to believe that some of our own countrymen would betray our country," Martha said.

"I know what you mean," said Sam. "But let's not forget that there are people who actually feel they are patriotic Americans who truly believe we have no reason to be in this war and that America is being led down the wrong path."

"Even after Pearl Harbor?" Martha exclaimed.

"Oh, they are in agreement that we should retaliate and even punish Japan, but for whatever reason, they do not think we have justification to allow ourselves to be dragged into Europe's problems," said Sam.

"Especially since many are sympathizers with Fascism and Socialism," Martha said.

"Yes, and quite coincidentally, these political beliefs just happen to agree with those of the Freemasons and the Illuminati. Of course, with all their wealth, they feel it is their birthright to assume that they will be the ones in power to control and think for all the rest of us," Sam said.

"Oh, yes of course," said Martha. "And just where did all of this wealth come from in the first place?"

"The individual freedoms that exist nowhere else in the world but in America. Somehow they seem to have lost sight of that," said Sam.

"So can we agree that our first plan of action would be to define, locate and take a serious look at the self-imposed hierarchy out on Long Island and assume Commander Boland or whoever he is has made his way into their protective bosom?

"Protective bosom!!" said Sam. "Well, aren't we the literary one."

"If you are finished, we can proceed," said Martha. "You know, Mr. Tyler, this is serious business."

"I know, honey," said Sam as he took her in his arms. "I'm really glad you are here to help me. We have got to get a handle on this whole case. I can't stop thinking about our boys over in France and how this traitor or a group of traitors hold their lives in their hands."

"I have some ideas," said Martha.

"Okay, let's hear them," said Sam.

"In my books, I always try to find the simplest or most plausible action to take to get the feeling that I am making headway. Any success, no matter how small, is better than no success at all."

"I'm with you so far," said Sam.

"I'm pretty sure Boland, let's call him that for now, had a good idea that he would not have left Veronica Lansing's home alive. I really think we should try to establish a link between them. I refuse to believe that he picked her name and home out of a hat. Something alerted him that he was in danger there. I really believe Veronica is totally innocent. But, we must find a link to put them together. On the other hand, I feel that we should put all the resources available to capture Commander Boland before he can escape and I just can't help feeling that he is at the Twin Eagles, the home of Margonette Provost. While you are at it, Sam, it just occurred to me that the Provost woman knows Veronica and that they possibly know each other. If that is the case, it's very likely that someone out there on Long Island was going to implicate her. A dead person cannot defend himself. And, even if she were not killed, she was set up to be a patsy."

"I love it," said Sam. "I was thinking along the same lines, but had not developed it to the extent you have."

"How on earth could you?" Martha asked. "You have been buried under an avalanche of information. It's a wonder you can think at all. So what do you think?"

"I think I am going to talk to Arlen to let him work the possible Veronica Lansing/Margonette Provost connection. Of course, they could know each other. Both are rich, from wealthy families, and the Provost woman would want to be associated with a star like Veronica Lansing. It would be so good for her image and as they are both wealthy, they would be extremely comfortable in each other's company. I'll get on Arlen right away.

"In the meantime, it would be very helpful if you could get together with Veronica Lansing. She really seemed to like you. Maybe you could get together with her and see if she knows anyone else out on Long Island who might figure into all this. I'll call Admiral Brown and have him give Detective D'Onofrio as much support as he needs to deal with this situation on Long Island, should it be necessary. Who knows, it may be necessary for the military to get involved. It may even require more than the Navy to intervene. Honey, I think we're really onto something. This is, if our suspicions are correct. I agree with you that it doesn't make sense that Boland would not have a very good reason to involve Veronica Lansing and choose to use a holiday meeting with no logical purpose.

Sam and Martha decided to take a chance and try to contact Arlen and Veronica. Both were shocked when they got immediate responses and found both of them readily available. They made plans to come back home as soon as their respective meetings were completed. There was a definite electrical charge in the air as each was confident that things were starting to go forward.

CHAPTER THIRTY-ONE

Martha took the Buick and drove down Rte. #154 to Old Saybrook. She made a left-hand turn at College Street. The busy thoroughfare dotted with shops, eating and drinking establishments, hardware and book stores gave way to wonderful old New England churches with their stately steeples before reaching Saybrook Point. She turned right onto Bridge Street and headed towards Fenwick. As she crossed over the causeway separating the waters of the mouth of the Connecticut River from South Cove, she was trying to balance the two emotions vying for her attention. She knew she must gain some helpful information for Sam's case from Veronica regarding possible relationships with the Long Island royalty. She was beginning to realize that keeping her focus on the task at hand was not going to be an easy one. In truth, she rather felt like an adolescent schoolgirl who would soon find herself alone in the presence of the legendary Veronica Lansing. It was all she could do to rein in her feelings of childlike anticipation.

Martha applied the brakes in front of the Lansing residence and realized that she was so deep in thought that she could not recall making the left hand turn onto Nibang Street, just the other side of the causeway, and passing the lovely homes of Fenwick before reaching Veronica's home. Any idea of serenity was quickly dashed as she was forced to find a place to park among the vehicles of the many tradesmen who were summoned by Veronica to refresh and transform her home.

"My dear, it is so good to see you. I was so delighted that you called," said Veronica.

Veronica hugged Martha then proceeded to lead her through rooms filled with painters, wallpaper hangers, carpenters and electricians.

"I've decided to change almost everything so that I will not be haunted by the ghastly images of that awful night," said Veronica.

Martha smiled as if she understood. Actually, she did. And truthfully, everyone would understand if Veronica chose to permanently vacate and sell her home. Just then a rather large woman, who appeared to be in her early fifties, wearing a grey maid's uniform with a white collar and buttons all down the front, asked if she could serve them.

"Yes, Louise," said Veronica.

"Please bring us tea to the sitting room. We will be up there."

They climbed the stairs to the second floor to Veronica's bedroom which was easily twice the size of any bedroom Martha had ever seen. Veronica led her past the oversized, specially made wrought iron bed to a walk-in closet filled with more clothes than Martha could imagine one woman would possess.

"She must have every outfit from every movie and play she has ever been in," Martha imagined.

"What do you think?" Veronica asked.

"I feel as though I'm in an exclusive women's clothing salon," said Martha.

Veronica laughed and bade Martha follow her to a sitting room just off the bedroom. Martha was happily surprised when she entered the room. She admitted to herself that she had envisioned a gaudy, glitzy Hollywood style room: mirrored walls, white furniture and perhaps a white bearskin rug in the middle of the floor.

Instead of what she had expected, she saw an exquisitely appointed room, with understated elegance. Beautiful lace curtains tied back by white satin bows framed a breathtaking view of the waters of Long Island Sound. In front of the windows Martha's eye was caught by a small bistro-like table and chairs. A linen cloth edged in delicately embroidered pink baby roses covered the table. An English tea set in very fine porcelain sat on a silver tray in the middle of the table.

On the wall opposite the windows was an eighteenth century ladies' desk from a Virginia antebellum estate with a matching chair. Its fine mahogany wood with inlaid cherry flowers and scalloped borders made it a perfect fit for the room. A painting of Fenwick hung above it. All this was complemented by a Victorian settee upholstered in mauve velvet. A portrait of Veronica graced the wall above it.

"Matthew bought it for me when we were first together," said Veronica pointing to the small table and chairs. "There was this lovely bistro on the Seine in Paris, where we went after we finished shooting the St. Louis story. Matthew was so romantic. It seemed as though we spent most of our time just sitting together gazing out at the boats going along the Seine. I told him how much I loved being there with him. After an exhausting filming, it was wonderful to just relax and share with someone whom you were wildly in love with. True to his nature, Matthew bought this set and had it sent to the States. He surprised me with it when we moved in together.

"When we came east it was the only thing I brought from California. Moving to Connecticut signified a whole new start, but this setting was the only thing from the past that I could never give up."

The women sat and gazed out of the windows to enjoy the view. Louise came in and placed the tea and settings before them. Neither took milk or sugar. They sipped their tea in silence for a few moments.

"To what do I owe this unexpected pleasure of your company?" Veronica asked, breaking the silence.

"Truthfully, I was looking for an excuse to invade your privacy," said Martha. "And then Sam and I began to realize that what happened in your home was no accident or a mistake in communication."

"Whatever do you mean?" Veronica asked.

"We have been trying to find any connection we can to all the information we have gathered, and until now, none of it connected. And then we hit upon an idea that would do that very thing," said Martha.

Veronica did not say anything, but it was obvious she wanted to know just what that idea was.

"The man posing as Naval Commander Boland specifically named you as a relative. We now feel that he was not trying to impress people. The only possible explanation can be that somehow, you were part of his plans. But, we are convinced that was not something he orchestrated. Sam and I are more inclined to believe that someone was going to implicate you in all of this," said Martha.

"Who would do such a thing?" Veronica asked.

"Do you know Margonett Provost?" Martha said.

"Of course; unfortunately we travel in the same social circles," said Veronica.

"Are you aware of her political views?" Martha asked.

"I know that Margonett is passionate about our staying out of a war with Germany," said Veronica. "But certainly she poses no threat to our government," she added.

"I'm not saying that she is," said Martha. "But, it is a well known fact that she has entertained a number of people who agree with her views and she is on the F.B.I. watch list."

"How awful," said Veronica.

"Sam and I are not one hundred percent positive, but we truly believe that Commander Boland and Margonett Provost are somehow connected and that everyone at your house on Thanksgiving, including Boland, was going to suffer the same end. We believe that the Germans were going to take possession of the documents Boland has taken and were going to leave no evidence or anyone alive to tell of what they had done. I'm sure that you were either going to be blamed or killed. As they say in the movies, you were being set up to be the fall guy."

A look of shock came over Veronica's face.

"Margonett Provost and I are not what anyone would mistake for friends. We've had some very heated discussions concerning Hitler's true intentions. She is very naïve and completely duped to think that Hitler is not the maniacal fiend that he is. Margonett is not from Europe and has a very limited understanding of conditions there. She is spoiled, self possessed and completely clueless when it comes to anything outside the boundaries of her precious Twin Eagles and social set. She has too much money and too few brains. If what you say about her is true, I can assure you that she is not the orchestrator of any plot against me, the country or anything else for that matter. That is way beyond the depth of her abilities."

Martha paused for a long moment. Veronica waited patiently.

"I don't want to think about what could have happened if you were here that day," said Martha.

"I never intended to be here that day," said Veronica.

"But what about all that food?" Martha asked.

"I planned to host a party for some very close friends living in the area on Friday evening, but everyone had previous plans and I certainly did not want to create a conflict for them. I was at the Taft and then attended Warren Carstairs' lovely party. I had no intention of entertaining anyone on Thanksgiving Day. I was looking forward to a nice quiet day with a script from a play I am contemplating doing. But I bet I know where the information concerning my so-called Thanksgiving Day party came from."

"I can't wait to hear this," said Martha.

"It was reported in the gossip columns. I tried my best to tell them that it was simply not so. The more I protested, the less they believed. I finally gave up. And now, my dear Abigail is gone and of course, that poor handyman. How terrible that they had to die for something that did not exist."

"So someone saw the news in the tabloids and decided to carry out their plans in sleepy Old Saybrook, where nothing ever happens. We are convinced that the killer or killers did not look forward to reporting back to their superiors that Boland never showed up. Whoever brutally killed those people in your home is no stranger to rage," said Martha.

"Well, something good actually came out of this awful tragedy. We got a chance to meet, my dear," said Veronica.

"I'm so glad you feel that way. I have been a fan of yours for so long. I never thought I would ever get the chance to meet you," said Martha.

"And now we are neighbors. How fortunate," said Veronica.

They spoke for another half hour about New York, the theatre, Long Island castles and, of course, Martha's books. Veronica had immense admiration for those who could craft the written word into something people wanted to see, hear or read. Veronica was sure that she was the chief beneficiary in this case. It was obvious that she found Martha totally delightful. They hugged at the door and then Martha descended the steps and went to her car. She drove home to meet Sam with a smile that lasted the whole way.

CHAPTER THIRTY-TWO

Sam and Arlen shook hands and said their goodbyes. Sam turned and walked across the courtyard to his car. As always, Arlen had much to tell him: things of importance and not just some frivolous hearsay. Not that Sam needed any more news to add to the pressure he was under, which seemed to be coming from all sides, but things were rapidly turning sour for Hitler who was becoming more and more unsettled and emotionally unstable as he also appeared to be facing a great amount of pressure. Hitler desperately needed to score some measure of victory in the war before the German people would begin to turn on him and deal with him as they had the Kaiser after World War I. This was not good news and only served to intensify the need to keep the secret military plans out of German hands.

Sam pulled up to Aunt Clara's back porch and entered the kitchen where he knew a fresh pot of her coffee would be waiting for him. He had just added his milk and sugar when he heard Martha's car approaching. Martha came through the door, hugged her husband and headed for her own cup. She and Sam took seats around the kitchen table. Sam bade Martha go first, which she did. He listened as Martha explained how she had informed Veronica of their suspicions concerning a possible plot to involve her and even murder her. Martha shared with Sam the fact that Veronica

147

had provided her with the names of two other members of the Long Island royalty set who were as gullible and adamant against our war with Germany as Margonett Provost. This revelation excited Sam as Arlen had told him that he also knew quite a few inhabitants on the Island who were violently loyal to America.

It just so happened that the Vanderbilt estate, Eagle's Nest, was closed up for the winter as W.K. Vanderbilt was spending the holidays in Asheville, North Carolina at his family's Biltmore Estate, the largest home in America. Arlen called a friend who was a close business associate of Vanderbilt, who in turn contacted Vanderbilt and gained permission to use Eagle's Nest as a place the F.B.I. could use to begin surveillance on the Provost estate. While Sam was still in Arlen's home, the F.B.I., with the aid of Admiral Brown and the U.S. Navy, immediately began to make arrangements for a move into the home, using a New York City field operative and his wife to move in. Three other agents would pose as the help staff so that anyone observing their actions would find nothing to alert them as to their real purpose.

Next, once again, Sam contacted Admiral Brown and informed him that Arlen had shared that the Olmstead Brothers of Brookline, Massachusetts, the famous family that designed Central Park in Manhattan, are a constant presence in the area. The Olmsteads were under contract to service many of the estates there and should be contacted to allow Detective Phillip D'Onofrio and his team of N.Y.P.D. detectives to use Olmstead trucks, uniforms and employees to take up positions as a perimeter around Oyster Bay, Cold Springs Harbor and Glen Cove.

OHEKA Castle, in Cold Springs Harbor, was now being used by the U.S. Military. It was decided that Admiral Brown and members of his staff would go there immediately to set up a command center to coordinate all surveillance activities. Admiral Brown was impressed by the rapid decisions made by Sam, decisions he was in complete agreement with. True, there were a lot of people involved in this undertaking, but Sam was counting on immediate results from his own "blitzkrieg". Admiral Brown got a good laugh out of that one. Now all that was left was for all of this activity to bear fruit. That was the tricky part.

CHAPTER THIRTY-THREE

The children exploded through the door and rushed into Aunt Clara's waiting arms.

"Six more days," shouted Thomas.

"Six more days, for what?" Aunt Clara asked, as if she didn't know.

"Oh, you know, Aunt Clara," said Thomas.

"It appears that Thomas has learned to count," said Mary, which brought an exasperated look from Lillith.

Aunt Clara was about to respond when she heard the door open.

"Well, I'll be," she said as she looked up and saw Arlen Templeton enter her kitchen.

"I hear you still make the best coffee in town," Arlen said.

"Well, set yourself down and I'll get you a cup," said Clara.

"Children," she said, "now go on home and change your clothes and get right back here to do your homework."

The children put their books and papers down and ran out the door yelling, "Come on, let's go."

Aunt Clara poured two cups of coffee and placed them on the table. She went to the refrigerator and took out the bottle of milk and set it down near Arlen.

"Okay, Mr. Big Shot, what brings you to my humble home?" asked Aunt Clara.

"Still shy and retiring, I see," Arlen responded.

"Well, what did you expect? I was sure you had eliminated me from your social register," said Aunt Clara.

"It sure has been a while. I apologize for not stopping by sooner. I took the liberty of picking the children up at school. It's been a long time since I've done that. I informed Injun Jim what I was planning to do. I see he is still hanging around. Why, I cannot fathom."

"Did you come over here just to beat up on a defenseless old lady?" said Aunt Clara.

Arlen almost choked as he started to sip his coffee.

"Did you say defenseless?" Arlen asked.

"It's a good thing you left out the old part," Aunt Clara said.

"I envy you, dear lady. I can only imagine how wonderful it is to see these children every day, and to be right here while they grow up," Arlen said. "But it is obvious to me that you are not wasting any of that time. Every time Betty and I have the opportunity to be with them, we are just so impressed at how warm and loving they are. Sam is so fortunate to have you. And speaking of Sam, I'm sure you can see the enormous pressure he is under. I swear the task they have laid on him is more than one man should have to bear."

Aunt Clara took all Arlen had to say in quietly while sipping her coffee. He had said a mouthful. "I just know Samuel is up to the task!" she responded, finally.

"To be sure," was Arlen's quick response. "They definitely made the right choice, the only choice as far as I am concerned. No one I can think of can touch all the bases like Sam can. And at a time like this, making great demands upon people without ruffling a few feathers is quite an accomplishment. But, the stakes are high and I can tell you that that nephew of yours has a whole lot of government people in his corner. It takes someone quite special to pull something like that off."

Aunt Clara just smiled and continued drinking.

"You've done quite a good job helping Sam become the person he is, and don't give me any of your false modesty, either. I'm not that far away that I don't know the part you've played. Sally told us all about you, Clara. Betty and I owe you so much for making her time as a Tyler a joyous one for her. Betty and I will never forget that."

Aunt Clara was speechless, probably for one of the few times in her life.

"Okay, okay," she said, finally, "now you just get along Mister, and take that silver tongue with you."

They both laughed and got to their feet.

"Have Sam call me when he gets in. I've got some news for him."

Before he could make his way to the door, the children came running in. He hugged each one and they all walked out to his car with him. Aunt Clara stood in the doorway while the children waved goodbye as the big black Cadillac sedan pulled away up Pratt Street.

CHAPTER THIRTY-FOUR

The green and white Chevrolet two-door delivery truck with no windows in the covered back section, one of the many in the Olmstead Brothers' fleet, made its way to a small bluff on the Eagle's Nest property that had a clear view of the Provost Estate. It was eight o'clock in the morning. Two men in grayish coverall uniforms bearing the green and white Olmstead crest got out and opened the rear door to the cab. They took out the tools they were going to use to dig out a small area that would house a bed of azaleas, tulip trees and rhododendrons that would be planted there as part of a new floral area to dress up that section of the property, which had a large amount of untended undergrowth among the many trees.

Soon, another truck, identical to the first and bearing the Olmstead crest, pulled up. More workers exited and they too went to the rear cab and began taking large azalea and rhododendron plants out. As they were doing this, the driver's side door to the first vehicle opened very slowly, almost imperceptibly, and a lone figure slid out, being careful to stay below the window so as not to be seen. He used the ground brush as cover and made his way over to a very large oak tree and began to climb it. He reached a branch that appeared strong enough, about fifteen to twenty feet up and making sure he could not be seen, pulled out field binoculars and began surveillance on Twin Eagles, the Provost estate, but not before he used a large leather harness to secure himself to the tree.

One short hour later, he spied a man with blonde hair cut short exiting the Provost mansion wearing a black leather coat and black leather boots. The man's height appeared to be just a little under six feet and he walked upright with authority. He made his way over to a black four-door Cadillac attended by a driver wearing a chauffeur's hat. The driver bolted to attention as soon as he noticed the man coming in his direction and did everything but salute him as he opened a rear door for his passenger. He rushed around and entered the driver's side of the car. The car made a quick advance to the long driveway leading to the main road. The man in the trees pulled a radio from the backpack he was wearing and radioed the car's departure to his command post. There were only two ways off the island, by car or by boat. A plane would attract too much attention.

The radio operator at the command post at OHEKA informed Admiral Brown, who had arrived there very late the night before, of the message. The admiral had him alert the two stations set up to observe that part of the island. Before long the command post received word that the automobile was heading for the water. A small fishing boat, manned by Coast Guard personnel dressed like local fishermen, made note of a large forty-five foot wooden cabin cruiser heading towards a cove at a relatively fast speed. The boat disappeared into the cove, but the fishing boat did not follow it. A lone radio operator, part of the radio corps being trained at OHEKA, sat high on a bluff wearing a camouflage uniform to blend in with the topography. From his vantage point he observed the lone man exiting his vehicle and boarding the large vessel, which was moored at the end of a long wooden dock where the water was obviously deep enough for the yacht to enter safely.

The man hurriedly made his way to the end of the pier and boarded. He was greeted by another man whose movements were also stiff and who, like the driver of the Cadillac, did everything but salute him. With little fanfare the large yacht made its way out of the cove and headed in a westerly direction towards New Haven. The Coast Guardsmen took down the name of the large vessel and radioed it to the command post at OHEKA. The name on the boat was the *One, One and One*. Built in 1935, it was a real wooden beauty. Its surfaces were hand-painted with the elegance of highly varnished teak exteriors. The inside furniture was walnut with leather upholstery. She had a crew of two and had three cabins which could accommodate six overnight guests. Her cruising speed was nine knots, but she could reach a maximum speed of 12.5 knots, which seemed to be her present speed. Such boats were commandeered by the government to help monitor the Sound. They were to be returned to their owners when the threat was gone.

Within minutes the admiral learned that the boat was in registry out of New Haven. Its owner was the German American Club of West Haven, an ethnic club with large numbers of people coming and going.

At this point, the military began an air to sea surveillance with various small craft flying overhead and at a distance to mark the progress and destination of the yacht. At about ten fifteen, the air surveillance noticed the yacht going slightly off course and heading towards a large, lone sailboat, anchored about five miles off the coast of West Haven. A small single engine craft, taking off from Tweed Airport, in New Haven, observed the two boats tied together. A plane out of Sikorsky Airport, in Stratford, took off a little later, just in time to observe that the boats had disengaged and were heading in two different directions. The yacht appeared to be heading towards New Haven Harbor, while the sailboat, the *Free Winds* out of Lloyd Harbor, Long Island, began heading easterly along the Connecticut coastline towards Saybrook.

The New Haven police were alerted to be on their watch for the *One, One and One* heading there and to keep a watch out for the man who was on board. Their orders were to observe his movements and to take note of anyone with whom he came into contact. Acting captain, Sgt. Varnish, was alerted to be on the lookout for the *Free Winds* which might be headed towards him and to work along with Captain Tyler to set up an observation network as far up the Connecticut coast as New London. Naval personnel would take over from there as this was the major submarine base on the east coast.

Varnish immediately contacted Sam, who told him to go to the Saybrook Yacht Club and sit tight until he got there. Sam was at the Essex Police Headquarters speaking to Trooper Coulson. Coulson had nothing new to offer concerning his surveillance of the First Methodist Church. Sam told him to keep his eyes open and direct most of his efforts on the church.

CHAPTER THIRTY-FIVE

Sam met up with Sergeant Varnish at the Saybrook Yacht Club. They spent a few moments discussing vantage points for observing the *Free Winds* when she arrived. The harbormaster had been alerted and assured Sam that he could arrange docking the *Free Winds* in a slip convenient for unobstructed police surveillance. Once that was done, Sam took his leave and headed back to Essex to check in with the family.

As Sam was heading down Main Street, he just happened to look to his left and noticed one of the large doors to St. John's Church was slightly open. It was usually closed at this hour. He pulled over to the curb and parked, exited his vehicle, crossed the street and began to ascend the stone steps. Considering that the Methodist church had been attacked, it would not be beyond the possibility that another church was about to suffer the same fate.

Sam carefully opened the door, just enough to gain entrance to the vestibule, looked in both directions and entered. Almost instinctively he placed his hand on his revolver. He took a few steps, then stopped and realized that he was about to draw his weapon in church. He was not pleased at the idea.

The center doors to the sanctuary opened noiselessly. Sam entered and closed them behind him very carefully. He placed himself against the wall and began to scan the dimly lit church from left to right. He remained as quiet as possible attempting to hear any noise. There was none. He very quietly made his way over to the far right-hand isle and began carefully examining each pew from where he was to the far left wall. He took his time, never taking his hand from his weapon which was still not drawn. He finally reached the altar and paused a moment to make sure it was clear. Next he climbed over the heavy wooden railing which separated the altar from the congregation and made his way to the rectory. It was empty. He went over to the door which led out the back to the rectory. It was locked. Finally, he made his way over to the door leading to the church basement, but not before checking the closets. The basement door was also locked. The key to open it was still hanging on the wall up above and to the right.

Convinced the church was empty Sam made his way back across the wooden railing and walked to the center aisle. He walked down about four rows of pews and suddenly felt the urge to sit down. He sat and allowed the atmosphere of this place of worship to surround and overtake him. He looked up to the large wooden cross that hung on the back wall of the altar. It was surrounded on both sides by huge stained glass windows depicting saints in full armor with large shields. The light from the outside came through, illuminating the altar with streams of light broken up by the metal casings which housed the stained glass. Sam noticed he had released his hand from his sidearm and looked down at his hands folded in his lap. He closed his eyes. After a few minutes, he sensed he was no longer alone. He opened his eyes and looked to his left where he felt someone's presence. Instinctively, his hand again went to his weapon.

"Good to see you here, son," came the gentle voice of Pastor Linus Foster.

Sam smiled and acknowledged him.

"Mind if I join you?" the pastor asked.

"Please," said Sam, who could think of nothing else to say.

Pastor Linus sat in the pew in front of Sam and to his left.

"What is it son?" he asked. "Why are you here?"

"The front door was open. I noticed it as I was driving by. It's usually closed and the church locked up tight at this hour. I came in to see if everything was alright, what with the two attacks on the Methodist Church and all."

"And?" Pastor Linus asked.

Again Sam was silent. It seemed he had no answer.

"And?" Pastor Linus persisted.

"And, I guess I felt that as long as I was here I might take some time from the outside world and sit here and maybe have God tell me why all this hatred and death seems to be covering the earth."

"Are you saying you are blaming God or that God had some part in this war?" the pastor asked.

"No, not at all. Actually I was just hoping to get some form of revelation. It seems the more information I get with regard to my investigations the more I see of the world's ills. There is so much corruption, hatred and inhumanity. I just don't know how we got here and why so many have to suffer. Why are we doing such terrible things to each other and where is God?"

Pastor Linus let out a deep breath. "Samuel, your family has been members of this church for many years. When you were young, you belonged to our youth group and studied the Bible all through your youth. And, all during that time, many things were explained to you concerning God."

"Care to share some of your wisdom with me?" Sam asked.

"I know you won't believe me, but you know just about as much as I do where the Lord is concerned," the pastor said.

Sam gave him a look of disbelief. "Explain this to me. God is omnipresent. So He sees everything and is where everything is happening."

"And yet, He does not intercede when bad things happen," the pastor interrupted.

"So it would appear," said Sam.

A period of silence followed.

"I'm not going to try to bowl you over with great words of wisdom, my son," said the pastor. "The truth is that since Adam and Eve, God has allowed man freedom to choose which path he will take, which actions he takes part in and which decisions he chooses. It all comes down to sowing and reaping. And believe me, in pretty much all that you choose 'ye will reap what ye have sown.' Simply put, this war and all the wars and horrible things that came before it are not things that came about by pure happenstance. Some people made some very bad choices that eventually led to terrible things happening. Remember the tree of the knowledge of good and evil. I truly believe that evil is done by those who possess that knowledge and know exactly what they are doing. And yes, there are many cases to be made that God is inconsistent. But, I will tell you this without a shred of doubt; God is faithful to His word. Man is free to choose and when he chooses wrongly, or maliciously or foolishly, God will not just come in and make it all better."

"The Bible is full of stories that demonstrate this. Each story requires much thought and desire to fully know and understand. Or, better put, to gain knowledge and wisdom where they are concerned. This is our faith, Samuel. The Bible says we will never know the mind of God. Anyone who thinks differently is self-deluded. I cannot tell you how the stars in the sky got there or how the oceans and rivers truly came about or how this small gem of a planet got to be so beautiful. But, I choose to have faith in the One I believe created it and to serve His wishes to the very best of my ability. And while we are at it, let me say I also choose to tell as many people as I can how great and wonderful He is and to provide a place for all who seek Him to find refuge.

"We are all so proud of you, Samuel for all that you are doing in such a difficult time. I have known you since you were a little boy and I have faith that you have been chosen for a time like this."

Sam got to his feet and Pastor Linus did the same.

"Anything else, son?" the pastor asked.

"Just that I would like to know where all the goodness and kindness are," said Sam.

The pastor smiled.

"I believe I am looking at a fine representation of it right now."

"Thank you for your kind words, Pastor," said Sam. "I will do my best."

"I would expect nothing less from you, son," said the pastor. "Come on, I will walk you out."

When they reached the front door of the church, Sam and the pastor shook hands. Sam began to walk down the steps.

"You know I will be praying for you," promised Pastor Linus.

Sam stopped and turned around. "Remember, where two or more gather...," said Sam. "I wonder what would happen if that were two hundred or more. Better call all your friends, Pastor."

Pastor Linus had a good laugh. "Will do that, son. I will do just that."

CHAPTER THIRTY-SIX

Aunt Clara had been waiting for Sam to return home. She kept looking out the kitchen window behind the sink that gave an unobstructed view of the driveway. When she saw his approaching headlights, she made her way out to the porch.

Sam exited his vehicle and waved hello.

"This is a pleasant surprise," said Sam.

"Got some news for you, Sam," said Aunt Clara. "Come on in and sit a spell."

Sam entered and immediately made his way to the coffee pot.

"I thought you might need some fresh coffee. I just made it," Aunt Clara said.

"What's going on?" Sam asked.

"Arlen Templeton wants you to call him as soon as you can. He's got something he wants to tell you."

"Did he call?" Sam asked.

"No, actually he came here to tell me," said Aunt Clara.

"Here?" said Sam.

"Yes, here," said Aunt Clara. "And, I gave him 'what for' for being such a stranger. I told him it was about time he brought his sorry upper crust self over here."

"I'll just bet you did," said Sam.

"Darn right," said Aunt Clara.

"Have you heard from Martha?" Sam asked.

"She called about a half hour ago. She was just about to head home. She should be home pretty soon," said Aunt Clara.

"Mind if I use your phone?" Sam asked. "Go right ahead, son. I'm sure it's important. Anyone else calling can wait," said Aunt Clara.

Sam placed his cup on the table and went over to the telephone and called Arlen.

"Hear you came over to Aunt Clara's to get me," said Sam.

"Just barely escaped with my skin intact," said Arlen.

Both men laughed.

"I think you had better not make your visits so infrequent," said Sam.

"I kinda' got that feeling," said Arlen.

"What can I do for you?" Sam asked.

"By now you know all about our mystery man heading either to New Haven or hopefully, Saybrook," said Arlen.

"Yes, I just got home from touching base with Varnish over at the Yacht Club. He and his men are ready. I haven't heard from D'Onofrio, down in New Haven yet, but I'm quite sure he's more than ready," said Sam.

"Well, don't get your hopes up yet, but a conductor on the Long Island Railroad is pretty sure he saw our Commander Boland two days ago heading out onto the Island. He's not one hundred percent sure, but he thinks Boland got off at Huntington Station. He says the only reason he noticed the man was that he was in uniform. The conductor tried to engage him in conversation, but he saw the officer seemed distracted and was in no mood to talk. If this person is our man, it's safe to say that would put him pretty close to the Provost property," said Arlen.

"Thanks, Arlen, but hope is just about all I've got at this point. I can never remember a case where I was going strictly on instinct and just a little hope to boot. I wonder if this so called 'mystery man' is part of a grand scheme. I'm also wondering if that fellow could be our killer who seems to have vanished. But I have to tell you, the mystery man's demeanor and dress sounds like S.S. to me. If he is, would Boland be safe? And, do you think the Nazis could be so desperate that they would send someone like that here?"

"I don't know about the Nazis, but from what I've been hearing, Hitler sure could be. We started bombing Hamburg in April of this year. They tell me the devastation is incredible. For months the German people have been fed all this propaganda about the glorious victories by the invincible German army and now these people are digging out their dead and wounded by the thousands. These people had believed that air raid drills were only a precaution. After months of bombing and the devastation they have seen with 'their own eyes,' I'm pretty sure those who are left are none too happy with der Fuhrer. And, just as a side note, son, intelligence tells us that the people in Hamburg have always voiced their opposition to Hitler's thirst for war. It's a darn shame they had to be some of the first German people to suffer. What this all means to me is that Hitler is feeling oppressive heat and is showing his cowardly self by no longer appearing in public making his imperial speeches. In fact, he has not been seen at all. It seems the Fatherland is losing its father."

"Yeah, and leaving everyone else to suffer the consequences," said Sam. "Well, I think we have to put our people on the Island on high alert to see if Boland is there. Time is not on our side, so I'm going to ask Admiral Brown to try to get someone inside the Provost mansion to see if he is there."

"Good luck, son," said Arlen.

"You take care," said Sam. "Anything breaks, I'll let you know."

"Much appreciated," said Arlen.

No sooner had Sam placed the receiver back into the telephone cradle, Sam heard Martha come through the door.

"What's going on?" Martha asked.

"We might have caught a break," said Sam. "Let's go over to the house and see how the kids are doing. I've got some calls to make. We'll clean up and get back here for dinner."

"Sounds good, but what was the good news?" Martha asked.

CHAPTER THIRTY-SEVEN

As they walked across the lawn to their home, Sam told Martha about the possible sighting of Commander Boland on the Long Island Railroad. Once inside the house, they instructed the children to get ready for dinner over at Aunt Clara's. As Martha and Sam freshened up for dinner, Sam filled her in on the mystery person spotted at the Provost mansion and that he was probably heading their way, if New Haven was not his destination.

There was much talk about the upcoming trip to New York at the dinner table. The children were very excited. As usual, Mary and Thomas tried to outdo each other with questions concerning what places they would be visiting. Would there be museums or churches or landmarks on the itinerary? Maybe they could go to see the Christmas show at Rockefeller Center? Would there be time for ice skating in Central Park? Each question was immediately followed by another before Martha and Sam had a chance to respond. But, it was Lillith who succeeded in capturing the moment.

"It's Christmastime," said Lillith. "I'm sure mommy wants to surprise us. I think that would make her very happy."

For a moment, there was stunned silence. It was obvious neither Thomas nor Mary knew what to say to follow that. In fact, they both seemed a little embarrassed by their younger sister's contribution to the conversation. Martha put her head down trying not to laugh while Sam sat with a look of total amazement at the words that had just tumbled out of Lillith's mouth. Lillith just sat there looking around the table at everyone with her amazing sparkling eyes. Aunt Clara sat back and smiled broadly at the wisdom spoken by her "little treasure."

"Wow, Lillith," said Thomas, who looked at his little sister with a look of total admiration. Mary managed to give Lillith a weak smile. She was not going to be outdone by Thomas. But there was something else going on in that pretty head. She could stand an occasional victory by Thomas on their never-ending war to have the final word, but now, to also have Lillith to contend with was something she neither anticipated nor appreciated.

After washing the dinner plates and helping Aunt Clara clean up the kitchen, Martha took the children home to get prepared for bed. Sam went back up to the Methodist Hill to check on whoever was watching the church property. When he got there he found William Meecham, the hardware store proprietor. Meecham told him that he had been there a few hours and no one had gone near the church. He also told Sam that Injun Jim was going to spell him around midnight. Injun Jim was always the last one because he could be counted on to stay awake and knew how to be somewhere and not be detected. After all, he was Injun Jim.

While the children enjoyed their time before bedtime, Martha made a phone call to Veronica Lansing. She had an idea she wanted to share and wished to see if it was something Veronica would be interested in. The excitement in Veronica's voice was all the answer Martha needed. She had a surprise for Sam, one she could not share until she had done what she was about to set out to do.

CHAPTER THIRTY-EIGHT

Martha headed out very early the next morning. She told Sam that she was going to visit with Veronica Lansing.

"Wow," said Sam. "Sounds like you two are really hitting it off."

Martha kissed him good-bye and took the Buick, then headed down to Fenwick.

Martha was met by a very excited Veronica Lansing at the front door, where they hugged each other.

"I cannot tell you what this means to me," said Veronica. "It is like going on a great adventure. My only hope is that we get the chance to prove Margonette is harboring a criminal and that we will help the police put her in prison where she belongs."

Martha turned towards the Buick and took a few paces.

"Oh, no, my dear, let's take my car. I am sure we will make much better time with it," stated Veronica.

Martha turned to see Veronica heading towards her garage full steam ahead. Walking as fast as she could, Martha attempted to catch up to her, but just as she was about to reach her goal the doors to the garage flew open.

Martha was stunned by what she saw. Veronica had a look of pure joy as she observed Martha's reaction to the 1936 Rolls Royce Phantom II staring back at her. The magnificent grey beauty with shiny black fenders and roof was very rare. Only a few had ever been made.

"Well, let's get a move on. We won't get very far standing here." Both women got into the two-seater with rich red leather upholstery and mahogany appointments of dash and console.

"This baby can really fly," said Veronica, as she hit the accelerator, forcing Martha and her to sink backwards into their seats.

"How long have you had this?" Martha asked.

"Errol gave it to me shortly after Matthew's death," said Veronica over the roar of the engine straining through every shifting of gears. Veronica proved to be an experienced driver.

"Errol Flynn?" Martha said.

"Who else?" said Veronica.

Martha did not answer. She just stared at Veronica who turned to see her.

"Oh for goodness sakes," Veronica said. "We were all the very best of friends. Errol and I knew each other when each of us was no one."

"But?" Martha questioned.

"Errol won this glorious beauty from Matthew in a game of poker, about a year before Matthew's death. He wanted me to have it as he knew how much Matthew cherished this lovely object. Besides, he confided that he took unfair advantage of Matthew by getting him drunk and then cheating him in their game. He told me he could not live with himself after Matthew died if not righting the wrong that he had committed. And, as far as your thoughts on Errol and me, let me just assure you, Errol is a rogue, a very naughty boy. He could never be satisfied with one woman and I, my dear, could only be with a man I loved and trusted."

"I have just one question," Martha said.

"What is it?" said Veronica

"You do have an American driver's license, don't you?" Martha asked.

"Oh, dear, no," said Veronica.

Martha had a look of astonishment as they barreled down Route #1 heading towards New Haven.

"Stardom does have its privileges, you know." Veronica said with a smile of pure satisfaction.

Veronica pulled into Tweed Airport in New Haven and made her way to a private hangar. Warren Carstairs was standing there as they pulled up. Behind him was a single engine Piper E-Z cub, William T. Pipers' brilliantly designed aircraft, which placed heavy emphasis on ease of handling, warmed up and ready to go. Even during the Great Depression, this plane sold. Veronica had told Martha to leave all the plans for their trip to her. There was quite a distance to travel and the plan was to return home safely before dark; and, of course, being able to confirm that Commander Boland was being given aid and shelter by Margonette Provost. Carstairs had arranged for them to land on a small landing strip in Sands Point on the property owned by the Guggenheim family. Their chauffeur would be waiting to take the ladies to Twin Eagles.

It was a little after noon time when Sam took a break from going over all the information in front of him. He decided to call home. There was no answer so he called Aunt Clara who told him she had not seen Martha since she had left early that day. He then placed a call to Veronica Lansing's home and spoke to the housekeeper. When Sam was informed that Miss Lansing was on Long Island, Sam could not believe his ears. When he inquired if she went alone, Sam was informed that Martha was accompanying her. Immediately Sam felt himself tensing up. When he inquired where on Long Island, the housekeeper became silent. He asked again and this time heard the phone disconnect. Without hesitation Sam burst out of the house, got into his cruiser, put on his flashing lights and sirens and headed down to Fenwick.

Sam pulled up in front of the Lansing residence, parked his car and ran up the porch steps. He pounded on the door until Lillian, the new housekeeper, opened the door reluctantly. When the woman refused to tell Sam the address of where Veronica and Martha had gone, Sam exercised every restraint he knew to keep himself under control.

"Have you ever been to jail?" Sam asked the housekeeper.

The woman just stood there appearing frozen in her tracks. Sam took out his handcuffs. The housekeeper grabbed his arm and pleaded.

"Please, please," she said, "Miss Lansing will fire me for sure if I tell you."

"And, I'll put you in jail for sure if you don't tell me and right now," said Sam.

Sam gave the woman a moment to consider her options.

"She is going to the Provost residence and told me not to tell anyone."

Sam was shocked by the news. He quickly gathered himself. "Alright, I'll make sure you are not fired," he assured the woman. Then, almost absentmindedly, "She has no idea how much danger she has put both of them in," came out of Sam's mouth.

"Oh, my Lord," said the housekeeper.

"Thank you for your help," said Sam as he headed for the door.

When Sam got into his cruiser, he phoned ahead to the barracks to get word to Admiral Brown out at OHEKA to be on the alert. He was surprised to hear that the admiral had already tried to communicate with him.

"Sir," said his desk sergeant, "I have a communiqué for you from Admiral Brown."

"Read it to me," said Sam.

"Veronica Lansing and a woman who fits the description of your wife, Martha Frost, entered the Provost mansion at eleven forty-five a.m. If they do not come out by four p.m., when it begins to get dark, we are sending forces in."

"Tell the admiral that it is my wife with Veronica and I have no idea what either of them is doing there. Thank him and ask him to keep me informed. I am heading out right now by boat. I should be there in a couple of hours depending on the currents."

"Will do," said the sergeant.

Sam called Arlen and asked for his help. Arlen had a friend with a 36-foot cabin cruiser, who would be more than happy to help. The friend lived on the shore in Lyme and would be able to meet Sam at Saybrook Point in thirty minutes. The thirty six foot cabin cruiser had twin **three hundred** horse power motors with a capacity to reach **thirty five** knots, making it possible for Sam to reach his destination in **ninety** minutes. Sam wasted no time heading to Saybrook Point.

It was getting cold; winter-like cold and the threat of moisture was in the air. Sam made sure he had a heavy state police issue winter surveillance coat in the trunk and decided that was enough. He did not have time to go home and get more suitable clothing to be out on frigid waters for an extended period of time. He made it to the Point and waited in his car until Arlen's friend came into view. Sam had called ahead to the Yacht Club and made sure they had their launch ready. Sam got in the launch and was transported out to the "Silver Lining" out of Lyme, Connecticut and introduced himself to Ortman Scully, its owner and a close personal friend of Arlen Templeton.

Scully wasted little time. He headed towards Cold Spring Harbor, where Captain Phillip D'Onofrio of the N.Y.P.D. would be waiting for him.

* * *

Along the way, Veronica had warned Martha what to expect once inside the Provost mansion.

"It is French medieval mish mash, darling; more dungeon-like than anything I have ever seen. The Provosts are old European money, but they clearly lack European taste. Margonette's father inherited a huge banking empire and had the good sense to leave all the financial affairs to his nephew, who truly can't stand him.

But the nephew is the son of Provost's brother Aaron, the other heir who is a genius. It should come as no surprise that Aaron considers his brother a witless ass. The Provosts of Centerbrook, Long Island, are some of the most clueless people on the planet.

Margonette's father spends most of his time traveling abroad squandering his money however and wherever he can. For everyone's protection, his family has placed him on a strict yearly budget. But these Provosts do not disappoint. He and his clueless daughter just manage to make it through the year. It always amazes me that people like that are so fortunate while there are so many good people in the world who seem to have no luck at all.

CHAPTER THIRTY-NINE

A huge display of faux affection was put forth as Veronica and Margonette hugged and feau kissed.

"And this is the one and only Martha Frost of literary fame," Margonette gushed. "How wonderful to meet you, dear."

Martha thanked her for allowing them to come on such short notice.

Two great iron doors gave way into the mansion which instantly lived up to everything Veronica had promised. Two large staircases, one at each side of the grand foyer, wound their way up twenty-five feet above the marble entrance flooring to be joined together by a balcony which seemed totally out of place with the rest of the decor.

To enter the interior of the home, one had to pass under the balcony. Before reaching the main atrium, Martha was sure that she counted at least ten statues of knights in full armor. With each step, Martha noticed that there was absolutely no thought given to order or balance where the furniture or appointments were concerned. Martha knew instinctively that everything she saw was expensive. It was just that nothing made sense to whatever else it was near. As a writer, Martha's thoughts immediately turned to envisioning this home in the center of a comedic movie or play. Somewhere in their disillusioned minds, the Provosts entertained the idea that huge stuffed bears, of which there were two, were needed to go with the stuffed animal heads that adorned the walls above an immense fireplace in the great room.

Veronica had used the excuse to visit her dear old friend while traveling to OHEKA to spend time with the boys being trained there. When Margonette invited Veronica and Martha to stay for tea, both ladies assured her that they would love to.

The hostess made up for her bad taste in interior decorating by serving a truly scrumptious and sophisticated high tea. Scones with jam and clotted cream, cucumber sandwiches, ginger cakes, cream pastries, fruit tarts. Veronica and Martha tried all of them, and were delighted by the array of sweets and the authentic English tea.

Martha looked up from her tea cup and was met by the handsome, smiling face of a manservant who just happened to be the man who had passed himself off as Commander Boland. She did all she could to make no gesture to arouse his suspicions. He poured the tea and then backed out of the room.

The three women sat and talked. Veronica encouraged Martha to answer at length any question Margonette made as she could not stand the sound of Margonette's voice. To her credit, and the great relief of Veronica, Martha took pains to fill up the time as best she could while telling the story of a country girl from upstate Vermont who found life in the big city, a life of celebrity and professional and financial success.

Veronica was forced to share the particulars of her upcoming return to Broadway. While she spoke, Martha was on the alert to see if Boland had become suspicious. To the contrary, he came into the great room to inquire if anyone needed anything. He exited as silently as he had come. He appeared at least two or three more times convincing Martha that he did not suspect anything.

Sam arrived at Cold Spring Harbor at about three-thirty. Captain D'Onofrio of the N.Y.P.D. was waiting. They immediately headed over to the Eagle's Nest and proceeded to wait on Route

#25 while in communication with the radio officer in the trees at Eagle's Nest. On the way, Captain D'Onofrio informed Sam that every known exit from Twin Eagles leading to safety was being covered by policemen from the nearby towns. As of that very moment, no one had left the Twin Eagles. But four o'clock was rapidly approaching and with it, darkness.

It was obvious that Sam was getting tenser by the moment. At the stroke of four, Admiral Brown sent a call to all units to make ready to converge on the Provost mansion. Just then the radio man, in the tree at Eagle's Nest, sent out a call.

"The two women visiting the Provost home were now leaving in a black limousine. They were already heading down the driveway and would be at the main road, Route #25 in less than a minute."

The driver of the limousine was startled by the large police presence as soon as he emerged from behind the wall of the estate and turned onto Route #25. He had to slam on his brakes to avoid hitting the first vehicle.

Sam jumped out of D'Onofrio's police vehicle and ran over to an equally startled Martha.

"What on earth were you thinking?" he shouted.

Martha looked around. Everywhere she looked she saw a large police presence.

"Yes," said Sam without being asked. "There must be fifty officers out here ready to storm the Provost residence. Fifty officers for a false alarm."

"Admiral Brown has been contacted, sir, and "he has ordered everyone to stand down," came the news from the radio officer.

Sam just looked at both women. He was grateful for their safety, but there was no love in his eyes.

The next sounds anyone heard was the hysterical laughing of Veronica Lansing.

"This is so exciting," she exclaimed. "I feel as though I am in one of those adventure movies."

Sam looked down at Martha, who could only shrug her shoulders and smile weakly. He opened the car door and pulled his wife out and thrust her body into his and held her as tightly as he could.

"You scared me half to death," he said. He began to say something else, but he was interrupted.

"He's here," said Martha

"What, excuse me. Who?" said Sam.

"Boland or whatever his name is. He is posing as a manservant," said Martha.

"Get me Admiral Brown, ASAP," said Sam.

CHAPTER FORTY

It wasn't much of a movement, but just enough to catch Acting Commissioner Varnish's eye. It was eleven P.M. and a welcome shift change was about to take place for a grateful policeman who had begun his day at seven A.M. Varnish had just looked at his watch to check the time and, hearing no footsteps and seeing no approaching headlights, he reasoned his relief was going to be late.

The *Free Winds* had come into port at four P.M. and after the crew made sure all riggings were secured to the dock, it appeared that everyone on board was settling down and making ready to spend the evening on board. Varnish's first thoughts were that the Free Winds was only going to be there until the following morning. The captain had talked to the harbor master and paid the overnight docking fee. After he waited for the captain to return to his ship, Varnish received confirmation that indeed they were only going to be there till morning. The captain claimed to be heading to Mystic Seaport.

The moon was at about three-quarters full and the skies were clear. There was enough illumination from the lights strung out over the docks to make visibility at least adequate for surveillance. Varnish observed the shadow of an object in the water at the far end of the pier and then it was gone. He waited to see if his relief had come, but no such luck. He unclipped his holster to be able to draw his weapon and then began to slowly head towards the end of the pier. He was sure that he heard the muffled sounds of an outboard. He hesitated, to try to locate where the sounds were coming from. He was sure that he was close and, after checking once more to see that his relief still had not arrived, he proceeded to move forward, crouching to melt into the shadows. All of a sudden, the motor became louder and the small craft it was powering cleared the pier and began to rapidly move out to sea. Varnish now stood and ran to the end of the pier. Suddenly, Varnish found himself covered in light coming from the small craft. For an instant he froze, but instinct drove him to the ground. It was not a second too soon. Bullets seemed to be flying all around him. It was all he could do to scramble on his stomach to a safe position between the large support posts. He never got a chance to draw his weapon and return fire. He was very lucky to escape unharmed.

Just as the small boat made its way around a peninsula-like property, Varnish heard footsteps coming his way very quickly. He whirled around, drew his weapon to defend himself and realized his relief had just arrived on the scene, ten minutes late! When Varnish looked back to the water, he realized that the boat carrying the shooters had disappeared. He slowly rose to his feet and began dressing down the police officer from Saybrook, who was late and of no help.

Varnish called down to State Police Headquarters looking for Sam. It was a pretty fair assumption that it was the mystery man who fired on him and that for some unknown reason, he was in the area. That thought was unsettling as it appeared that a very dangerous and very angry professional killer was in the area. There seemed to be no plausible reason why such a person would be there. Varnish and D'Onofrio had both been warned that this was no ordinary assignment. He was probably German S.S. and a highly skilled murderer. A mental profile of the kind of person chosen for the S.S. showed these people to have no regard for life, human or animal. They enjoyed inflicting pain and killed with no remorse. To display a complete lack of conscience and empathy, when the officers were in training and before the new officers' bars were pinned on them, each one had to prove that they were capable of committing any kind of cruelty no matter how vile. Varnish knew that the men on his police force would be no match for this man. He decided that until the threat of this man was past, all of his men would now travel in pairs. The overtime would be significant, but Varnish would have no use for a job or a system where those who served and protected were not served and protected by the very system that employed them. If the town council had objections, and they always seemed to have objections when asked to spend more even for the worthiest of causes, Varnish knew that his time on the Saybrook Police Force would be coming to an end.

CHAPTER FORTY-ONE

Sam was forced to wait patiently for the radio operator to reach Admiral Brown. His patience was being tested. It appeared that the admiral's attention was being sought by many. While he waited, Sam placed Veronica Lansing in the custody of two soldiers who were instructed to take charge of her and to protect her, even from herself if necessary; it appeared the lady was fearless and considered the whole proceedings to be great fun and adventure. Sam made sure he impressed upon the two young servicemen standing before him that she was never to leave their sight. He was waiting for a call from Mitchel Airfield in Uniondale to see if a plane was available to fly Veronica back to Deep River where Sergeant Varnish could be counted on to make sure she was taken home and safely locked in.

Mitchel Airfield in Uniondale, Long Island, was the U.S. Army Air Force headquarters for the U.S. Air Defense Command. Besides being the installation responsible for the training of countless numbers of pilots between World War I and the present war, Mitchel Field was given the responsibility of protecting the Northeast Coast, up to Nova Scotia by air while running anti-submarine patrol missions in the Atlantic. The planes stationed there were always at the ready and were capable of lifting squadrons airborne with very short notice. This was absolutely essential to protect

181

New York City and the neighboring coastal areas. Mitchel Field was named for a former New York City mayor, John Mitchel, who was killed on a training mission in Louisiana during the latter stages of WWI. Mitchel fell 500 feet to his death from the aircraft in which he was training.

At just 34 years of age, John Purroy Mitchel became the second youngest man elected mayor of New York City. Although he served only one term he was instrumental in championing the demise of Tammany Hall, the name of a powerful system of corruption, a system of patronage and profit that lasted some one hundred and forty-three years in New York. This Democratic organization wielded enormous power both in New York City and other parts of New York State.

Legend suggests and many believe Tammany Hall originally got its name from an Indian Chief, Tammend, who was believed to have dealings with William Penn. Chief Tammend was known as the benevolent chief, one who practiced rewarding those who aided him to get whatever he wanted. In the late seventeen hundred's he also appeared to have some sort of involvement with Aaron Burr. But it was with the election of Thomas Jefferson to the presidency in eighteen eighty-two that the real efforts of the system began to become a powerful tool for those already in or seeking power practice of patronage for votes, power and money to new heights. Tweed became like a king amongst his subjects. His power led him to become so brazen that his voracious appetite for all of what that power could give him landed him in prison where he died in 1878. Other bosses popped up to perpetuate the system until Fiorello LaGuardia picked up the torch, originally lit by Mayor Mitchel, and carried on the fight to diminish their power. But it was the present president who, being angered over their refusal to endorse him in his campaign for presidency in, ushered in the demise and collapse of the Tammany hall system.

In nineteen seventeen Mitchel presided over the first water tunnel in New York City's giant water supply system. A marble and granite monument in his honor was dedicated in nineteen twenty-eight. The monument is at the reservoir in Central Park at Fifth Avenue and 90th Street.

Sam finally received a call from the admiral. He could not believe it, but the admiral informed him that storming the house might not be the best approach for them to take. The admiral was concerned that Boland might be alerted and have an escape route already in place. Sam was informed that a twenty-four hour wait-and-see would give the admiral time to investigate the area around the Provost estate to make sure there would not be any chance of Boland's escape. No one wanted to be responsible for the plans Boland was carrying to find their way into Nazi hands. The admiral knew he had one chance and he was not about to compromise it by being in too much of a hurry. The other side of that coin was being overly cautious to the tune of taking too much time and allowing Boland to escape.

Sam decided to keep Martha with him rather than send her back with Veronica. Night was quickly advancing. It was getting darker by the minute. Sam and Martha joined Admiral Brown in his private quarters at OHEKA for dinner. Midway through dinner Sam received a call from Sergeant Varnish.

"What?" Sam exclaimed.

Martha and the admiral looked on questioningly. More bad news?

"Are you alright?" Sam asked the sergeant. Sergeant Varnish relayed all that had happened at the Saybrook Yacht Club and expressed his utter disdain for a certain town councilman who was greatly troubled by Varnish's decision to double up his men for their safety. As expected, the councilman nearly choked at the thought of the expense for the overtime. He questioned whether Varnish might be over-dramatizing the situation. The fact that Varnish had nearly been killed by a barrage of bullets by a shooter whose intentions were just that, somehow escaped the councilman's grasp. Sam told Varnish to calm down and proceed exactly as he had decided. Sam assured him that he agreed with Varnish's decision and that the situation would be taken care of. He also told Varnish to make sure Veronica Lansing was taken home from Deep River and to station someone there to see that she was safe until the mystery man was taken into custody. Varnish agreed, but was having a difficult time calming his anger over the certain councilman.

Sam explained what had happened over in Saybrook to Martha and the admiral. He told the admiral that Martha was one of the civilians helping with his investigation and that he could speak freely in front of her. One thing all three were in agreement on was the fear that Boland would find a way to escape to Germany with precious documents.

"You have read my books, haven't you?" Martha asked Sam.

Sam looked puzzled. "Yes, of course, I have," he answered.

"You read the Witches of Westchester County?" she asked.

Again, Sam seemed puzzled by the question.

He took a moment to reflect, and then it came to him.

"The plans in the assayer's office on public record," he nearly shouted.

Sam was referring to a chapter in Martha's book where the police had surrounded a home of three dangerous sisters claiming to be witches, who were suspects in a series of cult-like murders. To insure there was no possible way for them to escape the police went to City Hall to obtain blueprints of the property. Satisfied that they knew of every entrance and exit to the building, they then stormed the home and arrested the three women, the villains of Martha's book.

"Admiral, we need to get our hands on the blueprints of the Provost estate," Sam said.

The admiral smiled. That's some smart lady you have there, son," he said.

The admiral motioned to his attendant who brought over a large cylindrical leather case and placed it in the admiral's hands.

"The blueprints?" Sam asked him, anticipating his answer.

"One and the same," said the admiral.

Sam looked at Martha who was all smiles.

Sam paused for a moment, allowing Martha and the admiral their moment.

"Sir, do you know any Masons?" Sam asked.

Now it was the admiral's turn to be puzzled by a question.

"Not that I can think of," said the admiral.

"Wait a minute," said Sam. "I do."

Sam asked for and got permission to make a phone call to Connecticut. If anyone knew just exactly who to call it would be Arlen Templeton, himself a Grand Mason. Arlen not only furnished Sam with a name, but also an address, Dominick Bouchard of Mount Vernon, NY. Bouchard was not only a high ranking Mason, he was also the owner of a construction company. He was a builder. He had been commissioned by numerous wealthy clients, many of whom were enamored of the thought of secret passageways built into their lavish mansions. If anyone could flush out possible locations for such things, it was Dominick Bouchard.

While he had Arlen on the phone, Sam filled Arlen in on the shooting at the Saybrook Yacht Club. He asked Arlen to intercede on Sergeant Varnish's behalf before a certain Saybrook councilman suffers Varnish's wrath on him. Arlen laughed at that and assured Sam that Sergeant Varnish had nothing to worry about.

Sam hung up the phone and again, paused. Another thought suddenly came to mind.

"We need Injun Jim!"

CHAPTER FORTY-TWO

Karl Getman was a young boy of fifteen years of age growing up in Germany following the defeat of Germany after WWI. Bismark's ambitions had cost the German people dearly. Karl would rummage through the streets of Stuttgart, the sixth largest city in Germany, and the one closest to the French border, for scraps of food to bring home to his elderly mother. Karl's father was a casualty of the war and now Karl and his mother, like so many, were left destitute.

Europe made Germany pay a heavy price for the war bankrupting whatever was left of it. Because of its close proximity to France, the people of Stuttgart experienced a regular dose of French cruelty. By 1920 things had not gotten any better. If one did not have a farm, prospects were bleak.

On a dark overcast day in June of 1920, a policeman who had been a soldier during the war came across two young boys attempting to relieve Karl of the potato he had been fortunate enough to procure. Karl was long and lean in stature while the two young boys were rather large and stocky. After a few moments of talking and a little shoving, the two boys attacked Karl. The policeman was very tired, heading home after a long shift of duty. His inclination was to intercede, but his weariness slowed his response. To his surprise, Karl managed to hit one of the boys across the face, even though the other had him in his grasp. Karl dislodged himself from the one holding on to him and struck him several times knocking him to the ground. He turned to face the other boy who had regained his composure and landed several more blows also sending him to the ground. What the policeman saw next caught him completely by surprise. He expected to see young Karl run away. That would have been the logical thing to do. At that moment, he realized Karl was not one to do what most would do. Instead, Karl began kicking each of the boys who were on the ground and begging him to stop. Their cries for mercy only served to add fuel to Karl's attack. After he kicked one boy in the head, rendering him unconscious, Karl merely laughed and went on his way.

From that day on, the police officer who later would become a member of the S.S. in the Nazi regime found out where Karl lived and kept a close eye on him. Over the years, Karl grew up to be a thug who hung out with a very rough crowd and who always seemed to have money when so many in Germany did not. Whenever he was caught in a crime, the police found it difficult to get anyone to testify against him. He did manage to serve a little time in German prisons, but each time the warden was more than delighted to see him go. Karl could not be intimidated, and even if he were to lose a fight, he found a way to make his adversary sorry they ever crossed paths. He became a local legend.

When Hitler began his plans to thrust Germany into another war, people like Karl were considered useful to the cause. The policeman, now a member of the S.S., decided to recruit Karl and entertained him in high style. German officers enjoyed the best of the land and Karl soon learned that after all of his years of struggle, with little to show for it, his time of plenty had arrived.

Karl's talents were perfectly suited for the role of enforcer. Should anyone resist or oppose the new Germany under Adolf Hitler, Karl was dispatched to convince, discourage or dispose of them; it did not matter what form of action he took. His success by whatever means necessary was the desired result.

And now, Karl, a.k.a. the mystery man, found himself in the town of Old Saybrook hiding out and waiting for instructions from his superiors who were none too happy that he had not been able to kill a man posing as a naval officer, one Commander Boland and gain the valuable military papers Boland had in his possession.

CHAPTER FORTY-THREE

Injun Jim stepped down to the tarmac from the small single engine plane that had carried him from Deep River. Sam's call had been totally unexpected. But the urgency of Sam's voice made him gather a few of his belongings and hightail it to the airstrip. Arlen had his driver ready to take him and stay with him until the small plane that would take him arrived at first light the next day. No sooner had the plane touched ground, Injun Jim found himself inside, airborne and off to Long Island. When he told Aunt Clara what he was doing, and why, he was surprised to see that the woman was nearly speechless: nearly.

Even Martha could not believe it when Sam quite unexpectedly informed her and the admiral that Injun Jim's presence was absolutely imperative.

"We know that Bouchard can probably locate whatever tunnels are on the Provost property. We also know that the Masons were very tricky and filled their secret places with traps and false passageways. If Bouchard can get us in we'll still need to avoid using a lot of illumination. Bolan should be armed. We don't want any of our people becoming sitting ducks. Nobody can track as silently as Injun Jim. And he won't need much light. Bouchard should be able to get us in the right direction and Injun Jim gives us the best chance to keep Bouchard safe."

The admiral liked Sam's reasoning. Now all they had to do was to wait for the two men to arrive. The admiral had a room prepared for Martha and Sam to get some sleep. Tomorrow promised to be a very eventful day.

The next morning, as Sam and Martha made their way to join the admiral in the dining hall for breakfast their senses were treated to the smell of fresh brewed coffee hanging in the air.

"Well, you two are up early," said the admiral.

The admiral was seated at the huge dining table, but he was not alone.

"Sam, Martha, meet Dominick Bouchard," said the admiral.

Dominick Bouchard arose from his chair to greet them. Bouchard was a man in his mid-fifties who looked every inch a person who made his living with stone and lumber. He stood about five feet ten inches tall, with large arms and a very large neck. He had a barrel chest with a stomach that seemed to be connected to it. He was a big, robust man. His hands were quite large and calloused. He and Sam shook hands. His grip was strong and firm, but not overly aggressive. He was much gentler taking Martha's hand. One thing that was very noticeable about him was that he did not smile. By the time the soldiers located Bouchard, it was three o'clock in the morning. They pounded on his front door. Peering out from his bedroom window, on the second floor, Bouchard did not know what to think as he viewed the four New York City police cars and two army Jeeps, with their lights ablaze, blocking his street.

Bouchard had relocated and now lived out on Staten Island in a relatively new development. He was not happy to be rousted from his bed at such an early hour. He had just put in an exhausting day on his construction site in Parsippany, New Jersey. Actually, he had already informed his foreman that he might not be there the next day.

The officers told him only that he was needed by the military out on Long Island and to get dressed immediately and go with them. No matter how hard he tried, Bouchard could not get an answer from his escorts.

"I'm going to be the talk of my neighborhood," he complained. The officers appeared not to hear him.

A launch from the Brooklyn Navy Yard came to bring him across the Verrazano Narrows, which separates Brooklyn and Staten Island. Once in Brooklyn Bouchard was ushered into an army transport vehicle and with four police cars and two army Jeeps to clear the way. Bouchard and his convoy sped up through the streets of Brooklyn and over to Queens heading for the North Shore.

After finally arriving at five am and being informed of what the admiral wanted from him, Bouchard was not overjoyed. Helping the military to aid in the defense of the country was one thing, but he had serious reservations about the possibility of violating the Masonic code. When the admiral made the whole situation clear to him, Bouchard realized that finding the tunnels, if they did exist, was the right thing to do. He also knew it could be quite dangerous.

At that point, Bouchard sat down until Martha and Sam made an appearance. A scant breakfast of coffee and toast was served. The group quickly consumed it and then cleared the table and spread the floor plans out.

Bouchard spent some time looking them over and made his conclusions. He pointed to two possible areas that he was sure the Mason architects would use. This revelation was the Masonic code violation causing Bouchard some concern. Both areas Bouchard pointed to seemed to be nondescript and gave no indication that their location would be desirable. Bouchard ran his fingers over the plans to show the group where he would lay the tunnels. He assured them that when they finally did get inside the Provost home, he would be able to gain access. Sam and the admiral seemed convinced.

"Well, what's the holdup?" Bouchard asked
Just then two armed guards led Injun Jim into the room.

"Him," said the admiral."

CHAPTER FORTY-FOUR

Within thirty minutes after Martha and Veronica Lansing took their leave, the man claiming to be Commander Boland was busying himself in the immense dining room, laying out the china and silverware for the evening meal. He paused to take in the enormity of the space and its grotesque hodgepodge of furniture from different eras, none of which blended to create a space pleasing to the eye. A Louis XV style gilded dining table with matching tapestry tufted chairs lit up the dining area with golden hues. Margonette, however, had introduced dark, heavy Victorian pieces with carved bodies of animals, some still in their death throes, victims of hunters. These pieces, far removed from Louis XV's era, were completely out of context with the golden, elegant French furnishings.

Perhaps the most out of place piece in the room was an upright stuffed bear whose dark brown body stood against one of the few panels in the room not already covered with bad paintings and breakfronts. A few short feet to its left stood a massive stone fireplace, also, in complete contrast to the elegance of the French furnishings. This room seemed to have been decorated by someone who closed his eyes and indiscriminately placed objects all over the room, with absolutely no aesthetic criteria. To say it was ugly was to do it too much honor.

Margonette entered the dining room and observed Boland standing there.

"Just who are you?" she asked.

Boland turned to face her. He paused for a moment as if trying to decide how to respond. But instead of answering, he simply smiled. In fact, it was more of a sneer than a smile.

" And who was that scary man who was obviously looking for you?" Margonette demanded.

"His name is Karl Getman and he is a member of the Nazi SS," said Boland.

"Dear Lord!" exclaimed Margonette. "What does he want here?"

Once again, Boland did not immediately respond. But the look on his face was one of contempt!

"My name is Daniel Carson and I am a Seaman First Class in the United States Navy."

"I don't understand," said Margonette.

"Why am I not surprised?" said Boland/Carson. "Do you have any idea who Martha Frost's husband is?"

"No, I do not. And why would the identity of her husband be of any interest to me?" she asked.

"You really are as stupid as your ridiculous appearance," said Carson.

"How dare you!" Margonette said.

Margonette's fashion sense mirrored everything that was wrong with the interior of her home. Her eyes were made up for evenings at the opera, even at nine o'clock in the morning. She used a heavy rouge to paint her cheeks with no attempt to blend the color into the rest of her face. At first appearance one would be reminded of a "ragdoll". The only thing preventing her from looking like a clown was her hair which was fashioned like a queen who was attending some elegant function. She never changed it, no matter the time, season or circumstance. She dressed as one younger than herself, much younger. To many in society and unbeknownst to her, she was referred to as "a mess in a dress." This was the person standing before Carson.

Carson smiled and shook his head in disbelief.

"I wonder, do you ever read anything but the society news and maybe the comic strips?" Boland asked. "Or better yet, are you even capable of reading?" he said.

Margonette was speechless, caught completely by surprise by Boland's harsh tone and obvious lack of fear of her social standing.

"For your information, you absurd sow, Martha Frost's husband is Samuel Tyler, a captain of the Connecticut State Police and the man who has twice been decorated by the President of the United States for acts of heroism against plots to endanger America here on the home front. The man is a national hero and you have no knowledge of him. How amazing that you could miss such information as it was only plastered on the front page of every newspaper in America."

Margonette collapsed into one of the overstuffed Victorian dining room chairs she was leaning on.

She was about to say, "I had no idea," but thought better of it.

"Why are you here? What do you want from me and my family?" Margonette asked.

Carson leaned against the massive fireplace and drew his Colt revolver.

"I will tell you why I am here. Now let's see if you can pay attention long enough and grasp what I am about to disclose." Carson said.

"I am from San Francisco, the son of a man who makes his living at sea catching and delivering fresh seafood to the markets there. I knew that I would be drafted, so I chose to join the Navy. An easy choice as I have been out to sea my entire life."

"I was stationed in San Diego, California. As fortune would have it, the real Commander Boland was also stationed there. It was amazing, but the commander and I looked so much alike that we could easily be taken for twins. In fact, Boland took much pleasure in having me masquerade as him, never in uniform of course, on certain occasions when he needed to steal away for a rendezvous with one of his many lady friends. The man was a womanizer, and there is no end to the willing young women who seem to be only too happy to attract men who wear officers' uniforms. So successful were our deceptions that Boland became more and more active and, might I say, reckless in his adventures.

"It was easy for me to play my part. The moment he saw and met me, Boland took me on as his assistant. I became his right hand and easily learned all of his mannerisms. Our voices were different, but by speaking as he did, the deception was successful.

"When Boland received his transfer to Washington, one that had been expected for months, the people who were watching him, with the help of a few of his lady friends, decided the time was right to act.

"It was no secret that I had no desire to go to war and possibly die before my time. I had expressed my feelings on more than one occasion. I was approached by some gentlemen who said that as I was so successful in appearing as the commander, they had a proposition for me. They told me that the commander was never going to reach Washington, and that they could arrange it so that it was I who could go instead and assume his post there. Boland was born in Arizona, and had never traveled east. In fact, San Diego was the first place he had ever traveled to. All of his time in the service had been on the west coast. But, he was about to go east and assume control over a group that was responsible for secret documents pertaining to the war effort.

"At first, I was not too keen on the idea of committing treasonous acts against America, but when they told me how much they were willing to pay for my services, I began to change my mind. When they informed me that, should I refuse their offer, I would suffer the same fate as the commander, I quickly warmed to the idea. Seaman First Class Carson died in a boating accident and I, as Commander Boland, went to Washington to assume his post.

I surprised myself at how easily I was able to carry on the deception.

"And now, let me tell you how you figure into all of this. The Nazis were desperate to get their hands on secret war documents that were critical to allied troops in France. Germany's army was spread thin and growing smaller as the war progressed. I know all about your plan to disgrace and accuse Veronica Lansing as a traitor. It was your idea to have her arrested when the documents I was carrying were delivered to her. It seems you felt slighted by your unsuccessful attempts to include her in your social circle, for your own benefit, of course. Do you really believe she could not see through your foolish actions? Do you honestly believe that those two women came here on their way somewhere else? No, this was their destination all along. They were looking for me. That is exactly why Martha Frost was here. I'm not sure if she recognized me, but I have an important meeting to attend and you are going to aid in my escape. After all, it was you who made this whole thing possible."

Margonette was horrified by Carson's words. She searched vainly for some response.

"How?" came weakly out. It was all she could muster.

"When word of your feelings of contempt and humiliation reached those who employed me, a plan was put into effect to have all of this happen over the Thanksgiving Day holiday. A plan that had your approval. This was to be your early Christmas present to the vane and smug Veronica Lansing. How dare she spurn your advances, indeed!

"As plans for my involvement were being formulated, I became friendly with some of the participants who accidentally revealed that the person who would be at the Lansing home was a member of the SS and not some dupe who would take the blame with the Lansing woman. It was an Italian officer from Mussolini's personal guard who killed the handyman and took his place. I was pretty confident that once I arrived there I would never leave that place alive. When I did not show up at the appointed time, Getman went crazy and killed everyone he could get his hands on. He was not happy that the plan failed. He knew that as far as Hitler was concerned, that failure rested solely on his head. His prospects back home were not looking very promising. I am positive he is determined to find and kill me, get the plans and then get back to Germany.

"My plans are to escape through one of your tunnels that run underneath this home, meet up with those who hired me and then make them pay dearly for these plans which I have no problem relinquishing to them.

"Now get up and show me those tunnels. And do not try my patience. I have overheard you giggling with your equally foolish friends about the adventures of your youth down in them."

CHAPTER FORTY-FIVE

It was bitter cold combined with a nasty biting wind that swept over him as the nineteen thirty nine Riva run-about Getman was traveling in cut across the choppy water at thirty five knots hoping to make Savin Rock Amusement Park in West Haven before eleven pm. Karl Getman had set up a meeting with Peter Ziegler, the president of the German-American Club in West Haven. Ziegler had told him that he would not wait past eleven p.m. Getman wrapped himself with a blanket and huddled against the uncovered helm compartment the best he could to avoid freezing to death. Powered by a one hundred twenty five horse-power engine the run-about, built by the famous Riva family of boat builders in Italy, and fitted with the V-shaped bottom, a brilliant innovation courtesy of the American boat building Hacker Boats Company, allowed the run-about to hydroplane, skimming over the water, thus avoiding bumps and turbulence. It travelled on relentlessly in quest of a successful meeting with a group of German-Americans Getman hoped would aid his cause.

Three miserable hours later Getman caught sight of the lighthouse off Light House Point in New Haven, which sat directly across New Haven harbor from Savin Rock Amusement Park, a gargantuan repository of amusements that sat on a large strip of waterfront in the town of West Haven. Originally this section of beachfront was part of New Haven before West Haven broke away and gained it through a gifting from the city of New Haven. The first thing anyone would notice from Getman's vantage point was the huge wooden roller coaster, Roller Boller, the oldest and lone survivor of Savin Rock's many. Then came the ninety-two foot Thunderbolt in 1925. At the time it was the tallest and fastest roller coaster in the country. It burned and fell into the harbor during the Great New England Hurricane of 1938. The next, The Devil, also burned down in 1932, after only seven years of service.

Savin Rock has quite an interesting history. The brainchild of Colonel George Kelsey, a colonel in the 6th Connecticut Regiment during the Civil War, its original intent was to be a place of leisure and repose for the affluent. Kelsey made his fortune by following his entrepreneurial spirit. After the war, he began to buy into the West Haven horse-drawn trolley system, eventually gaining the controlling interest. He then turned his attention to building a large pier to accommodate ferry service on Long Island Sound. Its immense size of 1,500 feet guaranteed that the tides of the Sound would have no negative effect on its service and reliability. Next, Kelsey sought to build an amusement park to draw people to the area, but first he had the wisdom to build a grand Victorian hotel, the Sea View Hotel. Once that was completed, Kelsey used his influence to lure local businessmen to set up shop in a large tract of land he owned next to the hotel. The operative word was "amusement" businesses. That included any business that would attract visitors from near and far.

Taking its inspiration from the World's Columbian Exposition of 1893, Savin Rock became one of the largest and most successful amusement parks in the nation, featuring every conceivable attraction from roller coasters to giant Ferris wheels. No fewer than five carousels or "flying horses" as they were called were there. Every imaginable type of eating establishment from small hut like enclosures to elegant dining rooms could be found every-where. There were actual movie theatres, the Hippodrome and the Orpheum, to present picture shows for those hoping to escape the heat of summer. However, the movie houses did little to provide an escape from the heat. Stage plays and vaudeville acts, courtesy of the Poli family, that of Sylvester Poli, the movie and vaudeville theatre king of the northeast and resident of nearby Milford, Connecticut, were also very popular and attracted large crowds

Now the park was deserted, having ceased operations for the winter months. Claus Friedman, one of the caretakers employed by the town of West Haven to monitor and care for the West Haven beaches, sat in the tiny Spartan hut connected to a large maintenance shed near the water's edge. The caretaker was on his third metal mug of coffee when he saw Getman's boat approaching. The driver expertly slid alongside a small dock and secured the boat. Friedman was standing there waiting. He extended his hand to Getman, who took it and jumped onto the dock. Friedman shivered at the icy cold hand that gripped his. He introduced himself and led Getman and his driver to the hut where he offered them coffee, which both men quickly accepted.

"Ziegler is anxious for your meeting to take place. He does not keep very late hours and hates the cold," said Freidman.

Getman did not respond verbally, but gestured towards the door. Friedman understood and started to leave when Getman and his driver began to follow. Friedman stopped and told the driver he must stay here, only Getman would be allowed to the meeting. That settled, Getman and Friedman made their way to a 1934 Chevrolet coupe that would bring them to the clubhouse located on a lonely strip of land known to the locals as "no man's land" where the Sperry & Barnes Meat Packing plant took up most of what was known as Long Wharf, just to the south of New Haven harbor. It was the only industrial section of West Haven.

On a lonely deserted street that seemed to have no name, and completely overshadowed by the meat packing plant, stood a small two story structure where the German- American Club of West Haven had their clubhouse

After a short ride, Getman and Friedman entered the clubhouse where Ziegler and ten of his club members were waiting. The smell of beer was the first thing Getman's senses identified. It was your typical working men's clubhouse, all wood and mirrors with a large bar area to satisfy the drinking members of the German-American Club. It was bleak and non-descript with plain walls filled with pictures of the German countryside and famous German men hiding the many flaws.

Getman was introduced to Ziegler, a stout middle-aged man who appeared to have prospered in America. By the size of his considerable girth he had not missed too many meals in his time. As Getman looked around, he noticed that most of the men appeared to be well fed as well. He did his best to mask his feelings of contempt. Germany had endured many long years of suffering after World War I and most of its inhabitants were lucky to have meager supplies of food. In all of his travels throughout the Fatherland, Getman had not encountered many who could be described as overweight. If all of America was like this, he reasoned, it must be a place where laziness and over indulgence ran rapid.

"What can we do for you, friend?" Ziegler asked after he and Getman had taken seats around a small wooden table.

"I am in need of American currency and the means to reach a place called Block Island in the Atlantic Ocean," said Getman. Both men conversed in German to allow Getman to speak more fluently. Everyone there could speak German.

"What is your business here?" Ziegler asked.

"I was sent here to observe all that I could about this section of America and bring that information back to Germany," Getman lied.

"And you have no other reason?" Ziegler asked.

Getman was slightly taken aback by the question. He did not anticipate being suspected of any wrongdoing. Maybe Ziegler was just being cautious. Getman decided to throw caution to the wind.

"I am here solely to see if all the tales of rich treasures, buried by the pirates and religious orders are here, and if so, how vast are these treasures."

"And how may these treasures be of use to Hitler?" Ziegler asked.

"Once again, Getman was impressed by the questions being asked by Ziegler, a man Getman had obviously underestimated.

"May I speak plainly?" Getman asked.

"Of course," said Ziegler. "Are we all not of German blood?"

Encouraged by the response, Getman continued.

"I am to inform you that after Germany wins this war, we will use our considerable resources to obtain these treasures. I have been instructed by the Fuhrer himself to promise that those who aid in our cause now will be amply rewarded. The Fuhrer is intensely loyal to those who he considers friends."

"Even Rommel?" Ziegler asked.

Getman was stunned by the response. How could this man know about Rommel's increasing fall from grace and Hitler's plans for his death?

Ziegler folded his hands and placed them on the table. He looked Getman squarely in the eyes.

"I am sorry to tell you that the persons and the aid you are seeking are not here." Waving his hands at the others in the room, Ziegler continued, "We have come to this country to escape the Hitlers of this world, men who seek power at all cost. Here in America we have found freedoms those in Germany will never experience. Our families are allowed to thrive and pursue any course they choose. You speak of after 'Germany wins this war.' Surely, you are well aware that it will not. Hitler's quest for gold is merely a desperate attempt to save himself."

Startled by this revelation, Getman made an attempt to move his chair out and to retrieve his weapon from his coat pocket. He was met by the weapons drawn by all the men standing around him. He placed his hands, palms down, on the table as a sign of surrender.

Ziegler asked him to stand and when he did, one of the men came and took his weapon. He then checked to make sure he did not have another.

Getman was escorted outside by two burly men who with Friedman were to hold him until the West Haven Police, who had now been informed, came to take him into custody. But the locals had no idea who they were dealing with. No one had thought to see if he had any other type of weapon. Pistols were not the only weapon Getman had in his possession. Feigning cold, he shuddered slightly and pulled his arm close to his body, appearing to attempt to warm himself. He slipped his hand into the lining of his leather coat and drew a six-inch knife, standard issue for the S.S., and slashed the gun hand of one of his captors. The man screamed in pain. When the others looked to see why he was holding his wrist, which was now bleeding profusely, Getman grabbed the driver and with his knife against the driver's throat ordered the other man to drop his weapon and go back inside the building. He saw no choice but to drop his pistol. Then, he reluctantly took hold of his friend and retreated back inside. Getman picked up the Colt pistol the man had dropped and pulled the driver back to the driver's side door and opened it. He slid in backwards while holding onto the driver. He pulled him in, placed the barrel of his weapon into the man's throat and told him to drive. The driver did as he was told and accelerated the vehicle down the long alleyway to the boulevard. Within seconds, they were out of sight.

The two men Ziegler chose to escort Getman outside were much larger than him. They were big clumsy men who worked at hard labor. Getman was lean, but all muscle. The winter cold made it necessary for everyone to wear heavy clothing, making it possible for Getman to hide the knife. His captors had no way of knowing of his physical prowess. Their size made Ziegler confident they could overpower him if he tried to escape. He was wrong.

CHAPTER FORTY-SIX

Sam introduced Injun Jim to the admiral and Bouchard. By now, the two men understood the wisdom of Sam's sudden decision to call Injun Jim into the fray.

"You can find the tunnels and get us in there," Sam said to Bouchard while the admiral looked on, "but Injun Jim can make things much safer for us down there. He is a full-blooded Mohegan Indian and I'll feel a heck of a lot safer with him leading the way, especially because we won't be using much light for fear we'll make an easy target. Jim makes our chances of sneaking up on Boland much better."

After Injun Jim and Martha hugged, the two soldiers that escorted him took Martha to Mitchel Field to be flown back home. Martha knew what was going to happen next. Once in flight, she peered out the window to look down on the frigid waters of Long Island Sound. Her thoughts were of the plan Sam had laid out to the admiral. A large force of men, local police from the nearby town, Detective Philip D'Onofrio and about twenty New York City Police officers along with at least a dozen uniformed army personnel would be deployed all over the area near Glen Cove to attempt to cut off any escape by accessing the tunnels. No one really knew if there were any tunnels and if so, where they led. Admiral Brown called in Commander Mickelson, from Washington, to head up a network of boats along the shoreline to cut off any access to Long Island Sound on the north shore or the Atlantic Ocean to the south.

Three Coast Guard Cutters took up a perimeter presence to aid any boats who might come under attack.

Sam's plan was to have a number of men in stationary positions, while other groups roamed the area in hopes of finding entrances to the tunnels. It was a daunting task, but it was as efficient a plan as was possible. All Sam and the admiral could do was hope for the best and pray that those called in to carry it out were equal to the task. In any event, it would take the whole day to assemble their forces and coordinate everyone as to the overall plan and define each person's responsibilities.

D'Onofrio and the local police chiefs would handle the ground deployment while Commander Mickelson and Commander Thomas, out of Milford, coordinated the guarding of the shores. To complete the patrolling of the shores, which wrapped around Glen Cove to Oyster Bay to an outer section of Huntington Station, the Coast Guard had the three cutters placed in the outer perimeter. Two 80 footers stationed at Ditch Plains were positioned in the outer sections while the 125 foot CGC Yeaton, out of New London, but commissioned to patrol Montauk and Gardner's Island, sat in the middle. All were capable of gearing up speed to reach any section of the embargo-like set up when necessary. In essence, this was a naval version of a gauntlet. There was no way out.

At first light, Sam, Injun Jim, Bouchard and four army officers would enter the Provost estate. That meant everyone else would need to deploy during the evening and take up their positions. No one of the military personnel had to be reminded how important this mission was. An added incentive was the capture of a traitor, possibly one of their own. Every man was ready to do his part.

After a relatively smooth ride and flawless touchdown, Martha exited the army aircraft at Tweed, in New Haven. She was met there by Arlen Templeton's driver, who took her back to Essex.

She had to admit Arlen's Cadillac was the best ride she had experienced in quite some time. Indeed, Martha could not recall the last time she sat in the back seat of a chauffeur-driven luxury automobile. She had to admit, Arlen Templeton knew how to get around in style. Martha allowed her body to sink into the luxurious embrace of the rich leather interior, which seemed as soft as a pair of very expensive gloves. The chauffeur informed her that the interior of this American-made luxury automobile was fitted by an Italian designer who was famous for crafting the interiors of the yachts of the mega-wealthy, including those of the European royals and Arab princes. But the real story behind this oversized vehicle, the largest automobile of its day, was that it was a 1939 cloth covered beauty that had been completely refitted for its role of "Batmobile", in the 1943 Batman and Robin movie. While on business in Southern California, Arlen's hosts treated him to a visit to the on-location setting of the Batman movie. It was mid-1942 and the movie was about to wrap. It was scheduled for a release and premier in the summer of 1943. One look at that Cadillac and Arlen was smitten. He persuaded the producers to sell her to him for a hefty price. Once he got his hands on his new automobile, he had the entire interior refitted with leather, replacing the glitzy mohair and leather seating used for the movie. The mahogany dash and steering wheel completed the interior ensemble that guaranteed Arlen that his was a one-of-a-kind wonder.

Arlen's chauffeur knew the way to the Tyler homes and pulled into Aunt Clara's driveway and stopped at the back porch. He exited the car and came around, opened the rear door to allow Martha to do the same.

"Must I?" Martha said to the chauffeur who was pleasantly amused by the question.

Martha thanked the man and began to walk up the stairs just as Aunt Clara was coming out to see who it was that had just arrived on her property. As she and Martha stood there watching the chauffeur expertly back out of the driveway, Martha half jokingly stated, "Aunt Clara, we need one of those."

CHAPTER FORTY-SEVEN

It was just before dawn when the man driving the runabout returned to North Cove. As he pulled up to his dock, he saw smoke coming from his chimney. That could only mean one thing: Getman somehow had made it back. Getman's instructions had been to wait one hour from the time he left with Friedman. If he was not back, the driver was to leave him and head back. Getman assured him he would find his way back. It appeared he had not overstated his abilities.

When the driver opened the door to his small three room boat cottage, he was presented with the sight of a man all tied up and gagged in the middle of his living room.

"I put his car in the shed. Yours is in the back, well hidden from the water," said Getman.

"Do you think it wise to have a hostage?" the driver said.

"My choices were limited," said Getman. "I could have killed him, but I rather liked the company for the ride here. Luckily, I remembered how to access your road and where your cottage was. Besides, we may need him. Hostages are not volunteering right now."

"What now?" the driver asked.

"I have one more thing to accomplish," said Getman. "It appears that my mission here is a failure. I have only one other choice. I have been guaranteed a large sum of money to kill someone. I will go to Argentina and begin my life anew. I will reward you handsomely for your help."

"What happened in West Haven?" the driver asked.

"I am not sure, but the man I spoke to, Peter Ziegler, knew as much or more about what is happening in Germany as I do." Getman said.

"How is that possible?" the driver wanted to know.

"I have no idea, but I was fortunate to escape from that place. I was correct in my assumption that those Germans had grown soft in America. Foolishly, they underestimated my abilities." Getman continued.

"And you killed others?" said the driver.

"Of course not. They were no match for me. The most important thing now is that this search for hidden treasure is proof that Hitler is going mad and is desperate to seek some magical solution. As time and the war creeps on, many in the high command are beginning to see Hitler as delusional. There are stories that claim he was influenced by some mysterious mystic, who prophesied a god-like existence for him. When Hitler came to power, he rewarded the man by having him murdered along with every known occult practitioner that could be found. The Fuhrer was not going to allow any other prophesies that would be threatening to his control. And then, who do you suppose he chooses as his second in command?"

The driver gave no answer.

"Himmler, the head of the SS and a man deeply involved in the occult." said Getman. "There are rumors that some generals are planning to kill Hitler. Rommel, himself, may be one of them. There is no future for me back in Germany. Who knows? I could live very comfortably on one of the many islands in the South Pacific. If conditions were favorable, I might even proclaim myself a king." Getman said.

At first the driver was silent and then he said, "There is one thing I must know."

"Anything," Getman assured.

"Why did you kill the Italian? He was with us."

"Yes, but he was not German." Getman said. "When he saw what I did to that overweight house frau, he was horrified. I'll admit that I let my anger get the best of me, but I did not come all the way to America to fail. I can just imagine der Fuhrer's expression when he learned I had not gotten those documents. That foolish woman started shouting and began to shriek. I became so angry that, well, you know what I did."

"But the Italian?"

"He was a sniveling fool, a cowardly whiner. He just kept after me and before I knew it, my blade was in his stomach. At that point I decided to make him look like the first victim, hoping it would confuse the authorities. I had no idea this Captain Tyler was smart, that eventually he would figure this out. In any event, when I looked at the two of them lying there, I guess I got so angry at the way things turned out that I just started wrecking everything I saw. Eventually, I tired and regained my composure. What's done is done. No one will suspect you once I'm gone. You will be in the clear."

The driver looked over to the bound and gagged Friedman.

"Don't worry. He won't be talking. But, right now, I am going to get some rest. I have plans to formulate once I complete my task; I will disappear and you will be wealthier for your troubles. Unfortunately, our friend here has seen you. He is an ethnic German, but completely American. There is no way he would protect you. Sadly, his fate is sealed."

CHAPTER FORTY-EIGHT

At 8:00 p.m., after dinner, Sam and the admiral presided over a final meeting. Captain Philip D'Onofrio, Commander Mickleson and Commander Thomas, four police chiefs from the neighboring towns and Captain Michael Simmons, U.S. Army, a native of Charlotte, North Carolina, met in the large mess hall for a final briefing. A partial force had hastily been deployed over a large area in the hopes that Carson had not already attempted to flee. Each town had two police rescue launches and they were immediately positioned from Glen Cove, around Oyster Bay, ending at Huntington Bay separating Lloyd Harbor from Huntington Station. The Coast Guard cutters had arrived and secured waters by six p.m. It was already dark, but each had to be released from its present duty. The Coast Guard cutter Yeaton had gone back to New London for minor repairs and traveled at top speed to provide the final piece in place on Long Island Sound, just north of Caumset State Park, a huge tract of land north of Lloyd Harbor and the northern-most dividing point between Oyster and Huntington Bays. It was a safe bet that Carson would not be headed there. The landscape and terrain could be treacherous for someone not fully experienced in travelling there, especially on foot and with limited light. The police launches had begun searchlight surveillance and would continue to do so until dawn.

For the local police departments, the task was much more difficult. Road blocks had to be set up at all thoroughfares leading to Route 25, the main artery for that area and the most direct to travel to either shore. Two officers were positioned at each train station. But for those officers patrolling the beaches on foot, it was a wing and a prayer situation. The amount of sea access was nearly fifty miles. Working in four-man shifts, each group had flashlights, communication devices and heavy armament. Their orders were to search, contain and, if fired upon, return fire with extreme prejudice. Obviously, apprehending Carson was the best possible scenario. He would be able to identify Getman and those responsible for Carson's defection. Hopefully, he could furnish information necessary to find and arrest the other perpetrators. Meanwhile, three military Jeeps carrying five senior personnel were placed strategically in the middle of the three areas of the quadrant from one end of the surveillance area to the other. These would be counted on to respond immediately to any area necessary. The fourth part was all of the water surveillance. So far, luck seemed to be on Sam's side. Locating Carson was a major stroke of luck. And it was beginning to appear that he and Getman were not working together.

Captain D'Onofrio had been informed by his cousin of Getman's clash with the West Haven group. It was believed that Getman was somewhere in Connecticut seeking to find a way to reach Block Island. If Getman was attempting to reach that destination, it could readily be assumed that a Nazi submarine was in those waters. Upon hearing the news, Admiral Brown immediately notified Mitchel Field to begin an all out air search of that area ASAP It was a pretty fair assumption that Carson had been acting on his own. It was also reasonable to assume that he would have support somewhere in the areas already under alert. He had to figure that going any further on his own would be extremely difficult. Help had to be close.

Sam was told that Matt had sent word to Varnish, up in Old Saybrook, that in all probability, Getman was heading his way. His small force was put on highest alert. Sam called Mayor Tinsley to see if he could round up any responsible men in the area to help the local police and the few State Police personnel available to be on the alert.

The mayor quickly began making phone calls and convened a meeting at the Black Swan. The Meecham brothers were members of an informal local hunting club. Two of these men, of Native American blood, along with the others, had hunted for deer in season for nearly ten years. Their involvement would be to deploy with Officer Dolan, the State Police officer in Essex should Getman be spotted in the area. Sam gave explicit instructions that they were to do exactly what they were told by Dolan and nothing more. They may be expert hunters, but Getman was an expert murderer. Getman had been in a war and was battle seasoned. Even if some of the hunters had been in WW1, they would not exactly be youthful. The last thing Sam wanted was to have one or more of them become victims. The mayor broke the meeting up and sent the men home. But they were all told that they were to make sure that they were ready if and when they were needed.

Wanda Loomis insisted that the Black Swan be used as the local command post between Varnish and his men and the Essex group. It was a sure thing that the coffee would be constantly flowing that evening.

Mayor Tinsley became the self-appointed head of command and with Wanda and her brother, who now ran the ice cream shop, once known as Zuckerman's, began an all night vigil. They would take turns waiting while the others slept. Aunt Clara and Mary Ellen Tinsley, the mayor's wife, were given phone numbers to call to set up a chain of communication between the volunteers. Each man had the number of a member so that within ten to fifteen minutes of the first call, everyone would be notified and on their way to the command post. When Sam got the news from

Martha, he had to smile. Tinsley had stepped up to the plate and the townsfolk had shown up for support. Now, all anyone could do was to wait and see. It appeared that all that could be done had been done.

At ten p.m., Sam and all the group heads gave a final toast for success and then attempted to get some rest before tomorrow's action. Just as it had been done in Essex and Saybrook, every possible step had been addressed. The weather report called for fair skies with plenty of sunshine with temperatures in the mid-thirties. No one would have any trouble staying awake and alert.

CHAPTER FORTY-NINE

Martha woke with a start. She did not need to look over to the windows to know that the sun had come up. It was just a little after six-thirty am.

"It's begun," she said to herself as she lay there staring up at the ceiling.

And, indeed it had. Sam, Bouchard, Injun Jim and four U.S. Army infantrymen drove to the Provost estate at first light. They exited their vehicles and approached the front door. Sam rang the bell. There was no response. He rang again and again but there was no response. There were no lights visible anywhere. The house appeared to be completely deserted.

Sam instructed one of the soldiers to break the door down with a metal battering ram. Once done, Sam and the men entered. There was no response to the slamming of the battering ram. Sam instructed three of the four army men to make a search of the house to see if anyone was there. The Provost home had twenty-six rooms over two stories, with a third floor used as servants' quarters, which was another ten rooms. In all, there were eleven bathrooms, including a huge bath salon in the master suite.

Sam and his group adjourned to the dining room where Bouchard spread the house plans over the huge dining room table. Bouchard began to familiarize himself with the floor plan and walked from room to room to see if there were any obvious choices before he began poking around at the walls. After a half hour of investigation, he decided on two obvious places to begin. First was the library with one wall of shelving completely filled with books of every interest and content. Like the rest of the house, there seemed no rhyme or reason for their being chosen. The Provosts were not known for their intellects. It was apparent from the looks on the faces of Sam and the other two that one would easily suspect they probably had not read any of them. They were there strictly for show, or maybe something else.

Satisfied, Bouchard headed back to the dining room, the second most likely place. He walked over to the place where the most overpowering presence in the room stood, a huge stone fireplace. So large was the interior that four men of normal size, standing side-by-side could walk into it without lowering their heads. He was beginning to study it, placing his hands on it and feeling along its surface when he was interrupted.

"We found these people, sir," said one of the army officers.

Three very relieved-looking people stood before them.

"They were on the third floor, bound and gagged in a storage area behind one of the walls," said the officer.

Sam bade the three, two women and one man, all advanced in years, sit down at the table.

"What can you tell me?" Sam asked.

The man, obviously the one in charge of the home, spoke up.

"A man posing as a butler has taken Miss Margonette captive," said the man.

"Where did they go?" Sam asked.

"I believe they are down in some tunnels located below the basement," said the man. "I distinctly heard him tell our mistress that he knew of their existence and threatened to harm her if Miss Margonette refused to guide him."

"Did she comply?" Sam asked.

The man was silent for a long moment. Obviously, he was deciding what words to choose to offer a response.

"I am quite sure she complied with his wishes. The man was very scared. He appeared desperate and quite on edge. We were all frightened. There was no telling what he was capable of. A very dangerous looking man came inquiring about him. He held a gun on these two women in the pantry just off the kitchen and threatened to kill them if our mistress gave him up. He showed me a picture of the butler. I told him the man had never been here. He did not seem very pleased by what I told him. After a few extremely tense moments, he left."

"Was it the man posing as a butler who tied you up?" Sam asked.

"Yes," came the response. The two women shook their heads in agreement.

"You were on the third floor. Where was Miss Provost during all this?" Sam asked.

"Tied up on one of these chairs," said the man.

"That's it," said Bouchard. It's a safe bet the tunnel is right here."

"Okay," said Sam, "let's start here."

"You three are free to go." Sam said.

The three looked questioningly at Sam.

"What is it?" Sam asked.

"We cannot leave Miss Margonette or her home," said the man. "Our employer would expect us to be here when she returns or, heaven forbid, should anything happen to her, we would be obliged to care for the house until our employer arrived."

"Alright," said Sam, "but please do not remain on this floor. Feel free to go anywhere you like, but please know that this floor could be dangerous for you."

"We will do as you say," said the man. "Is there anything we can get for you?" the man asked.

"Coffee, perhaps?" Sam said.

"Coming right up," said the male who later informed Sam his name was Malcolm, while shooing the two females out.

Once again, Bouchard placed his hands on the ledge along the highest point of the fireplace and slowly inched along the surface.

"I'm looking for a pressure point," he said, looking over his shoulder to Sam.

"There should be a lever that is enacted by the thrust backwards that sets the releasing mechanism in motion. It is amazing, the devices these men came up with," he said with a tone bordering on reverence.

Sam and the group waited patiently as Bouchard inspected every inch of the surface. After a half hour, he made his way inside to begin pressing against the large bricks from one end to the other. He was also looking for possible handprints. He found none. It was beginning to appear that Bouchard was becoming frustrated.

At this time, Injun Jim decided to satisfy his fascination for the huge stuffed bear that was as tall as he was. Jim walked over and admired the preservation job. It was magnificent. He placed his hands on both shoulders.

"My, you was really somethin', weren't you, big fella," he said.

Just then the bear turned on its pedestal about 45 degrees to the right. At the same time, as Jim pulled back in surprise, the inside wall of the fireplace moved to its left, completely exposing a large passageway. Bouchard scrambled out of the fireplace to see what had caused the movement of the inner wall. He looked over at Jim, who was pointing to the partially turned bear. Next he got down on his hands and knees to examine the base.

"Unbelievable! I told you these people were masters," he said triumphantly.

Sam looked over to the four army men as he drew his pistol out of its holster. He nodded to the soldiers to draw theirs. Each man had a flashlight, all except for Injun Jim who walked into the tunnel and stood motionless for a moment, allowing his eyes to become adjusted to the darkness. Finally, he turned to Sam and waved him and the group in. Sam went first followed by Bouchard and the army officers whose job it was to cover their rear flank.

CHAPTER FIFTY

Martha showered and quickly dressed for the day. She gathered her hair back in a ponytail; it took three tries, but her hair was just long enough to make it. Her hair being wet made the task easier. She bounded down the stairs, went out the kitchen door and ran across the lawn to Aunt Clara's. She came up the backstairs and entered the kitchen just in time to see Aunt Clara taking her famous blueberry muffins out of the oven. Aunt Clara placed the large muffin tin on top of the stove and looked over at Martha.

"There aren't too many women around these parts who can wear their hair that way, you know." Aunt Clara said.

"My, but you are quite a lovely young lady, Missy," she said. "My nephew sure hit the jackpot when he lassoed you."

Martha did not respond. She just stood there completely embarrassed, but quite thankful for the compliments. She smiled as she realized that she should never be surprised by anything that comes out of that dear lady's mouth.

"Well, don't just stand there, get yourself some coffee and come sit a while with me," said Aunt Clara.

Martha went over and took a cup from the cupboard and poured herself a full cup and took a chair at the table where Aunt Clara had already seated herself.

"You're up kinda early," said Aunt Clara, knowing full well why that was so.

"It's begun," said Martha.

"Don't you go getting all frazzled. Samuel is going to do just fine. That man could always take care of himself. Besides with Injun Jim as his guide, I am sure he can handle the situation."

Aunt Clara finished and looked over to Martha who was smiling back at her.

"What are you smiling for?" Aunt Clara wanted to know.

"I haven't been here very long but that's the first time I've ever heard you say anything complimentary about Injun Jim," said Martha.

Aunt Clara began to smile herself. She looked to the left and then to the right.

"Now don't you go blabbing what I said all over town, dearie," said Aunt Clara. "Folks will start to think I am getting soft."

Again, Martha chose silence but could not hide her smile.

"Well, enough of this," said Aunt Clara. "That's all I'm going to say on that subject."

She got up and went over to the stove and gently touched the baking tin. She took two dish towels out of a drawer.

"Now why don't you use some of that inquisitive energy you seem to have all stored up and take these up to Wanda and the folks and see how they are doing?" Aunt Clara said.

Martha did just that. She wanted to do anything she could for the mayor and Wanda and anyone else who was pitching in to protect the town. The cool, fresh New England air was always inviting to her with her fur hat, huge wool scarf wrapped around her neck, her winter coat, woolen gloves. She hastened up Main Street to spend time with Wanda and the folks gathered there.

Everyone in town had taken an instant liking to Martha. Most famous people in the area, whether visiting or living there, carried themselves with an air of pomposity and importance. She was one of the most celebrated authors of her day, and certainly one of the most popular, but insisted everyone call her Martha Tyler, the wife of State Police Captain Samuel Tyler.

CHAPTER FIFTY-ONE

Sam had been assured that every inch of the home had been searched. Margonette Provost was nowhere to be found. It was a pretty safe bet that Carson had taken her with him for obvious reasons.

Bouchard had warned Injun Jim that the Masons were famous for using trapping devices to either trick or harm anyone who was not of their order. He also warned Sam that they might be led down false passageways, probably leading nowhere.

Carson definitely had the advantage if the Provost woman was with him. It was a pretty good bet that he would be waiting for dark before leaving the safety of his hiding place. There was the strong likelihood that those who had employed him would be the ones who would be coming to his aid. The truth was, the stolen documents were the only reason for these men to chance aiding his escape. They surely would not allow any more time to elapse before gaining possession of them. Time was precious, and for them, it was running out.

The group moved along cautiously. Every so often Jim would find a blind alley, but once he was sure no footprints were on the dirt floor, he made the group double back and begin anew. About two hours into the search, Injun Jim was sure he heard sounds, sounds like voices. He cautioned everyone to be silent. After a few moments of silence, he was positive he heard voices, male and female. Carson had removed Margonette's gag, a move he immediately regretted. Confident they were closing in on Carson, Sam joined Injun Jim and they began inching their way up the tunnel. Before long they caught sight of Margonette, bound and once again gagged; the sound of Margonette's voice had nearly driven Carson crazy. Sam started to move towards her, but was held back by Bouchard who was convinced of a trap. Bouchard insisted on going first into the area where Margonette was tied up. He moved slowly and cautiously. At just about the time he reached Margonette's position the ground beneath him opened up. Only the quick reaction of Injun Jim saved him from falling down a very long and narrow hole.

Carson heard the sounds and knew that his pursuers were near. He now realized he had to leave the tunnel and try to reach the place where those whom he was supposed to meet would be waiting. It was quite early. He had to hope they were already there and that the place was safe from detection. He knew his chances were slim, but his options were limited. If he allowed Sam and his people to reach him, it would result in a gunfight, one he had little chance of surviving.

Once her gag was taken away, Margonette began singing like Jenny Lind, P.T. Barnum's famous "Swedish Nightingale." Carson heard her hysterical ramblings and realized he had no choice. The time to go was now. He pushed open the wall and hunkered low to the ground to allow his eyes to adapt to the light. He realized he was not very close to the shore.

He had been told to head in a westerly direction until he reached West Neck Road, the largest blacktop in Lloyd Harbor and the one that ran from Chaumset State Park in the north down to Route 25A, the main highway through that whole section of the island. Once he reached West Neck Road, he was to travel north along that route, traveling in the bushes to avoid being seen until he reached a large beach at the northeastern tip of Lloyd Harbor. Less than one-half mile to the south was a small beach cottage.

There, he was to meet up with the men who would take him to safety.

Carson was no fool. He had three pistols on him to make sure any plans to kill him and take possession of the documents would fail. He had no idea what their capabilities were. But, he was an expert marksman and knew that he would have to take them captive as soon as he got on the launch. He began heading in the direction he had been given by those he was in league with. He was sure that if he could arrive there, he would be safe.

Just then, shots rang out.

"He's over here," came the cry of one of the Huntington Station police officers.

Carson dove to the ground and crawled to a cluster of trees. As he continued towards his destination, he caught sight of the small beach cottage. He ran with all his strength towards it and once he reached it, he found the door unlocked. He quickly went inside and used most of the sparse amount of furniture to barricade himself in. Almost immediately the police converged on the scene and began firing.

Sam arrived and told everyone to cease firing. He radioed his position and had everyone take up positions around the building. All three Coast Guard cutters took up positions at the mouth of Huntington Bay.

Sam radioed Admiral Blake to tell him what was happening. The admiral told him to sit tight and to wait for his arrival. The Coast Guard wired him the coordinates. Within a half hour he joined Sam at the sight. The admiral brought coffee and doughnuts. Within minutes a tent was set up as a command post. A folding table and chairs were set up and the admiral spread out a map of the area of Huntington Bay. The admiral radioed instructions to the three cutters to take up positions one mile out to sea and maintain alert status. He contacted the police launches and dispersed them one mile out, but half each to north of Bayville to the west and Eaton's Neck to the east. The plan was to further create a gauntlet, allowing anyone in and then sealing them in on all sides so there was no getting out. Both Sam and the admiral agreed that the only thing that made sense was that a boat would be needed to enter Oyster Bay, pick up Carson and head back towards Brooklyn where ships were constantly heading out to sea. If they could make it there they could possibly escape to meet up with a German submarine. But, there was also the possibility that they would head to Idlewild Airport, to board a flight to Europe. If they were successful, there was no telling what the consequences would be. It was quite simple. They must be stopped now, and the documents must be recovered. Nothing else was acceptable.

All of the boats that had been commandeered to aid in the search were sent home. The plan was to make the area look as normal as possible. A number of these boats were to be moored in their slips with lights on. It was important to make the whole area appear safe for the men who were attempting to steal plans for the American war effort in France.

Now, all anyone could do was wait. There were two and one half hours of daylight left. Much coffee was consumed and many nerves were on edge. But the plan was a good one. With luck, Sam's plan should bear much fruit. As if the situation weren't stressful enough, there were only three days left before the Tyler family Christmas trip to New York City.

CHAPTER FIFTY-TWO

As daylight faded, Carson was hanging onto the thinnest thread of hope for escape from a huge force that seemed to be everywhere; he was completely surrounded. Meanwhile, Karl Getman was formulating a plan to come out of this whole botched attempt to kill an American traitor and return triumphantly to Germany with strategic American military plans for the French/German border where the French resistance had thwarted the Nazi attempt to overrun the whole country. If the Americans and the British allies could push the Nazis back then Germany would be vulnerable for a back door advance that would meet with only token resistance. By now, Germany's forces were spread so thin, and due to huge losses of life on the Russian front, it appeared as though the allied forces could waltz across Germany to advance against a threadbare force in Berlin.

But this no longer concerned Getman. He had made up his mind to switch gears and direction, and commit an act that would be so pleasing to the Provost family that he would be handsomely rewarded. The Provosts knew nothing of his plans, but he was confident that they would be so pleased that they would richly reward him. He also was absolutely prepared to end their lives should they refuse him.

While the American military and intelligence communities believed Hitler was searching for great treasures and the coveted Holy Grail and all its supposed powers, Getman was fully aware of the actions of Heinrich Himmler, Hitler's right hand and closest confidant. While Hitler attempted to find the treasures of Captain Kidd and the Templars along with the Holy Grail, Heinrich Himmler had one agenda and that was to find and take possession of the Holy Grail. Hitler never suspected Himmler of any subterfuge. In the latter years of the war, Hitler seemed to be sinking into a dream world filled with fantasies and rampant paranoia. He was constantly at odds with his generals, thwarting their attempts at key military strategies at every turn. He spoke with great conviction and zeal expressing strategies that had little chance at succeeding and lacking even the remotest chance of success. The German high command could do little to thwart the ruinous desires of the Fuehrer knowing that many would lose their lives in futile campaigns.

Himmler was a student of the occult. He was also the leader of the most powerful and feared organization in Nazi Germany, the Nazi SS. Getman had firsthand knowledge of Himmler's maniacal thirst for blood, having witnessed firsthand the internment of countless numbers of the Jewish population, as well as anyone else labeled a dissident. He was also aware of a civilian historian who believed as Himmler did, that an ancient priestly order known as the Cathars were said to have spirited the Holy Grail out of Jerusalem and had taken it to a castle high in the French Pyrénées. Otto Rahn was hired by Himmler and paid a small fortune with SS money to find and secure it. Hahn was given a high rank in the SS even though he was a civilian. Himmler had created his own secret organization within the ranks of the SS that resembled the Knights of the Roundtable. Hitler was the Fuhrer, but Himmler had his own ideas of where the whole war was going. He envisioned a Germany that would rule Europe for a thousand years. The Grail promised immortality. Hence, once in possession of it, Himmler, not Hitler, would be its ruler. All this was happening under Hitler's nose while he was too preoccupied with his own insanity to even notice.

In truth, Getman considered Himmler a pathetic little man with Goliath-like dreams. Getman had played his part well as a dutiful loyal SS agent, but now the war wheels were coming off. Returning to Germany was the farthest thing from his mind. What Ziegler had said back in that dingy, laughable so-called clubhouse was all too true. Germany was not going to win this war, and the memories of Germany's last defeat were all too present in his mind. In his short time in America, he had witnessed the revulsion of the American people over the Jewish genocide being carried out in horrible concentration camps. He knew that the crimes of Nazi Germany were going to be severely dealt with once the war was over. All these atrocities were not going to be forgotten and anyone suspected of being SS was surely going to pay a heavy price with little hope for forgiveness.

The SS took great pride in its cold-blooded conduct during the war. There would be no mercy accorded to these people in the aftermath of the war. Getman knew the score and it was heavily stacked against him. He knew his only chance for escape and he was ready to take his action.

CHAPTER FIFTY-THREE

"Goodness gracious, Martha, you really need to calm yourself down," cautioned Aunt Clara.

By mid-afternoon, Martha had packed, unpacked and repacked all the children's clothes for the trip. She had made at least four trips over to Aunt Clara's to have a cup of coffee. As the day wore on, her movements actually accelerated. Martha stopped abruptly and rested against the kitchen sink.

"You might want to make your next cup some nice relaxing Chamomile tea," said Aunt Clara.

"Is it that obvious?" Martha asked.

"All the worrying in the world won't make the waiting any easier," said Aunt Clara.

Martha sat down at the kitchen table and watched Aunt Clara take the tea bags out of their special tin container. Two sets of tea cups and saucers were placed on the table, each with a tea bag placed inside the cup. Next, Aunt Clara poured the hot water and then placed the teapot back on the stove and took her seat at the table. After a few quiet moments Martha began to smile widely.

"What's so amusing?" Aunt Clara wanted to know.

"I was just thinking," said Martha. "Not too long ago a very successful, yet world-weary woman came here with no more expectations than to escape the life she had in the big city, a life of emptiness and loneliness. She came to this quiet town, tucked away along the Connecticut River, to seek refuge from the madness of Manhattan. She was seeking serenity and rejuvenation. And, what did she find? Only the man of her dreams who just happened to be the father of three adorable children, an aunt who she would give anything to have as her mother and a life she could only dream about or maybe read about in some romantic novel. However, along with inheriting this idyllic life, the man of her dreams happens to be a state police captain and along with him she found herself immersed in a life of murder and intrigue which began almost immediately from the time she arrived here and refuses to end. Trust me. No one could have come up with all these plots. Truth truly is stranger than fiction, and certainly a lot more dangerous."

Surprisingly, Aunt Clara said nothing. Suddenly, Martha hopped up and went over to the parlor where the children were studying. She ducked in and said, "Grab your coats and hats, kids, we're heading up to Zuckerman's for some ice cream."

As she ducked back out, the children stared in wonderment at each other.

"Isn't it too close to dinner time?" said Thomas. "I don't think Dad would….," he didn't finish what he was saying as he found himself staring into the defiant eyes of Mary and Lillith.

The girls got to their feet. "Well, are you coming?" Mary asked.

"Darn tootin' I am," said Thomas, who jumped up and made a mad dash for the kitchen with his sisters hot on his heels.

It had not snowed before Christmas, but the air was crisp and cold. Autumn was on the wane. Christmas was a scant ten days away and winter a mere eight.

Martha chose to take the children directly over to Main Street and then up to Zuckerman's. Along the way Martha laughed out loud as the children filled the air with one question after another concerning their New York adventure. They burst through the door to Zuckerman's and were met by the open arms of Wanda Loomis. Martha was relieved to see her friend, who knew exactly where Sam was and what he was doing. Being with Wanda was always enjoyable.

"Do they know?" Wanda asked as she moved her gaze over to the children who were already perched up on the high round seats ordering their favorite flavors.

"No," said Martha.

"Good," said Wanda.

CHAPTER FIFTY-FOUR

Sunset was four-forty p.m. The wait was on. The admiral had a late thought to have a police launch and two 35-foot cabin cruisers moored at Cold Spring Harbor. Theirs would be the task to slowly make their way north when given the signal. As soon as the gauntlet was put into effect, they were to advance north at full speed. Their job was to join the other crafts that would be responsible to make sure no one escaped by swimming. Realistically, for anyone to reach shore by swimming, would be an almost herculean task. The water temperature and then waves caused by all the action would render such an undertaking next to impossible. Unless the person in the water was quite close to land, they would require a motor attached to their feet. Attempting an escape by diving into the water to swim towards land was sure suicide.

At nine-thirty p.m., nearly five hours after sunset, there was no sign of anyone sailing towards Cold Spring Harbor. Sam and the admiral were nervously pacing. Gas heaters had been turned on to battle the cold while kerosene lamps supplied the light. No one was saying very much. Tension was mounting and nerves were becoming frayed.

"Where are they?" the admiral barked.

Sam simply shrugged his shoulders. There was no point in responding. Obviously the admiral was becoming impatient. He was absolutely sure that the stolen plans were going to be with Carson.

A long-serving military man, the admiral's only concerns were for those plans to end up safely in the hands of the American military.

As the time reached ten p.m., it began to appear that Carson was being abandoned.

"I don't care if we stay here all night," said the admiral. "We break off and stand down at sunrise. Until then, nobody better doze off. There are a lot of our soldiers depending on us and by God, we will not fail them."

Finally, at eleven o'clock, a twenty-seven foot Barrell Backed Chris Craft made its way slowly around the tip of Hampton Harbor and began entering the cove towards Lloyd's Harbor. Surveillance from one of the moored yachts passed on the news that there appeared to be two men on board.

Carson, who had dozed off, heard the rumblings of the massive eight hundred forty-five cubic inch, three hundred seventy-five hp motor. He grabbed his case that carried the plans and began to open the cottage door very slowly. He was surprised to find no lights directed towards the cottage. He crawled out onto the porch and slid down to the bushes. Still no lights or noises. He had no reason to believe that the large force that had him completely surrounded had left. He had but one choice: make his way to the water and hope that this was his rescue party. As he made his way he kept stopping to hear if anyone was in pursuit. He heard nothing. Everyone on land had been ordered to make sure he went nowhere but towards the water. So far, so good.

The escape craft slid against the sandbar about twenty feet out. The two men on board saw Carson running towards them. He moved as quickly and quietly as possible to the sandbar and then took hold of the craft and pushed it out off the sand. The motor came alive as Carson climbed on board. The driver was busy directing the boat backwards and then came around and began heading north towards the Sound. The other man, about Carson's height but slightly heavier, reached into his pocket. He was too slow. Carson drew his weapon, a Smith and Wesson revolver, and grabbed the man and forced him down on the seat. The driver pulled back on the throttle.

"What are you doing?" the man demanded.

"I'm surprised to see that it is you two who have come," said Carson.

"We could not trust anyone else," said the driver.

"That's funny, because I can't trust you," said Carson.

"Of course you can trust us," assured the driver.

"Then you will not have any problem giving me my money," said Carson.

"Your money is safe in our motor hotel room in Brooklyn," said the driver.

Without warning Carson shot the second man in the foot. As the man who was shot cried out in pain, the driver yelled, "Are you insane?"

Carson reached down and took the man's weapon. Then he looked up at the driver. "You will need to get help for your friend here."

"We cannot take the chance of going to a hospital," said the driver.

"Then I guess you will need to get us out of here and figure something else out, won't you," said Carson.

The driver looked down at his companion who was holding his foot and rocking back and forth in great pain. Carson went over to the driver and searched him for a weapon. He removed the Lugar tucked into the man's belt on his left side. With the barrel of his gun he then gave the man a tap on the back of his head to occupy him as he reached down the man's trousers to see if he had any more weapons. He did not.

While this was going on, the speedboat was under surveillance from the yachts resting in private docks. All of it was being transmitted to the admiral. The police boats and yachts from Cold Spring Harbor were heading up towards them at a moderate speed.

"Time to leave," said Carson.

The driver offered no resistance. He pushed up the throttle and began to make his way towards the Sound. Every boat in the operation had been alerted and had been moving into position. The admiral gave the order and the whole area lit up with blinding lights.

"This is the Coast Guard. Stop your engines and prepare to be boarded," the booming sound came from the one hundred twenty-five foot Coast Guard Cutter Yeaton.

Carson put his gun to the driver's head and pressed it hurtfully into his skull. The driver responded.

Once again the voice from the Yeaton made the same command. But the boat Carson was on did not comply. Then the Yeaton fired a warning shot across the bow. Carson's boat surged forward. Then, suddenly, the driver steered hard to the left and began heading in the opposite direction. It had not gone far when it was met by a wall of boats heading in its direction.

"Land," yelled Carson. "Head for land, it's our only hope."

Once again the driver swung sharply to the left and headed towards the shore which was a mere one hundred yards away.

"Bad decision," said the captain to himself. The Yeaton was closing fast.

Suddenly the front of Carson's boat was blown away by the guns of the Yeaton. It pitched forward and immediately began to sink. Shore was over fifty yards away. In the freezing water, Carson and the two men had little chance of making it. Actually, their only hope was to be rescued before their bodies were rendered helpless and sank to the bottom.

After a few moments, the men were surrounded by boats. The driver and his companion were taken out of the water, but Carson was nowhere to be found. The half-frozen driver told the police that Carson had been thrown against the side of the boat by the explosion and probably went into the water unconscious. Once again the air back at the command post was filled with apprehension.

"I don't care what you have to do," said the admiral to the Coast Guard captain, "find those plans and that miserable traitor."

The captain of the Yeaton barked his orders and men in diving gear plunged into the water. In and out they went at short intervals to avoid hypothermia.

"We have the plans," came the call from the Yeaton. "We have everything and they are intact."

The command post exploded. Everyone was shaking hands and hugging one another.

"Get Boland," yelled Sam into the microphone to the captain. "Don't stop until you get him or his body."

"Will do sir," was the captain's reply.

The admiral looked up from what he was doing and shot a look of admiration to Sam. Twenty minutes later they got the call.

"We've got Boland, sir. He's dead, but we've got him."

"Now you can go nuts," said Sam to everyone in the room. Then he looked over at the admiral who was smiling.

"Nicely done, son. Nicely done."

Sam put his hands on his hips and smiled.

"All in a day's work, sir."

CHAPTER FIFTY-FIVE

Four Star General Hyram 'Hutch' Hutchinson was seated in his office at the U.S. Department of War, located in the old World War I building, the Gregory Building. General Hutchinson was already experiencing periods of exhausted patience over the delays of the completion of the new war department building, soon to be known as the Pentagon. The Gregory Building was situated on Constitution Avenue on the National Mall. It was just one of many buildings housing detached departments of the military intelligence complex. Hutch was looking forward to the day when the whole "shebang" as he called it, would be housed in the four story pentagonal building which took up all of the space of the old Washington Hoover Airport, a land mass of twenty-eight point seven acres with a five point one acre courtyard at its center.

The president had much to say about every aspect of its construction, including its height, so it would not obstruct the view of the Capitol from Arlington National Cemetery.

It was in his cramped office space, at midnight, that the general was informed by Admiral Blake that the mission was a complete success and that the war plans were now safe in the hands of America. The general paused for a moment. He was obviously tired, never having left his office complex since the operation began.

"You say the two orchestrators of this thing are in your custody?" the general said.

"Yes, sir," said the admiral. "Unfortunately, Boland died before we could interrogate him."

"Never mind that," said the general, "squeeze those two snakes until we know just how deep this whole thing runs and if any other of our people are involved. Is Mickleson with you?"

"Yes, sir, he is," said the admiral.

"Good, feed them to him," said the general. "And Admiral, thank you for a job well done. Now drain those two you have there of everything they have. Don't let them eat or sleep until we know everything. Capeesh? (*Italian slang for understand?*)"

"Yes, sir, will do. And thank you General. This is going to be a pleasure."

"Go get them, Blake," said the general, who signed off.

Pandemonium broke loose as the general's staff, all thirty people, began to celebrate. They too had been there the whole time. No one wanted to be left out of the loop.

Carson's body was bagged and sent to Columbia University Hospital in Manhattan. Captain Phil D'Onofrio was charged with making sure it was protected until a team of military doctors could be transported there. These were the same men whose job it was to look after the health of the president. Captain D'Onofrio sent twenty hand-picked officers to the hospital. All were equipped with bulletproof vests and rifles. They were there to give aid to the ten marines who were bringing Carson's body there.

The two, as yet unknown Germans fished out of the water, were taken to Blake's command post at OHEKA. Mickleson accompanied them and immediately began his interrogation. Along the way, he informed the two of just what they could expect at OHEKA. The two men smiled, in an attempt at bravado. Mickleson exhaled loudly. He folded his hands, smiled and sat back against the wall of the transport truck they were traveling in.

Then he stopped smiling and looked deeply into both of their eyes. He leaned forward and spoke.

"I'm going to break you both. When I am done with you, you will curse the day you ever came to this country and attempted to harm us. Don't concern yourself with thoughts of firing squads. You'll be begging me to shoot you both before this is over. One thing I am sure of, by the looks of you two ragamuffins, neither of you is SS. But, that is exactly how I am going to deal with you. I am going to break you and then I am going to crush you."

Mickleson once again sat back, satisfied by what he had just said.

"Let's see if you'll be smiling when I get you back to OHEKA."

Once everyone was back at OHEKA, Mickleson told them that it would probably be a good long while before the men broke down. He advised them to get some rest. Sam and Admiral Blake remained. They did not want to miss a moment of this. Neither man had slept very much over the last few days. It was amazing what showers and lots of strong coffee could do to keep the adrenaline going.

Mickleson allowed the two men he was interrogating to sit and stew in the large room with only one wooden table, which they sat behind. After about an hour, which Mickleson used to shower, change into some fresh clothes and grab a light dinner, he entered the interrogation room. The lighting in the room was bright with no character. It would serve to wear on the two as time went on. It was bright and harsh.

Mickelson started with an attempt to learn the names of the two. They were not very forthcoming. Mickleson expected as much. He told them about his shower, change of clothes and delightful dinner. He also told them that when he got tired, he would take his leave, get some rest and repeat his shower and dinner ritual.

Two hours passed and the two men began to soften. Mickleson sensed their discomfort and decided it was time for a break. Two hours later he reappeared looking fresh and wearing a new set of clothing. During that time, teams of soldiers had been stationed in the room to make sure the two did not get any sleep. By now, their wet, dirty clothes were becoming more and more uncomfortable. Another two hours and Mickleson got up and took another break.

When he came back, two more hours had passed. The man who had been shot began to break. His wound had been attended to, but he was experiencing much discomfort. Against his companion's protests he gave Mickleson his first bit of real information.

"Boland is dead," he practically yelled.

"We already know that," said Mickleson.

"Do you really?" said the man.

"The real Boland is dead and has been for over a year."

This caught Mickleson's attention.

"You don't know, do you?" the man said. "The man posing as Boland is Seaman First Class Daniel Carson. We killed the real Boland, in his place, over a year ago. Carson has been posing as him all this time."

For the next few minutes, the wounded man told Mickleson of how Carson resembled Boland and of all the times Carson impersonated him. He relayed how they had approached Carson and recruited him. At Mickleson's request, the man gave the exact time and method used to kill the real Boland. He even furnished information concerning Boland's family and life in Arizona. Mickleson took another break to find out if what he was being told was the truth. Less than one hour later, verification of the testimony came in. Everything the man had said was true. Sam and the admiral were stunned by the revelation.

The news served another purpose. Sam and the admiral had gone to their quarters to get some rest. It did not seem possible that this whole bizarre case was becoming even more so. Mickleson had decided to take another two hour rest period giving Sam and the admiral at least three hours of rest. When they were awakened, it was mid-morning. Like Mickleson, they showered, changed, and took a light meal with strong coffee.

When all three men reentered the interrogation room it was with little doubt both men were ready to talk. The last thing Mickleson had said to them was that he would be willing to make a deal if they told him everything. Thirty plus hours with no sleep, no food and wearing the same clothes for almost two days had convinced the men things were not going to get better or easier. The stench of their own bodies was turning out to be a magic elixir for the loosening of tongues.

Walter Bunn and Erik Houser were their names. Houser wasn't even German. He was an Austrian businessman who was merely trying to make a big score. He had no affection for either side and all he had to show for his efforts was a bullet hole in his foot. Bunn was a Canadian citizen of German descent, who, like Houser, was trying to make a big score. The difference between the two men was that Bunn was capable of murder. It was he who killed the real Boland and who would have killed Carson if he refused to go along with their plans. They had no intention of paying Carson. They had alerted certain parties in Germany of their plans and were promised a king's ransom if they could deliver. Their hearts were not large enough to cut Carson in and share in their reward. After another hour, where they divulged Kemplar's name and membership in the SS, Mickleson concluded the interrogation.

"Thank you, gentlemen, you have been most helpful," said Mickleson.

"And you will help us with the authorities?" Houser asked.

"Not a chance," said Mickleson. "But don't worry, you will be bathed and have clean clothes on when you face the firing squad."

241

CHAPTER FIFTY-SIX

Sam and the admiral took lunch together with Commander Mickleson. The two conspirators were being taken to Fort Dix in New Jersey, before being transferred to Leavenworth Prison in Kansas. The United States Disciplinary Barracks, part of the Leavenworth Prison Complex, was built at Fort Leavenworth and completed in 1921. It housed not only military criminals, but anyone convicted of crimes against our national security. It was a maximum security facility that would be the last place on earth Erick Hauser and Walter Bunn would inhabit.

"That was quite a job you did in there with those two, Commander," said the admiral.

"Where did you even learn that technique?" Sam wanted to know. "I have never seen anything like it. Is this some new technique out of naval Intelligence?"

A wry smile spread across the commander's face. "You can give the credit for that technique to Commander Arnold Mickleson," he said.

A look of confusion came over the faces of Sam and the admiral.

"My father," said the commander.

"Your father was with naval Intelligence?" the admiral asked.

"No, Sir, he was not," said Mickleson. "Please allow me to explain. When my younger brother and I were just little boys, our father would try to get us to admit to and explain why we had done something wrong. He would ask us and we would be afraid to admit any wrongdoing for fear of being punished. When we did not own up to our guilt, he would make us sit at the dining room table while he would leave the room and make himself a nice sandwich, which he would eat in the kitchen while we just sat there afraid to move. Of course, he would tell us beforehand what he was going to do. He would come back sometime later and sit down looking very content. Then he would talk some more and then, if we had not responded, he would tell us that he was going back into the kitchen and get a big bowl of ice cream and sit down and enjoy it. Then he would get up, go into the kitchen and make a big deal out of scooping the ice cream into his bowl. When he was done, he would stand in the doorway with his bowl, take some on his spoon and eat it so that we would know that what he was doing was very real. Then he'd close the door and go back into the kitchen. He would usually sit in the kitchen for a half hour or so, which for us felt like an eternity. He would then come back in and sit down at the table with us and not say a word. We finally realized that he probably knew of our guilt and that we were going to be punished anyway, so why prolong the agony? The longer it took us to admit our wrongdoing, the more time that added to the punishment because actually the whole interrogation was part of the time of punishment. As we got a little older, we knew the drill and realized there was no escaping the inevitable."

"That's some story," said Sam.

"Yes," said Mickleson, "and I came about using it quite by accident. I was interrogating a supply sergeant who was suspected of stealing and selling goods and equipment from his warehouse to anyone who would pay the price to line his pockets. It was rumored that everything was for sale. All anyone had to do was to meet his price.

"The sergeant was well aware of what the penalty would be if he were found guilty, so he fought me every step of the way. After about three hours, I found myself losing my edge while the sergeant was holding up just fine. I excused myself to go to the bathroom and throw some cold water on my face. As I headed back to the interrogation room, I suddenly remembered the times with my father. I started to smile, but then it struck me: his method of interrogation nearly drove my brother and me crazy. I stopped in my tracks and told one of my guards to go back into the room and tell the sergeant that I was taking a break for dinner and would be back shortly. Under no circumstances were the guards to let the men rest.

I returned on hour later and found the sergeant quite agitated, but still not ready to talk. So I proceeded to ask the same question, over and over, and he in kind, kept repeating the same answers. He had no idea that instead of frustrating me he was actually playing into my hands. After a few hours of cat and mouse, I took another break. As I left I informed the sergeant that I was going to refresh myself. Again, he was not allowed to sleep or even put his head down on the table. I, on the other hand, took a quick nap, had a nice long hot shower, and ate a light meal. I had one of my men drive me over to my quarters so that I could change into some fresh clothes to put on after my shower. When I returned to the interrogation room I thought the sergeant was going to come out of his skin. The look on his face was hysterical. It was all I could do to keep myself from bursting out laughing.

"After a few more moments of jockeying, and getting nowhere, I informed the sergeant that I was going to break him mercilessly and laid out every step of the way for him. Within minutes, he broke and confessed everything. I had him give a full statement to a stenographer who recorded every one of his illegal activities. He also told us where he had hidden his money and how he had been able to get large amounts of money to a cousin who was holding it for him. The cousin gave him up in less than sixty seconds and we retrieved all of his ill-gotten gain, a sum of twenty thousand dollars. To him it was a king's ransom. For me, it was an incredible victory. This technique has served me well over the years. Not one person has been able to defeat it. But, I must add that I have to be very confident that the person I am questioning is guilty. I am not here to harm the innocent. In this case, we already knew, beyond a shadow of a doubt, what the sergeant had done. He paid dearly for his actions."

CHAPTER FIFTY-SEVEN

Martha and the children were seated around Aunt Clara's kitchen table eating lunch when Sam called. Martha shouted for joy at the good news. Sam told her that he would be flying into Tweed around four P.M. and one of his troopers would be there to meet him and drive him back to his barracks. He would be home for dinner at five-thirty. After dinner and some time with the children, he would take Martha up to Wanda's place and relay all that had happened in the past few days to her, Wanda and the mayor.

No one had seen or heard from Getman. With the death of Carson and the documents safely in government hands a very large piece of this problem had been eliminated. But, until Getman was apprehended, no one was going to rest easy. The New York trip was only three days away and might be in jeopardy.

Sam returned to Connecticut on time and went to the state police barracks. He held a meeting with a group of his officers. Sam filled them in on all that had happened over on Long Island. His new main point of concentration was going to be the shoreline from New Haven all the way up to New London. Troopers would be immediately dispatched to each of the coastal towns to aid in coordinating a giant coastal surveillance operation. The fact that Getman had not been seen made a strong argument that he had not been able to reach Block Island as he had planned. Sam made it very clear that every minute he was out there, the degree of danger from him would increase. He reminded them that a cornered animal is the most dangerous kind.

It was obvious just how pleased Sam was to be home with his family and to experience the joy of sitting down to a meal in the safety of one's home. He was aware that there were many places in the world where families were being torn apart. There was so much to give thanks for. The thought of that was never far from Sam's consciousness. Men like Getman had to be stopped at all costs. And, those he represented, the Hitlers' of the world, were the most dangerous of all. If Getman bought into Hitler's lunacy, it only proved how depraved he was.

Sam spent a good half hour with the children, laughing and listening to them share their time in school and their anticipation of the New York adventure, one Sam was hoping to be able to provide.

Wanda cleared out a small section of the dining room so that Sam could fill everyone in on what transpired out on Long Island and where everything rested as of this moment. Mayor Tinsley said what everyone was thinking.

"Good Lord, Sam, once again you've done a marvelous job."

"Thank you, Ezra, but we are not out of the woods just yet. We were confident that Getman was trying to get to Block Island, but we have no way of knowing if that is still his plan. Remember he is a member of the Nazi SS and believe me, those people are extremely dangerous. I, for one, will not be satisfied until we have him all wrapped up and put away for good."

The mayor told the group that there had been no further incidents at the Methodist Church, but that the pastor and his wife were staying at the Griswold Inn. The innkeeper at the Gris would not accept any payment. The man was a good Catholic who was a parishioner at St. Mary's Roman Catholic Church right next door up on Methodist Hill.

The two churches enjoyed a very warm relationship with one another. It seemed only natural that every courtesy be extended to the pastor, especially at Christmas time. If things did not change, there would be no celebration of the Christmas pageant or service this year. The Methodist congregation was not the only group saddened by this. The good people of Essex could not believe such a terrible circumstance was happening in a town so proud of its reputation for being neighborly.

Sam told the mayor that he would have Trooper Dolan continue his vigil and suggested the mayor maintain his schedule of the men in town who were volunteering their services. Injun Jim came back with Sam and would take up his station in the morning. Jim had gone straight home to bed. Sam told the group how valuable he was in flushing out Carson from the tunnels beneath the Provost mansion. Jim even got to save a man's life from a trap set by the Masons' builders when the Provost mansion was erected. Sam verified the fact that everyone involved both here and on Long Island had done their part. He was proud of his neighbors for the way they were handling things at such a difficult time.

On the way home, Sam and Martha walked down Main Street holding each other close. It was a clear night with moon and stars showing off their beauty in the heavens. It was cold, but it felt good. There was a clean fresh smell in the air. Unbeknownst to Martha, Sam never stopped surveying their surroundings as they made their way. It would not surprise Sam that Getman might attempt to capture or harm the very man who had orchestrated the operation that, up until now, had frustrated his attempts for success. Where Getman was concerned, Sam was taking nothing for granted. Walking down Main Street allowed Sam to keep Martha to his left, leaving his right hand free to draw his weapon, if necessary.

They climbed the porch to Aunt Clara's to say goodnight before heading over to the house. Sam put in a call to Varnish and had him send two of his men over to patrol the property. He hoped he wasn't allowing himself to be drawn into a state of paranoia, but, realistically, there was no way of telling just how desperate or reckless Getman had become.

CHAPTER FIFTY-EIGHT

Patrolman Wil Hopkins was a third generation member of the Hopkins Farm family, which had come over from England and settled in Saybrook in the late eighteen hundreds. Wil was not tall but his body defined the term sturdy. He was twenty-six years old when he came onto the police force. The tireless life of working the soil had worn out its welcome to young, unmarried Wil, who wanted to know what it was like to wake up with clean fingernails in the morning.

Wil's blonde hair, blue eyed farm-boy good looks made him quite popular with the local young ladies. His police uniform merely served to enhance an already attractive package. Wil was lost in his thoughts of one pretty young lady, whom he met at the yearly Saybrook Halloween Barn Dance. His thoughts kept returning to the most beautiful pair of lips he had ever seen. He so wanted to know what it felt like to kiss those lips.

Wil was shaken from his reverie by the sight of a man walking towards him from the direction of the waters of North Cove. The man waved to him as he made his way towards Wil's police car parked in front of Veronica Lansing's home. Wil didn't recognize him, but he seemed friendly enough. Finally, the man made his way up to Wil.

"Hello, Officer," he said. "Is this the home of the famous Veronica Lansing?"

Without thinking, Wil answered, "It surely is."

"Do you think you could get her to open her door and let us all in?"

"What?" said Wil. Startled by the question he slowly lowered his hand down to the leather strap that secured his weapon.

"I wouldn't do that," said Getman, who had quietly made his way around to come up from the rear.

Wil turned to see Getman's German hand weapon pointed right at his chest.

"Keep your hands down," he said. Getman's companion slowly walked over to Wil's side and lifted his weapon out of the holster as gently and inconspicuously as possible.

"Now, let's go say hello to Miss Lansing," said Getman.

Wil had no choice. He walked with the men up to the steps and approached Veronica's door. He knocked and waited for Veronica to answer. When she did, he informed her that it was he at the door. She opened it slightly only to have the door kicked open by Getman, who pushed Wil into the house with his partner helping secure Wil's involuntary cooperation. Once inside, Getman instructed Veronica to be silent. He had Wil sit in a chair in the dining room and then took the rope he had wrapped around himself and under his jacket and tied him securely up. He then stuffed a handkerchief in Wil's mouth.

"Cooperate and you might just live through this," said Getman.

"Who are you and what do you want?" Veronica asked.

"Ahh, Miss Lansing, we finally meet. Fortunately for you, you were not here the last time I was in your home. Unfortunately, others were. I am sorry for the mess I left. But I am sure that you are well aware of how upset I can get when things do not go as I desire."

Veronica found herself sitting at his words. She didn't even remember it happening. Getman's words were all she needed to know that he was the most dangerous person she had ever encountered. No villain on the stage or screen was able to strike her with the suffocating fear assaulting her body.

"I need you to perform a very simple task," said Getman.

Veronica's eyes said "what?" Something her voice was unable to accomplish.

"I want you to dial up Margonette Provost. Get her on the line and I will handle the rest," said Getman.

Veronica looked over at the telephone that was set on a small table just inside the dining room off the kitchen.

"Yes," said Getman. "Now please do as I ask. I would hate to have to force you to do it. I am quite able to inflict much pain, Miss Lansing, without taking someone's life. Believe me you would not be happy if I were compelled to do so."

Veronica raised herself out of the chair she was sitting on and dialed the number. The Provost manservant, Malcolm, answered the phone. Veronica informed him who it was that was calling. After a few short moments of light banter, Margonette got on the line and said hello to Veronica, who then handed the receiver to Getman.

Getman took the receiver and introduced himself to Margonette. Just the sound of his voice struck her with terror.

"What do you want from me?" she asked.

Getman informed her that he had abducted Veronica and wanted two hundred thousand dollars, immediately, as a reward for killing her.

"Killing her!" yelled Margonette who nearly passed out. "What on earth makes you think I want her dead?"

"Your warped sense of self and the humiliation you believe she caused by rejecting you over time."

"Dear Lord, you've got it all wrong. I don't want her dead. You must believe me, please do not harm her," Margonette pleaded.

Now it was Getman's turn to sit down. He rubbed his hand across his forehead and back through his hair. He had to think fast. He did.

"Since you seem to have such affection for her, I've changed my mind. The amount is still two hundred thousand dollars American, but now, that is what it will cost you to save her life. Otherwise I will kill this charming lady in a not so pleasant manner," said Getman.

Just then, a male voice came on the line. "Please, sir, don't do anything rash."

"Who is this?" Getman demanded.

"I am Gustav Provost, Margonette's father. My daughter is in no position to help you with this."

"Well, she sure was in a position to begin this whole affair when she got in league with the men who contacted Germany to include her in an act of treason that was meant to destroy the Lansing woman's reputation," said Getman.

"What my daughter did was inexcusable and foolish. I would gladly pay your ransom, but we simply do not have that amount of money available to us at this time of the year. It would take too long for us to sell some of our valuables, which I would gladly do," said the elder Provost.

Getman was ready for Provost's excuse. "We Germans are well aware of your relationship with the Windsors, who are close to the Fuhrer. I'm confident they would give you whatever you need."

"You are quite mistaken, sir," said Provost. "The royal family cast them out. The Duke is now the governor of the Bahamas and has been for some time. He and his wife are living on a monthly budget and fortunate to have that. The whole world is aware of this. Churchill has seen to it that they are paying dearly for their affection for Germany.

Getman's mind was racing. He was reaching the point of no return. If the Provosts could not supply him with what he needed to escape, he would have to kill Veronica and the young police officer and take his chances.

"I have an idea," said Provost. "Please give me two hours. I will contact my family in Europe and tell them of this urgent situation. I am sure they will be willing to loan me the money as an advance. Please allow me to try. You have nothing to lose. As of right now, we are at a stalemate. Please give me a little time. I am sure we can work this out. I promise I will exhaust every avenue to get you what you want. I implore you, please, do not hurt Miss Lansing. She is completely innocent in this matter."

Getman liked what he was hearing. After all, what Provost said was the truth. They were at a stalemate and any chance at pulling this ransom off would be well worth the effort. But, he could not stay where he was. He was sure that the police would be coming to see what happened to their officer, who would not be checking in at his allotted time.

"I will have to move on from where I am. I can't stay here. I will give you two hours and then call you. I will need to reverse the charges. Do you agree?" Getman asked.

"Yes, yes, absolutely," said Provost.

"Fine, two hours," said Getman who slammed the receiver down.

"Take the woman," said Getman to his accomplice.

"What about him?" the man asked while pointing to Wil.

Getman walked over to the police officer and hit him in the head with his weapon. Officer Hopkins was rendered unconscious.

"Does that answer your question?" said Getman with a tone that made his accomplice very uneasy.

"Do not question me again," said Getman.

The other man gave no response. His silence was sufficient to convey his new found understanding of just how dangerous and unstable a man his partner in crime really was.

CHAPTER FIFTY-NINE

Getman told Veronica to get her coat, which she did, as though she were walking in a dream. He then spirited her out the front door, down the steps and across the lawn to the place where he had Dietrich Ekhard, his accomplice and constant companion, park the automobile they would be using to make their getaway, Ekhard's 4-door non-descript 1938 grey Chevrolet Master. The Master model came equipped with an 80 horsepower 6 cylinder engine with standard transmission. Ekhard was a mechanic by trade and made a few adjustments. He installed a three hundred eighty three cubic inch Chevy Stroker, three hundred sixty horse-power engine under the hood. He added a rear end used for auto racing and heavy supporting shock absorbers to stabilize the car when driving at excessive speeds. The suspension was a welcome addition when speeding along the narrow winding country roads of Saybrook and Essex.

Getman sat in the backseat with Veronica Lansing. His hand-gun was lying on his lap. It occurred to him that none of his plans had met with even the slightest degree of success. Because the time to activate a plan had been so short, Getman found himself constantly having to amend his plans. He was anxious to leave America, in fact, euphoric at the prospect. Never had he failed on so many levels. And now he found himself having to pin all of his hopes for rescue on a strange man who just came into the picture.

It was not a very comforting feeling. The one thing Getman had going for him was his all out, hold nothing back attitude no matter what the task or dilemma. He vowed that he would either succeed or die trying because he was absolutely determined he was not going to be taken alive and die a humiliating death before an American firing squad.

In his haste to secure Veronica Lansing and a large amount of money, Getman grossly underestimated Wil Hopkins's strength and rock solid body. Wil lifted himself up with the chair he was in and threw himself backwards on the floor. The back of the wooden chair cracked and broke away from the base. Wil got up and made his way into the kitchen to retrieve a knife. He cut away some of the rope and freed himself. He ran to his car and radioed to Varnish. Within moments the main roads would have roadblocks.

"You cannot be serious," said Sam when he got the news from Varnish. He immediately called headquarters and had all cruisers within twenty miles converge on all roads heading north, away from Old Saybrook, along the coast.

Meanwhile, Ekhard drove west up Route 154 away from the causeway and parallel to the main road of Old Saybrook, being careful to obey the speed limit. His route took him along the shore of Long Island Sound, past the castle at Saybrook Point, a home built to rival the great mansions of Newport. When he got to the intersection of 154 and the Old Post Road he and his occupants were greeted by the sight of Saybrook police vehicles speeding up toward north Saybrook.

"How could they know?" Getman said.

"Maybe it's something else," said Ekhard.

"Yes, and maybe it's Santa Claus coming to town just a little early, causing quite a stir," said Veronica, who had slowly come out of her stupor to lend her two cents worth with words bathed in sarcasm.

For a moment, Veronica's words succeeded in separating Getman's focus from possible danger.

"I can see why that Provost woman wanted you dead," he said.

"Oh, don't be silly," said Veronica. "Margonette Provost is a weak, sniveling, lame, brainless tart who hasn't the nerve to wish me dead."

"That may be so, Madame, but you being dead is now something I am giving serious consideration to," said Getman.

"And miss out on all the beautiful music we could make together?" Veronica said.

So completely taken aback by Veronica's immediate comeback line, Getman almost found himself laughing. It would have been the first time since he came to America, a place that was frustrating him at every turn.

"Karl," came the sobering voice from the front seat.

"Forget the coast. Head up to Essex, you know where," Getman ordered.

The driver responded by putting the car in gear and driving in the opposite direction away from the frantic police activities.

Sam rang Varnish up again and told him how he deployed his men. Varnish told Sam that he had sent a few of his officers to go to the yacht club to keep an eye on the water. Sam had already called Commander Thomas down in Milford to begin heading up to Saybrook to make sure Getman was not heading back that way. The roads were already under police control. The one hundred twenty-nine foot Coast Guard Cutter Yeaton and the two eighty foot cutters were traveling full speed ahead across the Sound towards New London and Block Island. Admiral Blake had planes in the air out of Mitchel Field on the slim chance Getman was traveling on the water in broad daylight.

Sam burst through the door of Aunt Clara's kitchen and ran to his cruiser. He backed out onto Pratt Street and headed up to North Main Street with sirens and lights blazing. He made his way over to Route 154 and made a left-hand turn, heading for

Saybrook. One mile later he flew by the modified Chevrolet of Dietrich Ekhard doing the speed limit heading up towards Methodist Hill.

CHAPTER SIXTY

The pastor of First Methodist was a kindly old gentleman who had grown up in Deep River and had been a member of First Methodist from early childhood. After high school, he served three years in the army and was greatly impressed by the chaplains who had to be well versed in the major religions: Catholic, Protestant and Jewish, to provide aid and comfort to the wounded. Having been brought up a Methodist, he was very familiar with the Old Testament writings of the Bible. One day, as he was observing a chaplain speaking to a young man who had been severely wounded and was in danger of never being able to walk again, the thought occurred to him, "I can do this." As time went on his thoughts changed to "I should be doing this." He spoke to the chaplain about it and was given the name of a seminary in northern Connecticut where he spent two years after his time in the armed forces.

Now, in his late fifties, he found himself saddened at the thought that someone had found a reason to harm his church and its parishioners. Having the church closed at Christmas time was placing a heavy weight on his soul. He was wondering if it were possible that he was somehow responsible for this. When he got to the church he was met by Trooper Dolan who told him that he would be leaving to join in on the hunt for the Germans who had succeeded in abducting Veronica Lansing and were probably heading towards New London. The pastor wished him well and unlocked the door for the chapel and entered. It was beginning to appear as though the limited Christmas season was going to be salvaged.

About twenty minutes later the pastor was sure he heard someone come into the sanctuary. He came out from behind the altar and started heading down the main aisle to see who was there. The doors at the entrance to the sanctuary opened as a man, moving backwards, used his back to open the doors. The pastor was about to greet him when a female also entered, being pulled in by the man. As the pastor reached the two he was met with the large bore of the Luger being held by the man who raised it and pointed it right between his eyes.

"This is a house of God," said the pastor.

"And I am a desperate man," said Getman.

"I can see that, my son. You have no need for a weapon here. Is there something I can do for you?" asked the pastor.

"I am afraid it is much too late for that. All I ask is that you give me no reason to fire my gun in God's house," said Getman.

The pastor did not answer immediately. For a brief moment, all three just stood there. No one said anything. Then Ekhard came rushing through the door.

"I hid the car down in the boatyard. I don't think it will interest anyone there," said Ekhard.

Just then, Ekhard noticed the pastor. "Oh no," he said. "What are we supposed to do now?"

"Keep as calm as we can. No one knows we are here. We can get some rest here and try to figure out a way to get to Block Island."

"How do we know that the pastor will not do something to prevent that?" said Ekhard.

"Like what?" Getman wanted to know. "Have you never been to church? This man is a man of God, you fool. Let me worry about things here and you just concentrate on not irritating me enough to find fault with you.

"Forgive me, Pastor, but I will have to detain you for just a little while until I can find a way for me and my annoying friend to take our leave," said Getman.

"Are you the one who created the two incidents this past week?" the pastor asked.

"Regrettably, yes," said Getman.

"Why would you do such a thing?" the pastor asked.

"For a time such as this," said Getman. "If all else failed, I wanted to have a place to fall back on," said Getman.

"I take it that all else failed," said the pastor.

"I am afraid so. That is why I wanted to make sure the church would not be used. I wanted to make sure it was abandoned so that I would have a place to hide and hopefully not have to involve anyone else. As you can see, that is now impossible," said Getman.

"I suspect this situation might last a while. Most probably, you are aware that there are food and provisions in the hall downstairs. Please feel free to partake in all that we have here and hopefully no one else needs to suffer any harm," said the pastor.

"Thank you, sir. I truly am sorry you have to be involved in all of this, but as you can see, the situation here is pretty desperate. I'm sure you know this lady," said Getman, pointing to Veronica.

"Yes, your hostage is well known and revered in this area. I am thankful that you have not seen the need to harm her," said the pastor.

Getman motioned for Ekhard to head over to the doorway which was the entrance to the church hall. Everyone descended the stairway down to the hall. The pastor helped Getman make the area comfortable for Veronica. But there really was no way for any of this to be comfortable for Veronica. She could not remember the last time she was not seated in the finest of furniture. Strangely, she did not complain. It was as if she knew that to portray herself as a weak, helpless woman would not work to her advantage. She studied Getman and his accomplice and followed their actions and decided not to give them any reason to harm her. It was obvious to her that Getman was a dangerous man, but still, he seemed composed, for the moment, at least. Anyway, Ekhard, on the other hand, looked as though he might fall apart at any moment. He was sweating and pacing nervously around. Getman noticed, but chose not to deal with him at the present time. But how long Getman would put up with him was becoming a concern.

CHAPTER SIXTY-ONE

A little over an hour had passed since Sam had called out the troops. No one had sighted Getman or Veronica Lansing. Sam was beginning to become concerned. All of the roads leading south towards New Haven had been under the surveillance of the local police departments. Still, there was no sign of Getman. Commander Thomas had been heading up towards Saybrook at a steady ten knots. He had commandeered three cabin cruisers from Port New Haven, each manned by five U.S. navy personnel, all armed and prepared for a possible gun battle with a German S.S. officer. As of Thomas's last report, there had been no sign of Getman or his party. The planes out of Mitchel Field reported the same. It appeared that no one was out on the waters leading to Block Island. There wasn't a single highway, single one lane or single dirt road that was not fully under the control of combined state and local police surveillance. As impossible as it seemed, Getman had disappeared. Reporting this to Admiral Blake was something Sam was not in a hurry to do.

Things had remained relatively calm in the basement hall at the First Methodist Church. But Ekhard was beginning to pace nervously as the time for Getman to call the Provost estate was getting near. Getman was skeptical that Provost would actually come through or that he even intended to. Meanwhile, Ekhard's pacing was not sitting well with him. But Getman knew he must control his emotions until he had spoken to the elder Provost.

When the time finally came that two hours had passed, Getman called the Provost estate. He reversed the charges. Contrary to Getman's fears Provost told him that he would be able to meet his demands. But, now there was one thing standing in Getman's way. He would have to go back across the Sound to get his money. Taking a boat out of Essex would be very risky. No, he and his party would need to get down to Saybrook and secure a craft from there to travel across the Sound to the island. Getman estimated the time and told Provost to meet him somewhere safe. Provost told him that it would be wiser to head into Glen Cove where there would be less chance of his being seen. From there, Provost would take him back to Twin Eagles to contact the men who had set this whole episode in motion. Neither man had any idea that those men were now in the custody of the U.S. military. The allotted time was agreed upon. Now all Getman had to do was to wait for dark before attempting his escape.

Martha had been busy writing notes for her new novel in an attempt to keep her mind off all that was happening. She decided to take a break and head down to the harbor. Over time, Martha had come to find solace from her daily cares by visiting the inviting waters of the Connecticut River. She bundled up and made her way down to the water. The boat yard was fairly deserted except for a few workers who were in the main building busy rebuilding the motor of a seventy-five foot, twenty year old Chris Craft holed up in dry dock. Martha loved wandering among the boats all taken out of the water and hoisted on steel cradles waiting out the cold weather until the time when they would be placed where they truly belonged, back on the Connecticut River. The river traveled hundreds of miles from the Canadian border to pour into Long Island Sound.

As she made her way along, Martha noticed something odd, definitely out of place. A lone Chevrolet four-door vehicle was parked between two dry docked sailboats. Martha stopped and looked to see if anyone was in the vehicle. It was locked and empty.

"Kinda strange, don't ya think?" came a male voice that startled Martha.

"Hi," she said to the old man standing about twenty feet behind her.

"You're Captain Tyler's wife, aren't you?" the man asked as he approached.

"Yes, and Martha," she said as she extended her hand. Martha recognized him as one of the marina workers.

"Vincent Graham," said the man as he took her hand in his.

"Do you know who the owner is?" Martha asked.

"No idea," said Graham, "but I can tell you this, I'm sure it does not belong to anyone from around Wolf Harbor."

"Why is that?" Martha asked.

"Well, first off, no one from around here would do such a thing, except for some young ones trying to spend a little time keeping each other company away from disapproving eyes. If you catch my drift," Graham said with a slight twinkle in his eye. "And, secondly, I saw the man who put it there."

"You saw him?" Martha said.

"Yes, I did, and I can tell you he was not a local. Never seen him before, but he sure looked like he was hiding. He got out and looked around real good before locking and abandoning the car and then he headed up towards North Main Street at a full gallop."

"Really," said Martha.

"Vincent, would you happen to have a pen and a piece of paper?" Martha asked.

"Hold on a minute and I'll get it for you," said Vincent. He went inside the building and emerged moments later with a paper and pen.

"What are you thinking?" he asked.

"I'm not sure, but I'm going to write down the license plate number and then call Sam. It sounds a little fishy that someone who is not from around here would abandon their car and head out on foot unless there was somewhere around here to go."

"I agree, young lady," said Vincent. "Sounds to me like you might be on to something, and then again, it could be nothing."

"Better to find out. Don't you think?" Martha said.

"Couldn't have said it better myself," Vincent replied.

CHAPTER SIXTY-TWO

It took a few calls, but Martha was finally able to reach Sam. She relayed the story of the suspicious circumstances behind an abandoned automobile in the boat yard opposite the marina. Sam took down the information and put in a call to the Department of Motor Vehicles in Hartford, choosing to bypass the local offices. When told that the information he was looking for would take some time, he hung up and called the governor's office. Jefferson Fine, the state's attorney general took the call and spent a few minutes on the phone with Sam to decide what course of action to take. He agreed with Sam that as of right now, no stone could be left unturned. He told Sam to give him some time, an hour at most, and he would get the information Sam was seeking. The governor was not available, so it was up to Fine to make the decision. Fine called the central offices of the Department of Motor Vehicles, in Hartford, and put the full weight of his office into play to make sure that the information Sam needed would be forthcoming without delay. Forty-five minutes later, he received the information which he immediately gave to Sam.

The automobile in question belonged to one Dietrich Ekhard, an auto mechanic who lived in Lyme, just across the river from Essex. Immediately, Sam's senses began to come alive. He thanked Fine and after promising to keep him informed put in a call to Admiral Blake. Sam had only one question. Was Dietrich Ekhard a German name? When told that it was indeed a name of German origin, Sam's mind switched gears into overdrive. He hung up the phone and began to attempt to analyze Ekhard's actions.

Just then the phone rang. It was the mayor. The pastor was almost two hours late for a meeting with him at the Griswold Inn. The innkeeper had called the rectory, church and anywhere else the pastor could be. No one had seen or heard from him. He informed the innkeeper that he was going up to the church to check to see if everything was alright and then head to the Gris. The innkeeper assured the mayor that the pastor was known for being punctual. The mayor had told Wanda, who immediately began to call everyone she knew in the Methodist parish to see if the pastor was visiting. She put in a few calls to the nearby hospitals, but no one had seen the pastor.

"The church," Sam yelled so loudly into the phone that the mayor nearly dropped his receiver.

"That's it," said Sam. "Mayor, get everyone you can and meet me at Wanda's. Tell them to bring their weapons."

"Sure enough, Sam," Said the mayor. "I'll get right on it."

Sam called Varnish and told him to come up to Essex and bring half of his force. He then called twenty of his own men to converge on Essex as soon as possible.

It wasn't long before Main Street in Essex was overflowing with the mayor's local militia and state and local police. Sam took the mayor, Varnish, Trooper Dolan and Bill Meecham and Injun Jim into the Black Swan to instruct them on how to deploy the large group waiting outside to insure that Getman would have no way out. Once everyone understood their instructions, they wasted little time going up to Methodist Hill and completely surrounding the church.

Once Sam was satisfied that everyone was in place and that there was no possible room for escape, he used a loudspeaker to get Getman's attention. No response came from the church. It was still light. Sam went over to see Arlen Templeton to fill him in.

"Are you sure?" Arlen asked after Sam told him all that had happened.

"As sure as my instincts will allow," Sam replied.

"There's only one way to be sure," said Arlen.

Sam knew where Arlen was heading.

"There is no way that I am going to involve you in this," he said.

"But, it's the only way to know for sure if the German refuses to acknowledge his presence," said Arlan.

"How far is it from here to the church?" Sam asked.

"About a quarter mile," said Arlan.

"Straight line or winding?" Sam asked.

"Two sharp left turns. You go straight for a good piece, then left, then straight again on a diagonal to about one hundred feet from the end where you make another left. It's a straight run from there," said Arlan.

"Where does it access?" Sam asked.

"There is a small storage room just off the entrance to the downstairs meeting hall. The room contains things used for special religious occasions such as Easter, Christmas and the like. It is not a place of constant use so I'm pretty sure it would not be a concern to someone hiding in the hall. Besides, there are no windows in the foundation. It would be very difficult to know if anyone was in the hall. The stairwell from the main sanctuary would be the only place someone from the outside could come from," Arlan explained.

"Is the pastor aware of the existence of the tunnels?" Sam asked.

"I don't think so. The previous pastor might have been, he was quite old, but he passed away suddenly and had no contact with this man. The pastor's family has been members of this congregation for three generations. That is why he was brought in. There is always the chance that someone else would have known and passed that information along, but I think it's highly unlikely," said

Arlan. "And besides Sam, no one knows how to access my tunnel. The only one who does is me, and now you will know. At best, for the church's purposes, that tunnel is a blind alley. However, he just might know of the tunnel that leads to Our Lady of Sorrows. You might want to widen your circle. There is a short tunnel from Our Lady of Sorrows to a small shed about two hundred feet from the church. It could be accessed and used for an escape, as it was for the Underground Railroad."

"Wait here," said Sam, "I'll be right back."

CHAPTER SIXTY-THREE

Pandemonium broke out the moment Sam's voice, with the aid of his state police bullhorn, was heard in the basement of the Methodist church. Getman stood perfectly still and silent as Ekhard exploded with a hysterical exhibition of fear. Veronica Lansing shrank within herself fearing the worst, but maintaining enough composure so as not to add any more fuel to the fire. She rightly was concerned that Ekhard's hysteria would ignite Getman's dangerous temper. Based on the description she received concerning the carnage of her home, shooting Ekhard may not be sufficient to satisfy him.

Meanwhile, the pastor took a few steps in Getman's direction and held up one hand as a sign that his actions were not of aggression. Getman responded that he understood and then moved to intercept Ekhard as he paced back and forth. Getman placed his face very close to Ekhard's.

"You will calm down right now or I will end your pathetic life right here," he said, leaving no doubt that he meant what he said.

Ekhard appeared to deflate as though the air were suddenly vacuumed out of him. He looked down at the ground and paused to gather himself.

"I am sorry," he said. "Whatever happens, I will cause you no more problems."

"Good," said Getman. "Now position yourself near the stairway and do not hesitate to shoot anyone coming down them attempting to come at us."

Ekhard did as he was told.

"You did well, son," said the pastor.

Getman turned to face him and respond.

"I don't have any idea how many are out there and losing Ekhard would greatly diminish any chance I have of surviving this mess," said Getman.

The pastor accepted Getman's response, but he sensed a change in Getman.

"It will be dark soon. There are only a few windows down here. Once the lights go on, those who are trying to capture you will know you are here," said the pastor.

Getman acknowledged that what the pastor said was the truth. But, he did not speak, allowing some time to pass.

"What is it, son?" the pastor asked. "Please come and sit for a while," he said as Getman's demeanor inexplicably seemed to soften.

Getman checked to make sure no one was looking in the few windows that existed in the church foundation, then he took a seat near the pastor.

Without prompting, he began to speak to the pastor. "When I was a young boy, I was the only one who could make sure my mother and I would have anything to eat. After the Kaiser's war failed, we Germans suffered horribly. There were so many reasons to grow angry, and fearing starvation and abandonment after my father's death in the war, it forced me to become someone I never intended to be. As a child, I was very happy, enjoying my doting parents at a time when Germany was a place of families and parties and happiness that seemed to be everywhere.

"The Kaiser's ambition and foolishness brought us to our knees. Germany, once a place of unity and peace, became a battleground for those who survived the war's aftermath. We were persecuted from all sides and soon began to war with each other: those who used to be our friends, anyone who would steal our food and threaten our very existence. I learned to hate and to kill, first for survival and then as a way of life. After my mother died, I found no more reason to love anyone or anything. When I was recruited by the S.S., I experienced something I had never known, joining in a cause that I believed would restore Germany to the place I remembered as a little child. Many of my compatriots believed as I did. But after a time, we all began to realize that we had been lied to and that Hitler was not someone who wanted to protect Germany from the aggressions of the outside world, but a man, much like the Kaiser, who believed Germany's only hope for peace and prosperity was to rule the world.

"Go on, my son," said the pastor, when Getman momentarily grew silent,

"I soon learned that there were many among us in the S.S. who felt just as Hitler did. When I learned of Hitler's answer for dealing with the Jewish people, the horrors of the gas camps, I was shocked. Over time I realized how many of my fellow S.S. officers actually enjoyed killing these people and being able to treat even our own people so cruelly. I was greatly disturbed. I did not know what to do. Fortunately, I was able to join an elite group that was held out of such evil practices to be used as enforcers or assassins when needed. Thankfully, there was more preparation and less action necessary. People were terrified and the mere mention of coming under the wrath of the S.S. kept most people in line.

"I gladly volunteered for this opportunity to come to America. I was positive that it would be a simple matter of aiding two men who were going to obtain military maps and strategies of the American forces in France. This information is vital to the German forces in France along the German border. German intelligence needs to know just how much of a threat there is and how many troops to deploy to insure that part of Germany is not overrun, thus paving the way for an assault on an undermanned Berlin.

When I got to America I found that everything I had been told and had planned accordingly for had changed.

"The first thing I found when I arrived was that these people who sent for me did not have the information. They were waiting for a member of U.S. Naval Intelligence to steal it and bring it to them. I planned to meet with all parties once that happened. They assured me that the wait would not be long. Then I had another meeting with these men who informed me that, once again, the plans needed to be changed. Their new plan called for me to travel up to Connecticut to the home of a famous American actress." He motioned to Veronica Lansing. "I was to be met there by a member of the Italian army. When I asked why that would be necessary, they informed me that they wanted me to kill the American traitor and injure the actress and plant information at her home accusing her of being in league with the Germans. I was not happy with this, but when I contacted my superiors, I was told to do whatever these men asked. They wanted those plans. The Italian would have the necessary documents needed to accuse her of treason."

Up to this point Veronica had been listening, but not very involved. This new revelation got her attention, to be sure.

"When I got to the Lansing residence," Getman continued, "neither the Lansing woman nor the man who was to give me the plans was there. I found only the housekeeper and the Italian. When I was informed that the Lansing woman was not present and was not even expected until the next day, I became furious. Now, I was exposed and had no idea what to do or where to turn. The Italian and I began to engage in a heated argument. The housekeeper picked up a pan and tried to attack me. At that point, I confess, I was beyond rational thinking. I deflected the woman's attempt to hit me and slammed her into the wall. She turned and started screaming. Instinctively I took my knife and stabbed her. She fell to the floor in pain. Once again, the Italian started to yell at me. At this point I had no idea how to deal with him. I found myself stabbing him many times. He too fell to the floor. He died almost immediately. The woman started to moan and try to move. I pounced on her and began stabbing her repeatedly. I then began to search for the papers to be used to accuse the American actress. I found myself tearing and ripping everything in sight. I destroyed the place, but found no papers. Then I washed the blood off my hands and weapon and left. Later I was contacted by the men who informed me that it appeared that the traitor had a change of heart and was now asking for much more money than had been agreed upon. They had no idea where he was, but when he contacted them for the exchange, they would make sure that I would be at whatever place that meeting was to take place. Their intention was obvious to me."

"Pastor," Getman said wearily, "it looks as though I am not going to escape to some idyllic life on a tropical island. For what it's worth, I want you to know that I am prepared to accept whatever fate has in store for me. As for you, Miss Lansing, I am glad I did not have to harm you. Frankly, I am sick of all the killing. But, I will not allow myself to be captured. They will have to kill me now, not later."

"Why tell me all of this?" the pastor asked.

"In the short time I have been here in America, I have seen how the American people live. It is vastly different from the stories I was told. I have observed much kindness and civility everywhere I have gone. I wish that were the case in Germany. My people are saddled with a terrible existence. War has ruined us. I know we have no chance of winning this war. And believe me, the world will be all the better for it. Now, I must await my fate."

"What are you going to do?" the pastor asked.

"That remains to be seen, Pastor," said Getman, "remains to be seen."

CHAPTER SIXTY-FOUR

Sam left Arlan's residence and made his way back up the hill to the churches. Just as he arrived there, an army transport vehicle pulled up twenty soldiers had climbed down and stood waiting for orders.

"We are stationed down at Yale, sir," said one of the soldiers to Sam. "We are at officers' training, but have not seen any action yet. But, I assure you we are well prepared and ready to engage any enemy here."

Sam was glad to hear that. "I am Sam Tyler, Connecticut State Police Captain and acting commander for this area."

"We know who you are, sir," said the soldier. "General Hutchinson has given us his direct orders to follow yours to the letter."

"We're glad to have you. I have just learned that our perimeter is not wide enough," said Sam. "Follow me. I need to take a look inside that shed, over there," he said, pointing to a small harmless looking shed that was probably used for lawn and maintenance tools.

Sam and the twenty military men made their way over to the shed and at Sam's silent command, surrounded it. Sam walked cautiously towards the door. At this point, all twenty soldiers had their rifles pointed directly at the shed. Sam opened the door, very slowly and then all the way. Just as he suspected, it was a caretaker's storage area. Sam went in and realized that the only possible opening had to be in the floor. He took a few moments to feel around and then discovered a latch. He lifted it slowly, opening it all the way. Indeed, it was the entrance to a passageway underground. He took a flashlight and pointed it down the ladder-like device that went down approximately ten feet. He very carefully lowered his head into the opening and discovered the tunnel that headed back towards the Catholic church. It was empty and by the looks of it, it had not been used for a very long time.

Sam motioned for Injun Jim to have a look. Injun Jim made his way into the tunnel and found no signs of its being used in the last few days or even the last few years for that matter.

"How good are your men?" Sam asked the army spokesman.

"I have five sharpshooters here, if that is what you are asking," said the soldier.

"Alright," said Sam. "I am going to take your five sharpshooters and deploy them strategically. Have the rest keep watch over this shed, but be ready to come as quickly as possible if shooting begins elsewhere. And, I will need you to come with me. If I need your men, I prefer it is you who give the order."

"Yes, sir," said the soldier.

Sam took the five sharpshooters and deployed one at each exit of both churches. He explained that there were at least two hostages and Getman would probably use them as a shield to get away. Sam was assured that every precaution would be taken to avoid any harm to the hostages. Sam liked their confidence. He was hoping their ability to produce matched it.

Sam made his way around the whole area to make sure Getman had no way of escaping. Once satisfied, he took Injun Jim and went back to Arlan's home.

* * *

"I apologize for bringing Injun Jim with me, Arlan, but I will need his talents to get me into the Methodist church without being discovered," said Sam.

"Don't concern yourself, Sam" said Arlan, "Injun Jim and I have known each other for quite some time. I have complete confidence in his discretion."

Sam was surprised that these two men, from completely opposite spheres of society, knew each other.

"Come with me," said Arlan as he led the two men into his study. He went over to the bookcase and after taking two books from the third shelf, pressed a latch that released the bookcase from the wall. He pushed it completely open, exposing the entrance to the tunnel.

"I heard rumors, but..." said Injun Jim without finishing his statement.

Arlan smiled in amusement. "I am sure your people have passed down the stories of the possibility of tunnels underneath this land."

"But I thought they were just old Indian tales," said Jim.

"They may be old, but I assure you they speak of things that are very real," said Arlan. "When you get to the part of the tunnel that goes beneath North Main Street, you will notice some rather modern improvements to insure the tunnels don't come down on you, courtesy of the modern automobile that came many years after they were built. I enlisted the aid of some of my fellow Masons whom I trust without question to never reveal their existence."

"Well, what are we waitin' for?" Injun Jim asked.

With that, Arlan ushered both men inside the tunnel. Then he placed his hand on a section of the wall that appeared to be the end of the tunnel that led down to the water. He gave it two short pushes and then pushed and held until the wall moved.

"Well, I'll be," said Injun Jim.

"I've told you the way, Sam. So, good luck and be careful. This man's actions speak volumes to how dangerous he is. Knowing the Germans, I am sure he is one of the smartest, as well as capable. Good luck," said Arlan.

Sam led Injun Jim into the tunnel.

"Remember what I told you. We're in no hurry," said Sam as he handed Injun Jim a flashlight.

"Same as Long Island?" Injun Jim asked.

"Yes," said Sam, referring to a very minimal use of light to reach the other end. For this, Injun Jim was well equipped. He was an excellent tracker. He proved that out on Long Island pursuing the traitor Carson.

It didn't take long for them to reach the point directly under North Main Street. They realized that they were probably no more than ten to twelve feet below the tarmac. The walls had been fortified with steel buttresses. Two of the men who performed the construction had worked on the New York City subway system. They made sure that the tunnel was well protected from any possibility of caving in, now, and in the future.

It was obvious from the gradual rising of the path that they were now going up to Methodist Hill and their destination. It didn't take long. Entry to the church closet was made easy by a handle which when turned counterclockwise, at 45 degrees, would engage a latch that would release and the doorway could be easily opened. The release inside the closet was quite different. It too was activated by pressure exerted against a certain spot on the wall that was not easily discernible. Arlan had given Sam all the instructions he needed to get in and out without fear of being discovered or trapped.

"Ready?" said Sam.

Injun Jim responded by acknowledging with a nod of his head. Sam opened the entrance way very slowly, just enough to place his ear in the opening to listen for voices. He attempted to see what was in the closet so as to not step on or knock over anything to create noise. Convinced that it was safe, he unholstered his weapon and went inside. Injun Jim followed. Injun Jim very carefully pressed his ear to the door. He could hear talking from a room that was beyond the one close by. There was nothing to suggest any anger or hysteria.

CHAPTER SIXTY-FIVE

Under most circumstances Sam would have been reluctant to involve Injun Jim, a man who possessed neither military nor police authority, to take part in such a dangerous undertaking. But he recalled a conversation with Jim less than a month ago about that very topic. Jim was quite adamant, declaring that he and his native American brethren were the truest of Americans, born here of ancestors who had been here for centuries, not people who came here from other countries adopting America as their new home. Any question concerning his advanced age as a reason for his being ineligible was nullified by the actions of many prominent American men who, though above the drafting age for military service, had voluntarily enlisted for duty. Famous movie stars like Jimmy Stewart had joined up, refusing to use age or stature as a reason for exclusion.

Injun Jim had suffered a brutal injury to his leg while working as a young man on a fishing boat out in the Atlantic, north of Block Island. A harpoon-like pole, used to pierce the body of large fish to aid in bringing them onto the boat, had ripped through his leg during a violent storm. From that moment on, Injun Jim walked with a pronounced limp. That alone would have made his status unfit for military duty, no matter what age. But, it now appeared that the fight had come to America, and that trumped any argument that would leave him out of the battle. Jim had every right to defend his country, and now Sam was gladly honoring that right. Still Sam was concerned for Injun Jim's welfare and did not want to involve him in anything that could be life threatening. But the plain fact was that this situation was indeed a threat to America and it was the duty of everyone, regardless of their age or physical condition, to defend her. Sam would take every precaution to shield Injun Jim from harm, but there were no guarantees.

* * *

Sam very carefully made his way over in the direction of the large room beneath the church where Getman held his hostages. To insure his movements were undetected, he moved forward lifting each foot a few inches parallel from the floor stepping down flat-footed, an old Indian trick Injun Jim had taught him. This assured a very secure footing in the quietest possible way. Sam made his way to the large opening to the room and very carefully entered it. At first, no one noticed him. They had their backs to him and had no reason to suspect anyone would be coming from that direction.

It was Veronica who first noticed Sam's presence. Soon, everyone else, sensing her attention fixed at something across the room, turned to see Sam standing there with his service Smith and Wesson pointed at Getman whose weapon was in his belt.

"Who are you and how did you get in here?" Getman demanded.

"I am Captain Samuel Tyler of the Connecticut State Police and you are under arrest."

"Ah, the famous Samuel Tyler is here to save the day," said Getman.

"Tell your man to lay down his weapon," said Sam, referring to Getman's accomplice, who had turned his attention from the stairway to Sam.

"I am going to take my gun out of my belt and place it on the ground," said Getman, who slowly drew his weapon, while holding it pointed towards the ground. "I envisioned myself going down in a hail of gun fire, Captain. I have no desire to stand before a firing squad. Surely you can understand that. We are both soldiers and if we must die, it would be to our honor to do so in combat, not standing weaponless in some barren place blindfolded with our hands tied behind our backs."

"I am not so sure that would be your fate," said Sam.

"Let's not be naïve, Captain. What possible reason could there be for my being spared that miserable death?" Getman said.

"I'm sure you have vital information, such as the identities and locations of German spies in this country. I am sure we, like the English, could use you to turn on them and aid us in flushing them out and preventing any harm they might be attempting to accomplish."

"That is an interesting theory, Captain. But, I doubt the American government could forgive murder so easily. The Italian was with me, but that housekeeper was an innocent American citizen. I'm afraid I don't share your optimism that I could be of such value to the military that it would forgive and forget that. No, I think not. Why don't I make this easy on you and attempt to kill Miss Lansing. You would have no choice but to shoot me to stop that," said Getman, as he slowly lifted his weapon towards Veronica Lansing.

Sam went to say something to stop him, but was prevented from doing so as two gunshots exploded. For a few seconds everyone stood frozen. Then Getman fell to the floor, the result of two bullets striking him in the back from the gun of his accomplice.

"I shot him, I shot him," Ekhard shouted. "I saved Veronica Lansing's life. You saw that."

Just then there was a strange sound of something streaking through the air, followed by a shrieking scream. Sam looked over to the man who had shot an arrow through Ekhard's shoulder. Ekhard was down on the floor crying out in pain. His gun was lying a few feet away. He made no attempt to retrieve it. Sam looked back to see Injun Jim standing there with a bow in his hand.

"Better get his weapon," said Injun Jim.

Sam was looking at Injun Jim in disbelief, but recovered and went over and picked up both fallen weapons.

"Watch him," said Sam to Injun Jim as he pointed to the man Jim had wounded.

Sam turned Getman over to see if he was still alive.

"Sorry to disappoint you, Captain. This is not the way I had envisioned for my life to end," said a coughing Getman whose breath was labored. "Imagine, killed by a coward," were the last words Getman would ever speak. Sam checked for a pulse. There was none. He rose to his feet just as Veronica Lansing flung herself at him.

"Thank God you came, Captain. Not for one moment did I believe that lunatic would spare my life," said Veronica.

"Pick him up," said Sam to Injun Jim, who pulled a crying Ekhard to his feet.

"Pastor, are you alright?" Sam asked.

"Yes, son, I believe you have seen to that. Allow me to go on up first and make sure those waiting outside know that this affair has reached a successful conclusion."

Within moments, everyone was standing in the open space that divided both churches. It appeared as though half of the townsfolk had heard what was going on and came out to see for themselves. After all, Essex was a small town. News, any news, traveled fast in these parts.

Martha had been standing with the mayor and Wanda Loomis. When Sam appeared, having Ekhard firmly in tow, all of the people began to applaud and cheer. Jim had broken off the arrow in Ekhard's shoulder, but the tip was still inside. Sam called for the medic, who appeared instantly.

Sam turned Veronica Lansing over to Martha and the mayor. They took her over to the Black Swan for some tea and escape from the crowd, who recognized her and began a small riot. Veronica appreciated their efforts and opted for "a good shot of whiskey." Acting Captain Varnish had arrived on the scene and took charge of Getman's body. Admiral Brown had flown into Deep River and was met by Arlan, who spirited him onto the scene where Lieutenant Leonard Michaels, U.S. Army, stationed at Yale, was already present and organizing all the activity.

The pastor took Sam aside and told him about his conversation with Getman. The pastor was convinced that Getman was merely a soldier thrust into an impossible situation. The whole affair had been poorly planned and Getman had serious regrets over all that had taken place. The pastor told Sam that Getman had spoken of only two men who seemed to be in charge and who had convinced the Germans their plan was full proof. Sam told the pastor that the two men he mentioned were now in custody of the U.S. Army. It was obvious that Getman had no more real information to give the military. He swore he would not be taken alive. But, he never suspected that Ekhard would be the one to end his life. The pastor made no pleas for Ekhard's case. Simply put, he was a traitor and a coward. He had willingly joined and given aid to Getman.

CHAPTER SIXTY-SIX

It was pitch black as Sam made his way down the stairs from the bedroom on the second floor. He glanced into the living room where the luggage for the New York trip was assembled and ready. There was a lot to do before the limousine would be idling in Aunt Clara's driveway, at nine-thirty a.m., waiting to drive the family to New Haven to catch the ten-forty a.m. train to New York. All showered and shaved, Sam would be taking his cruiser down to Westbrook to the State Police barracks for some last minute instructions to Trooper Dolan, his officer in charge, while he was away for the next four days. Dolan would make sure the waiting coffee would be freshly made. Small consolation for the fact that no matter what time Sam was there, the coffee was horrible. Nevertheless, fresh was better than nothing; or was it?

Sam was going over all the notes for his report to make sure every detail was correct and in its proper order. This was the most important report he had ever been responsible to assemble. Three copies would be required in addition to the one that would be on file at the barracks. One would go to the chairman of the Joint Chiefs of Staff, another to the governor and still another to none-other-than the president of the United States. It was almost six-thirty a.m. when he sealed all three and gave them to Trooper Dolan, with instructions to make sure all three would be delivered to the Commander of the U.S. Army at Yale. It would be the commander's duty to make sure all were immediately and successfully delivered to their intended destinations.

As Sam was making ready to leave for home, he was informed that he had a telephone call. He took the call and immediately recognized the voice of Arlen Templeton on the other end. After a few pleasantries, Sam agreed to Arlen's request that he come to Arlen's home before returning to his own. Sam reasoned that he could easily be there for seven a.m. with plenty of time to spare. Martha and Aunt Clara had seen to everything on their end. All Sam had to do was show up and get into the limousine with the rest of the family. He was confident that he would be able to achieve that. Still, he thought it strange that Arlen would insist he come there before leaving for New York. He had no idea what Arlen had on his mind. But, there was one thing he knew for sure, there would be a great pot of coffee waiting for his arrival. That alone was enough to make Sam amenable to Arlen's request.

Betty Templeton greeted Sam at the door with a hug and a gesture to fetch his cup of hot coffee, courtesy of the wonderful beans of Puerto Rico. Sam swore he could smell them from the outer courtyard of the Templeton's home. Arlen was in his study working on his own cup of that wondrous brew.

"Glad you could make it, Sam," he said.

"I figured it must be something pretty special," said Sam.

"Have a seat, son," said Arlen, who instructed Betty to bring the pot of coffee and cream and sugar in and place them on his writing desk. An electric hot plate was already set in place to assure that the coffee maintained a proper temperature.

"I know that you will be leaving in a short time, but I wanted to fill you in on some things before you leave. First, you, Martha and the children will be flown to Washington sometime next week for an audience with the president. What you were able to achieve under the most trying circumstances made my old card playing buddy just simply ecstatic. The military is going to honor you and he insisted it be performed at the White House. No way was he going to miss that. Admiral Blake has not stopped extolling your accomplishments. Let me tell you, Sam, that alone should merit you an award. The military community is reluctant to share honors with anyone outside its family. More than one ranking officer has trumpeted your name. And, that makes me very happy. You know that I have always considered you the son I never had. It goes without saying that there can be no compensation for losing our Sally, but your willingness to share the children with Betty and me and my relationship with you, one that you have had much to say about, has been a great comfort to us. I would venture to say that our relationship is not the norm. And, we are just so pleased that someone like Martha has come into all of our lives. We are reaping many blessings from above. We are truly blessed."

Sam took in all Arlen had said, and it was a lot to digest. Sam had lost his parents at such a young age that it was natural to consider Arlen a second father. They had known each other since Sam and Sally were in seventh grade. Once they reached high school, there was little doubt that there would be no room for anyone else in their young lives. Only death could part them. And, when it did, Sam did all he could to involve his family with Arlen and Betty.

"I know all about your plans this weekend," said Arlen, "but I have to tell you that recent events have made it necessary for some changes to be made."

"Changes?" said Sam.

"Now don't worry. I have already talked to Martha and she is fully aware and in total agreement."

"Changes," said Sam, once more, motioning to Arlen to explain.

"For one thing, your accommodations at the Plaza have been upgraded to the "Presidential Suite," said Arlen. "Martha insisted that any changes had to be done at the Plaza due to all the plans she had in that area of the city. The Waldorf Astoria was offered, but I understood her reluctance completely. You and the family will have your own private car for your train ride to the city. It has a kitchen with dining facilities and a man servant to see to your needs. What you may or may not see is the Secret Service detail that will be with you, however discreetly, during the whole time you are in Manhattan."

Arlen immediately sensed Sam's objection. "Sam, hear me out. This was not my decision. The president has decided that you are to receive the same treatment as the First Family, as well as that of the vice-president and cabinet members, at least for this trip. And also, because a case could be made that you are entitled."

"Entitled, how?" questioned Sam.

"Tippecanoe and Tyler too," said Arlen.

"Our tenth president, if I do recall from my American history class in high school."

"Well, there you have it," said Arlen.

"How in the world can you come to that...," said Sam, stopping himself at mid-sentence. Sam paused for a moment. Arlen said nothing. "You can't be suggesting...?" Once again he did not finish.

"Your great-great uncle, I am afraid," said Arlen. "He was your great-great grandfather's brother. President Tyler was neither a popular nor successful president. The Tyler family worked tirelessly and quite vigorously to distance themselves from him. I'm sure your Aunt Clara could fill you in from a family perspective. I'm also sure she won't have much good to report and might allow herself to rise to a level of anger that might be difficult on the ears."

Sam just smiled and shook his head in disbelief.

"Sam, those Secret Servicemen are highly trained. They will in no way interfere with your family's good time. Their very lives are dedicated to absolutely making sure that every possible thing be done to insure that a good time does not get interrupted or hindered, no matter the cost. You could not be in better hands. Sam, you have got to get used to the idea that you are a national treasure. Your good press has given much comfort to the president and the American people. It would be terrible if something bad were to happen to you right on the heels of your great success."

"And, Martha is alright with all of this?" Sam asked.

"Actually, she thought it was great. That's some gal you have there," said Arlen.

Sam had to agree.

"I understand that Injun Jim showed his prowess with the bow and arrow," said Arlen, changing the subject.

"Yes, how about that," said Sam.

"Doesn't surprise me one bit," said Arlen.

"Care to explain?" Sam said.

"You're well aware of those annual hunting trips Jim makes with some of the townsfolk. But, what you might not know is that, from time to time, some of my friends and I go hunting up near the Massachusetts border. Jim always goes with us. Of course, we use our rifles, but not Jim. He is quite something with a bow and arrow. You got a real good firsthand look at that, didn't you?"

"You can say that again," said Sam. For a moment both men sat in silence.

"I need to know something," said Sam, finally.

"What?" Arlen asked.

"Arlen, I think it's time you leveled with me. You are not just some wealthy man of industry who happens to have a few friends in high places. I'm sure you did play cards with the president, and maybe you still do, but to quote Dickens, 'there is more gravy then the grave to you," said Sam.

"Dickens," said Arlen who allowed a broad smile to spread across his face. He paused for a moment. Sam could see that he was wrestling with something.

"Please don't take offense at what I am about to tell you, Sam, but this absolutely must stay between you and me. You will understand, I am sure. For the time being, you are not to share any of this with anyone. That includes Martha. Once the war is over, that will probably change."

Sam sat silently waiting for Arlen to continue.

"I am a member of a secret group of individuals code named, 'The President's Council.' Very few outside of the immediate group know of its existence, nor the reason for its existence. There are twenty of us. Ten captains of industry, of which I am one, and ten very influential businessmen, all Bonesmen, as a matter of fact."

"Yale?" asked Sam.

"Yes," said Arlen.

"The president is Harvard and Cornell," said Sam.

"And you are wondering why Yale?" Arlen asked.

"I'm thinking that is kind of strange, disengaging from one's roots," said Sam.

"You know the philosophy by which the Skull and Cross Bones are said to be governed?" Arlen asked.

"They believe it is their sworn duty, their sacred duty for that matter, to protect this country according to their beliefs," Sam answered.

"Very well said," said Arlen. "Can you think of any other fraternal organization on either of those campuses that has taken the same stance?"

"No," said Sam, quietly.

"This war caught us completely by surprise. The American public wanted no part of it. It was delusional to think that a war that was taking place everywhere but here was something we could avoid. We had no choice but to respond after Pearl. We needed to construct military manufacturing capabilities never before known in this country. And, we had to do it fast. We twenty were summoned by the president to make sure that happened, overnight! Bridgeport was our logical and overwhelming first choice. What has happened there and in Stratford has been nothing short of amazing. But you must believe me, 'the President's Council' was a stroke of genius. Only by our combined efforts, intelligence and commitment to work together to achieve that end could it have happened. There will be no awards for me or any of us. Each of us knows what we are doing and we are satisfied to know how much we have contributed to our country's well-being. Besides, we have made friends for life.

"A residual effect is that some of us, myself included, have healed old wounds with each other. That is a remarkable and immensely satisfying accomplishment. Some of us, who were at odds for years, are now looking forward to a rich, long lasting relationship. You have no idea how grateful I am for all of this.

"Mary, Thomas and Lillith share an amazing lineage. What you and I have done, Sam, has made the prospects of their future very bright. In that we share a common bond. No man can be happier than that."

Arlen got up from his seat. "Now go and join your family and have a grand time in the City. Martha has set quite an amazing itinerary. I look forward to your return and our trip to Washington."

Sam and Arlen hugged and then Sam got in his cruiser and headed home.

By now the children were up, fed, and were operating at a fever pitch. Aunt Clara could not have looked happier. Injun Jim had brought the luggage from the house to Aunt Clara's back porch.

"I see you and Arlen had a nice little discussion this morning," said Sam to Martha.

"Oh Sam, Arlen is such a love. We got it all worked out. The only thing for our plans is that they just got a little better. I am so proud of you. I never thought my life could be this wonderful. Let's go to New York and have the best time ever."

Just then a car horn was heard along with the screams of three beyond-excited children. Sam and the family hugged Aunt Clara good-bye. Martha and the children got into the limousine while the chauffeur and Injun Jim saw to the luggage. Sam thanked Injun Jim for everything and entered the car.

"I'll take care of everything here while you are gone," he told Sam.

"I have no doubt of that," Sam said.

The limousine moved steadily up Pratt Street towards North Main, turned left and headed for Route 1 and New Haven. As it turned onto North Main, Sam noticed a black four-door Chevrolet sedan with four occupants slowly pull away from the curb and maintain a two car distance. The vehicle had government license plates.

Martha inched closer to Sam and pressed against his side.

"Our guardian angels have joined us," Sam said.

Martha smiled and looked up at Sam with a sense of happiness and relief. "Merry Christmas, Honey."

THE END

ACKNOWLEGEMENTS

With great appreciation and endearing friendship, I would like to thank the following invaluable contributions to this book.

Pat Cucuzza - For keeping me on point.

Tina Laychak - For diligent monitoring of the text.

Arthur Shulz - For constantly building me up and encouraging me on.

Bishop Jay Ramirez - For inspiration and unwavering friendship.

Raquel Torres-Del Monte - My wonderful daughter who never seems to think I can't do it.

Special thanks to Toula Magi without whose help this project would never have gotten off the ground.

To all of the above, I extend my most fervent appreciation for all you have done, valuable time spent and cheering me on.

About the Author

Alan Del Monte is a successful hairdresser and salon owner in Milford, Connecticut. A former high school history teacher, Alan also spent ten years in New York City entertainment venues and recording studios as a musician and sound engineer. Today, Alan spends his time writing novels in many genres. Alan and his wife, Jan live overlooking the waters of Long Island Sound, in the Woodmont section of Milford. Alan has two children and seven grandchildren.

OTHER BOOKS BY ALAN DEL MONTE

Merchant Prince - 2019

Avenging Angel - 2018

Dance of the Masters - 2016

The Pirate's Island - 2011

Wolf Harbor - 2010

COMING SOON

Jim Smith "Born Again" - 2020

Now, It's War - 2020